"Don't cross me, [...] be sorry."

As the words came [...] snapped around to the other side [...] boat jibed and the boom came crashing around. A stinging blow to my head sent me flying sideways. As I fell over the guardrail, my feet too far off the floorboards to gain purchase, Egan's hand clamped down on my arm.

He leaned over me, staring down into my face. As I stared back, I saw that his eyes were the same deadly shade of blue as blade steel. His grip was all that stood between me and the cold gray water, which lashed at my hair and spattered icy drops on my neck.

Through my sick dizziness and the pain in my head, I knew I was helpless and in deadly danger. "Egan, don't!" I tried to cry, but the sound stuck in my throat. All I could do was stare into his eyes until my very soul seemed to drown in the lightless depths of his pupils. I felt his hand loosen slightly. I knew he was going to let me fall.

ABOUT THE AUTHOR

Like her heroine, Jane Silverwood is from the Detroit area and loves the Great Lakes region. She's always been fascinated with that romantic but dangerous era—the 1920s, with its bootlegging and wild times. She's combined both in this story, with a spine-tingling mystery, as well. Jane lives with her family in Baltimore.

Books by Jane Silverwood

Don't miss any of our special offers. Write to us at the following address for information on our newest releases.

Harlequin Reader Service
901 Fuhrmann Blvd., P.O. Box 1397, Buffalo, NY 14240
Canadian address: P.O. Box 603,
Fort Erie, Ont. L2A 5X3

Silent Starlight
Jane Silverwood

Harlequin Books

TORONTO • NEW YORK • LONDON
AMSTERDAM • PARIS • SYDNEY • HAMBURG
STOCKHOLM • ATHENS • TOKYO • MILAN
MADRID • WARSAW • BUDAPEST • AUCKLAND

To Linda, for all her patience

ISBN 0-373-22270-X

SILENT STARLIGHT

Copyright © 1994 by Louise Titchener

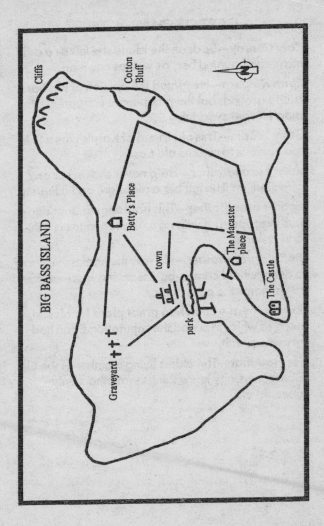

BIG BASS ISLAND

Cliffs

Cotton
Bluff

Betty's Place

Graveyard ✝ ✝ ✝

town

park

The Macaster
place

The Castle

CAST OF CHARACTERS

Katy Conroy—Back on the island she left as a child, memories haunted her, as well as one man.

Egan Halpern—He turned the opinion of Big Bass Island around, but the prosperous entrepreneur didn't forget everything.

Betty Wiblin—This old friend of Katy's was a little too anxious to resume old ties.

Katy's grandfather—He'd never shown her any affection, until he left her a mansion, and a legacy.

Egan's grandfather—This hotdogging bootlegger had disappeared with no explanation to his wife and children.

Betty's grandfather—He was the hapless victim of a decades-old crime—but the speechless man could never name the perpetrator.

Rex Halpern—Egan had great plans for his son, none of which included the reputation Egan had grown up with.

Flo Hadditer—The oldest living member of the Big Bass community knew things that others only guessed at.

Chapter One

A perfect day for a funeral, I thought. The April wind, heavy with chill water scooped from Lake Erie, whistled past my ears. Overhead, naked branches raked at the leaden sky.

"We are gathered here to bid farewell to our dear friend, Nathan Conroy."

While the preacher sing-songed a final prayer over my grandfather's casket, I stole a glance at the crowd. It surprised me that so many island people had come. To be brutally honest, Grandfather was a miserly recluse with an ice-pick tongue. Yet a third of Big Bass's winter population had put on their somber Sunday best to remember him. Or maybe they just hadn't had anything better to do. Winters are solitary confinement on Big Bass, and it would be weeks before the tourist season started.

When the ceremony ended and the mourners started straggling off, a hand tapped my shoulder.

"Good to see you back on the island, Katy. It's been a long time."

"It certainly has." I smiled at the familiar face, plump and pretty. "Betty Wiblin, is that really you?"

"Well, yes and no." Betty laughed. "My last name is McKenny now, and I'm fourteen years older and twenty pounds heavier. I guess that makes me a different person than the one you knew. Though, to tell you the truth, a lot of times I still feel like the dumb teenager I was that one summer we two palled around."

I couldn't answer right away because some people stopped to shake my hand and condole. It was all very stiff and uncomfortable, and some condoled less than others.

"I won't say I'm sorry Nate's gone. By my lights, the old coot was luckier than he deserved. At ninety-two he lived as long as any human being's got a right to and was spry as a monkey to the last. Having your heart stop on you while you're falling down a flight of stairs isn't a half bad way to go," declared old Mrs. Hadditer, the town's retired librarian.

When the old woman had stalked off, planting her cane in the scrubby grass like a pole-vaulter, Betty struggled not to laugh. "I know it sounds awful, but she's right. Your grandfather was independent to the last and died suddenly. Isn't that how we'd all like to go?"

"I won't feel qualified to give an opinion on that until I'm ninety-two, myself." Wanting to get away from this subject, I cocked my head. "Did I hear you say your last name is McKenny? Does that mean you married Bob McKenny?"

"Yes, but before you start congratulating me, Bob ran off three years ago and left me with two kids to support. Usual story."

Betty's sudden bitterness caught me by surprise. Impulsively, I hugged her. "Oh, I'm sorry. But it's still great to see you. I can't believe it's been fourteen years."

"Well, it has," she said, extricating herself. "And a lot's happened. Want to know who married who and how many kids they've got?"

"Of course I do."

While we walked back to the road, the April wind whipping our hair around our faces, Betty filled me in on the decade's marriages, births and divorces. I exclaimed every now and then and asked questions. But all the time, I was waiting for one certain name to crop up. When it didn't, I dug my cold hands into my pockets and asked.

"And what about Egan Halpern? Is he still on the island?"

"Oh, sure. In fact, I thought I saw him at the back of the church at the funeral. He and Nate were pretty palsy, you know."

That made me blink. "I didn't know. When did that happen? There was nothing like that the summer I spent here with Grandfather."

"Well, maybe their friendship developed later. I guess that's right. They probably got to know each other better through the historical society. Somewhere along the line, Egan developed a passion for Lake Erie history. In fact, I hear he's writing a book. Egan is still the world's sexiest, most contrary man, but in other ways he's changed a lot since you knew him." Betty shot me a sideways glance. "You had quite a crush on him that summer you were here, didn't you?"

"You know perfectly well I did. Seems to me just about every girl on the island was crazy over Egan's muscles and wicked blue eyes."

Betty chortled and then winked. "You should see the female tourists do a double take when he strides past. Hey, all this time I've been talking about myself and the other islanders. What about you? I don't see a ring on your finger. Don't tell me you never married."

"Never did."

Betty stepped back and put her hands on her hips. "Well, Katy Conroy, it can't be because you haven't had a million offers. You know, you haven't changed much at all. I recognized you right off."

"I'm not sure whether I should take that as a compliment or an insult."

"It's definitely a compliment. Any thirty-year-old who's got the same figure she had at sixteen deserves a medal." Betty hesitated. "I promised myself I wouldn't ask. But seeing you has really brought back old times and you know what a nosy parker I was. How come you never came back to the island after that summer?"

"Oh," I replied vaguely, "life got complicated. And to be honest, Grandfather never invited me back."

"He didn't?" Betty's eyebrows shot up. "Well, I know Nate Conroy got more ornery with every passing year, but that does seem unfriendly, even for him, you being his only grandchild, and all."

I shrugged. "To be honest, the last thing Grandfather ever wanted on his hands that summer was a spoiled sixteen-year-old girl. My father only parked me on his doorstep because my folks were going through a messy divorce."

"Where's your dad now? Was he here for the funeral?"

"My father died last summer of a heart attack."

Betty grimaced with sympathy. "You *have* had a rough year, losing both your father and your grandfather."

"Yes, I have." I could only think in silence about just how rough it had really been.

"But," Betty pressed, a calculating light coming into her brown eyes, "that must make you Nate's only surviving relative."

"Yes, I believe I'm the last of the Conroys now."

"Does that mean he left you his place?"

A gust of frigid wind sent leaves scuttling down the street. Shivering, I pulled up the collar of the cashmere coat I'd splurged on when things were going well in my life, and crushed it closed against my throat. "I have no idea. Tomorrow I'm seeing his lawyer. For all I know, Grandfather left everything to the Big Bass Historical Society."

Betty rolled her eyes. "Actually, you may not be so far-off. He was nuts about island history. Collected all kinds of stuff."

"What stuff?"

"Papers, documents. All I've heard are rumors, but word is he could have blackmailed us all. This is my car." Betty paused in front of a rusty pickup. "Can I give you a lift?"

"No, thanks. It's only a few blocks to the house. I'll walk."

"I hate to think of you rattling around in that spooky mausoleum all alone."

"It's not so bad. I have a lot to do to keep busy, dusting and sorting."

"I can imagine. Everyone knows Nate was a pack rat. Well, listen, if you're going to be around any time at all, how about coming for dinner?"

"That would be great. I'd love to meet your family."

We exchanged a few more words and then Betty got into her truck, waved and drove off. I waited until she was out of sight, then set off toward town.

As I braved the wind, scenes from the summer I'd spent with Grandfather paraded through my memory. That first week, I'd been the loneliest, most resentful sixteen-year-old in Ohio. The other teenagers on the island had been standoffish, not wanting to consort with a stuck-on-herself kid from the mainland. Betty had worked the cash register at the little corner grocery. With her puppy-dog smile and infectious giggle, she'd cut right through my stiff shyness and we'd struck up a friendship. We'd gossiped and confided through those long, hot summer evenings.

I still remember the grassy smell of them, the feel of my shorts rubbing against the smooth flesh of my tanned thighs, the pull of my thong sandals between my toes and the satisfying rhythmic clop they made as I strolled on warm cracked pavement. Betty and I would amble down to Mercer's Ice-Cream Parlor for a double dip chocolate cone or bowl duckpins at the Colonial. We'd been so painfully young, so tender in our hopes and fears.

I sighed, glancing from side to side at the freshly painted Victorian frame houses lining the street, noting the raked lawns and trimmed bushes. I remembered Big Bass as pleasantly shabby, a getaway place known to relatively few. Now it had the look of a trendy vacation spot.

When I'd stepped off the ferry earlier that afternoon, I'd hardly recognized the place. New restaurants and floating docks had appeared in the harbor which, according to the local paper, teemed with tourists in summer. Even now in early spring, bright yellow pedicabs roamed Main Street.

"Want a ride, lady? For two dollars I'll take you anywhere on the island you'd like to go."

"No, thanks." I smiled at the dark-haired boy in a red windbreaker who'd pedaled up to me, and I nodded my head at Grandfather's house. "I don't have much farther to go."

As he followed the direction of my glance and fixed his gaze on the sprawling Victorian mansion, which dominated a point on the left side of the harbor, the boy's jaw dropped.

For an instant, I saw the place through his eyes. Against the menacing sky, it threw up a jagged outline of shingled brown towers and turrets. I almost expected to see a bat fly out of one of its narrow, shuttered windows. Even without the bat, those windows seemed to frown down at the world with malevolent suspicion.

"You're staying at Old Crazy Nate's place? But he died!"

"I know. I'm just coming back from his funeral. I'm his granddaughter."

The youngster, who I guessed to be about ten, closed his mouth and eyed me. "Oh, yeah. I heard you arrived on the ferry early this morning."

Somehow I managed not to roll my eyes. Gossip had always sped around the island like an out-of-control sidewinder rocket. By now, everyone must know that Crazy Nate Conroy's uppity granddaughter had come back to bury him. Safe bet they were also waiting with bated breath to see if he'd cut me out of his will.

"You going to be staying in the castle all by yourself?" the boy asked, using the name the islanders had given Grandfather's Gothic domicile.

"For a little while, anyhow. Until I've got things sorted out."

He slanted his head back so the late-afternoon sun glanced off his square young jaw in a way that struck a familiar chord in my memory. "Then maybe you'll want to clean the place up. If it's the junk pile people say, you'll need some help. For three dollars an hour, I'll lug things to the dump, and such."

"Three dollars? You just said you'd take me anywhere on the island for two dollars."

"Pedaling is a lot easier than hauling junk around."

"Then why not stick to the business you're already in?"

He waved a hand at the empty street and then looked at me with scorn for my lack of perception. "You kidding? Not enough tourists to be worth diddly yet."

I had to laugh. This kid was obviously Big Bass-born and bred and running true to form. Isolated and with no yearlong work, generations of islanders had neverthe-less managed to persuade their daily bread out of what-ever and whomever came to hand. Yielding to his forthright logic, I said, "In a couple of days, I'll know better what my plans are. Come around then and maybe we can work something out."

"Thanks. See you around."

He'd already started to pedal away when I called after him. "Better tell me your name."

"Rex, Rex Halpern."

SHOULD HAVE GUESSED, I chided myself as I climbed the veranda's sagging wooden steps and then unlocked the paneled mahogany door. *By now, Egan probably has half a dozen kids*.

Heavily, I hung my coat on a brass hook. Running a hand through my hair, I walked into the living room and was instantly overcome with an eerie sensation.

Outside, clouds scudded before the wind. It riffled the grass, scattered last autumn's leaves and picked at the loose edges of roofing. Inside Nate Conroy's house, the wind was muffled. It seemed to murmur outside a castle preserved in the dusty spell of a dead necromancer. The only things moving were the hands on the clock ticking next to the piano.

It, like everything in the house, was an antique. So far as I could tell, nothing had changed since I'd spent the summer here fourteen years ago. Even the musty smell of decades of well-cultivated mildew was the same. My eyes moved from the massive needlepoint sofa with its lion-head arms, to the veneered radio cabinet, a relic of the thirties, to the threadbare orientals scattered across the dusty hardwood floor.

Five generations of Conroys had lived, accumulated and died here. Everywhere you looked, their tastes were memorialized.

I walked through the frigid living room and headed for the kitchen in back. It was a good thing I had learned how to light a gas burner in my misspent youth. After I'd gotten a blue flame going on Nate's antediluvian stove, I put water on to boil and then headed upstairs to unpack a sweater from the suitcase I'd dropped off before dashing off to the funeral. I was just warding off the house's damp chill with a hot cup of tea when the phone rang.

"Katy, is that you?"

"Yes, Edward, it's me." I'd recognized his voice at once.

"Are you all right?"

"I'm fine."

"I worry about you. To have to deal with this on top of everything else."

"I know, but really, I'm all right." Briefly, I described Grandfather's funeral.

"I don't know whether to hope he left you his place or not."

"Why? Don't you want me to be an heiress?"

"Yes, sure, if I could feel certain you'd sell out and come back to Detroit where you belong. I'm just afraid you might decide to stay there."

I dropped onto a kitchen chair and rubbed my forehead. A year ago, I'd never have considered living in this house. I would have laughed at the idea. Now... "Well, it's true I don't have too many options at the moment."

"You can always come back. We can still work this out. You know that, Katy."

I knew we couldn't, but I was too tired to tell my ex-fiancé that all over again. "Listen, Edward, I appreciate your calling. Really, I'm all right. I'm just tired. It's been a long day."

"All right." His heavy sigh weighed down the phone line. "Take care."

Take care, I thought. All my life, people have warned me to take care. Why don't I ever listen?

LATER THAT EVENING in the small back bedroom, I fingered the wool blanket I'd found on the bed. It smelled of having lain there untouched for too many years. Probably no one had bothered to clean it in half a century. I glanced around at the paneled walls and low ceilings. This was the room I'd stayed in as a teenager.

Prehistoric blankets hadn't been a problem that hot summer. Most nights, I'd opened the windows in hopes of catching a breeze. I'd lain on the bare sheets in my briefest nightie and dreamed of Egan's kisses falling on my fevered skin like hot rain. My gaze strayed to the window opposite. It was the one I'd climbed from when Egan Halpern and I ran away together.

Scenes from the past refused to stop playing through my mind as I lay awake that night. Some of them were pleasant. Some not. Almost all of them involved Egan.

The wind had died down, but the house still groaned and creaked. Settling, I told myself. Old houses settle. I thought of Grandfather—old, frail and pathologically stubborn—living alone here decade after decade. This house had seen so much Conroy history, and so much of Nate Conroy's long life, that it almost felt like an extension of him. I imagined the big old house crouching over me and wondered if it regarded me as an intruder. I shivered and fought the vulnerability of sleep. Finally, however, it seized me and dragged me down.

Just after 3:00 a.m., I awoke with all my senses stretched and a powerful knowledge that something was wrong. Intently, I listened. Although I heard no unusual sound, I couldn't ignore the tingling at the back of my neck that had yanked me from sleep. After pushing into a sitting position, I rubbed my arms through the flannel sleeves of my long nightshirt and strained my ears.

The wind had died down. Nevertheless, the house was like a great sounding box, every creak and snap magnified. It occurred to me that after sheltering—one might even say cocooning—Nate Conroy for most of his nine decades, this house had killed him. Mrs. Perkins, who came in once a week to clean and shop, had found Grandfather's body at the foot of the cellar stairs.

"He must have been going down to check on something and taken a tumble," she'd reported when she phoned me in Detroit. "It must have happened the day before I came, because the doctor said Nate hadn't been there that long."

Repulsed at the images filling my mind—Grandfather pitching forward on the stairs, clutching his heart, perhaps screaming in pain and terror—I hadn't paid much attention to the details. Now I wondered what he'd gone down to the cellar for.

It couldn't have been to see to the furnace or water heater. Like most dwellings on Big Bass, the house had no proper basement. Originally, its stone fireplaces had been its only heating system. The small cellar under the kitchen had been dug purely for storage. So far as I knew, there'd never been anything much stored there except highly suspect jars of preserves. Surely Grandfather, who'd lived on shredded wheat and frozen dinners, hadn't been after one of those.

A noise that didn't fit the house's usual repertoire of nocturnal moans and groans made me sit up straighter. Had I imagined it? Was someone or something down there? Who? What? I ran a hand through my hair.

Whatever had caused the noise, I wasn't going to get back to sleep any time soon. Maybe a quick investigation and a glass of sherry from the dusty decanter on the sideboard would help. I swung my legs over the edge of the bed and reached for my robe.

Out on the landing, I stood hugging myself. Leaving the familiar little guest room felt like stepping from a safe island into a sea of danger. In the dark, the house opened its throat like some cavernous hungry beast. I knew my imagination was overacting, but how the hell had Nate managed to live alone in this vast collection of turrets and stairways without suffering from paranoid fantasies? Maybe he hadn't. Maybe that's what had sent him to his death in the basement—a noise, a nighttime terror.

Despite their age, the stairs didn't creak. Their worn oak treads slid silkily against my slipperless feet. With the aid of a faint shaft of moonlight from the small octagonal window on the landing, I felt my way down. Not wanting to alert the alleged intruder, I opted against switching on the lights.

I found the sherry decanter in the dark, as well. As I padded back through the dining room to the kitchen, I thought of all the mice, beetles and spiders that probably ventured forth at night. Suddenly, I regretted my lack of slippers and squeamishness about turning on lights. I flashed back on an experience I'd had as a child of nine.

It happened during a family vacation on North Carolina's outer banks. While my parents slept, I stole down to the beach with a flashlight to take a midnight walk on the hard-packed sand.

Over the whoosh of the crashing waves, I heard a faint scrabbling. At first, entranced by the scenery and my daring at doing something forbidden, I'd ignored it. When the noise persisted, I switched on the flashlight to investigate. To my horror, sand crabs carpeted the beach so thickly that it had become a wriggling mass. With every step I'd taken, they'd scuttled just out of reach of my toes. In the light, they froze, staring at me with tiny beady eyes. Now when I tell the story, people laugh and I laugh with them. But I'll never forget my horror—the feeling of having stumbled into something alien and terrifying.

I pushed open the kitchen door and instinctively reached for the light switch. A second away from switching it on, my fingers froze. There was already light in the kitchen. Its cold gray thread seeped under the door that led to the cellar.

While my mind raced, my eyes stayed fixed on the filament of light. Burglars? What would they be doing in the cellar? And did I really want to find out? I seriously considered sneaking back upstairs, barricading my bedroom door and not coming out until morning. But this was Big Bass, not New York City. Lone women lived all their lives on this island and never had to bother locking their doors.

Even so, I snatched up a meat fork from the countertop before pulling the cellar door open. "Who's there?"

The noise stopped. Dead silence. Then footsteps dragged against the earthen floor. A shadow fell over the foot of the wooden stair. I heard breathing. I saw long simian arms with heavy balled fists, a distorted torso. The shadow flowed up over the steps, and I opened my mouth to scream.

A well-built man wearing jeans, a black turtleneck sweater and an old pea coat replaced his distorted shadow and stood looking up at me.

My heart stuck in my throat.

"Hello, Katy." His voice was deep. His eyes, as they fixed on me, strangely somber.

"Egan?"

"Yes, it's me."

I flattened a hand against my breast and tried to hear above the roar in my ears. A pulse battered the hollow of my throat. As my hand crept up to it, I remembered that I wore only a robe and nightgown. My hair had to be wild around my face and my expression terrified. "What are you doing here at this time of night?" I quavered.

"Looking for something that belongs to me. Seems I'm not going to find it." He began to climb the stairs, each step slow and deliberate, as if he was mulling over something he might or might not do. Egan was a big man, even bigger than I remembered, and his body filled the narrow passage. The smell of earth from the damp cellar came up with him. "Sorry if I bothered you."

"You might have called and asked," I said, forcing firmness into my voice, despite my racing heart and quivering nerves. I stood aside as his dark head came level with mine and then towered over me as he took the last step.

He walked past me into the unlit kitchen, then turned and gazed down at me. As we regarded each other, the silence between us stretched much too thin for comfort. But then neither of us had ever expected to receive comfort from the other. A thousand memories beat through my head, and I found, suddenly, that I was having a hard time breathing.

"Guess I didn't think you'd be here," Egan finally drawled. "I've been a pretty frequent visitor to Nate's place these last few years. Fact is, the old man had no one else to help him. It didn't occur to me I'd be trespassing."

"I have to stay here to settle Grandfather's affairs," I said lamely.

Egan shrugged. "No need to stumble around in the dark like this." He switched on the kitchen light. As it shone down on us, we couldn't stop looking at each other. While I struggled for control, we each assessed what the years had wrought. Egan looked rougher and craggier. Premature silver threaded his black curls and his face had weathered. Lines showed at the corners of his deep-set blue eyes and ran from nose to mouth. He was still greyhound-lean, but under his coat his shoulders appeared broader. I dragged my gaze from his. His expression only increased my nervousness.

"The years don't seem to have done you much harm," he said.

"What would you know about that?" I replied, attempting a light tone.

"Nothing at all, little Blondie," he murmured, using the name he'd once had for me. "Nothing at all." And with that, he turned and stalked out the back door and into the night.

Chapter Two

Two days later, I sat on the uppermost deck of the *Maiden,* one of the three ferries that connects Big Bass with the mainland. I was on my way to Sandusky.

"Leaving us already?" a querulous voice demanded in my ear.

I turned and saw Mrs. Hadditer settling stiffly onto the bench across from me. I hadn't spotted her getting onto the ferry, but I'd boarded early and had been lost in my thoughts for the last ten or fifteen minutes.

"I don't often leave the island," she said over the noise of engines shuddering beneath us. "Once a month, I have to visit my doctor for heat treatments."

"Heat treatments?"

"Rheumatism." She narrowed her beady eyes and used her cane to beat a tattoo on the painted metal deck. "Someday you'll have it, too, young lady. Then you'll understand the miseries that flesh is heir to."

"Yes, I suppose I will. Sorry it's giving you so much trouble."

Her fierce expression softened slightly. "You haven't answered my question. Leaving us?"

"Just for the day. I have an appointment."

"Who with?"

"A man named Kandefer." I didn't expect the name to mean anything to her, but she surprised me.

"Ah, yes, your granddad's lawyer."

"How did you know?"

"Not much I don't know that goes forward on this island, young lady." Again, she thunked her cane. "Going to find out what mischief that old coot made in his will, I suppose."

Assuming that she meant Grandfather and not his lawyer, I shrugged. "He had the right to leave his property where he pleased."

Mrs. Hadditer aimed her rheumy gaze out at the lake. "That's a matter of opinion. It's a fact that Nate Conroy did just as he pleased all his life, and what he pleased wasn't always what was right." She squinted and, stacking her gnarled hands over the ivory handle on her cane, hunched forward. "Now what's that young fool think he's doing? Racing the ferry?"

My eyes widened as I followed her gaze. In order to get a better look, I stood and walked up to the railing. No more than fifty yards away, a sloop with a black hull cut on aggressively racy lines was slicing across the ferry's bow. The sloop heeled at a dangerous angle. Her sails, sheeted tight, strained against the wind like overfilled bladders. Though the ferry blasted its airhorn, the man at the black sloop's helm ignored the warning. I stared at Egan Halpern's profile. The wind had lashed his spray-damp hair into an ebony froth. His jaw jutted at a stubborn angle, and I caught the flash of white teeth between his parted lips.

"Having a high old time, isn't he, now?" Mrs. Hadditer commented with asperity.

I had to agree. Egan looked like a man enjoying himself immensely. As the sloop shot past the ferry with room to spare, he slanted a cocky grin our way. Our gazes locked for just the briefest instant, and my stomach tightened. I caught the name painted in bold gray script on his boat's transom. *Nighthawk*. It certainly was appropriate.

"Always was a daredevil," Mrs. Hadditer commented behind my back. "Got into the worst scrapes when he was a youngster. Now that he's made such a success with his boat-building business, you get to thinkin' he's outgrown his devilish ways. Then you catch him pulling a stunt like that one yonder..."

She shook her head, and I nodded wordlessly. I had reason to know that Egan had been wild. My hands tightened on the ferry's railing, and I remembered Egan as I'd first seen him that summer long ago. It had been my second day on the island. Abandoned to the dubious care of my taciturn grandfather, not knowing a soul on the island, frightened by my parents' bitter breakup, lonely and resentful, I'd wandered through the park and down to the waterfront.

Then I'd seen him—a bronzed young god, loading a truck near one of the docks. "Hello, Blondie," he'd called out when he spotted me staring at him.

"Hi," I'd replied shyly. He'd worn only cutoffs, and I'd been unable to take my mesmerized eyes off the muscles rippling in his naked arms and shoulders. I thought I'd never seen anything or anyone more beautiful than this eighteen-year-old Adonis. I knew I wanted Egan, and that somehow I would get him. At sixteen, I didn't really understand what that meant. I soon found out.

"Ferry's about to dock," Mrs. Hadditer said.

"What?" I turned to her, my thoughts swimming in the past.

"I said, ferry's—"

"Oh, oh yes..." I smiled. "Can I help you with your things?"

"You could carry my bag and take my arm. I never feel too steady on my pins going down those metal stairs. Wouldn't do to pitch forward and land on my head, now, would it?"

An image of Grandfather doing exactly that flashed through my mind. "No, no, it wouldn't," I stammered.

I confess that once I'd guided Mrs. Hadditer across the gangplank, I was anxious to be on my way. But she seemed reluctant to let me go. "Are you off to your lawyer's now?" she asked, peering up at me from the open door of the cab I'd hailed to take her to her doctor's.

"No. My appointment's not until later this morning. I caught the early ferry so I could get in a bit of shopping. If I'm going to be spending any time on the island, I'll need a few odds and ends."

"Do you think you'll be staying?"

"I won't know until I speak with Grandfather's lawyer. But I'm willing to risk buying some shampoo and toothpaste on the off chance."

She reached out and patted my hand. "I never got to know you when you stayed with Nate that summer, Katy. But what I've seen of you, I like. I hope you do stay on and that you'll come see me. Will you?"

"Of course. I'm flattered by the invitation." I was touched.

Secretively, she glanced from side to side. "One other thing, Katy. If you do stay on, be careful."

"Careful? Of what?"

She pulled the door shut. "Just be careful," she repeated through the crack of the open window. Then she tapped the cabdriver's shoulder with the handle of her cane and the taxi moved off.

I stood in its exhaust, gazing after it as it disappeared around the corner. Finally, I shook my head, got my bearings and strolled the few blocks into the main part of town. As I walked, I kept a lookout, half expecting that I might run into Egan. It seemed likely that he and the *Nighthawk* had been headed for Sandusky, too. I mused on our meeting the night before. The terror that had streaked through me when I'd seen that light in the basement door still shook me. I was even more shaken by the reaction I'd had when Egan had climbed the stairs toward me.

Sleep had evaded me after Egan stalked back into the night. For long hours, I'd huddled on the couch in the living room. My weary eyes had stared through the window at moonlit shadows, and I'd listened to the rhythmic *shush* of the water on the rocks—listened and remembered. But it wasn't just memories that kept me from sleep. Every now and then, I'd go to the window and search the darkness. Though I'd seen nothing, I hadn't been able to shake the feeling that someone or something watched me—watched and judged.

I spent the next hour in Sandusky going from drugstore to hardware store to grocery. Though I kept an eye out for Egan, I never saw him. Finally, it was time for the lawyer's office.

Since I'd given up on the idea of a meeting with Egan, catching sight of him coming out of Kandefer's building came as a surprise. Obviously preoccupied with some none-too-pleasing thoughts, he didn't notice me half a block away.

As he let the glass-paned door slam shut behind him, a frown cut deep grooves between his black eyebrows. He'd slung a dark sportcoat over his jeans and sweater. Under his arm he cradled what looked like a black metal shoe box. As he strode off down the street in the opposite direction, I gazed after him. Why was he there?

A few minutes later, Grandfather's lawyer surprised me, as well. I had expected an older man, but Fred Kandefer had to be close to my own age. He had a head of thinning, sandy hair and a curious, darting gaze that looked me up and down with disquieting attention.

"Ah, Ms. Conroy," he exclaimed after his receptionist showed me into his paneled office. He came out from behind his desk with his hand extended. "I'm delighted to meet you, though sorry it has to be under such sad circumstances. I've heard a great deal about you."

"You have? From whom?"

"From your grandfather. On the occasions when I've crossed to Big Bass to help him with legal matters, he's talked about you at length."

"He has?" I couldn't have been more amazed if Kandefer had informed me that Grandfather's hobby was pole-vaulting.

When I stayed with him my sixteenth summer, he'd ignored me. Since that disastrous two months, he'd never contacted me in any way. No birthday or Christmas cards, no phone calls to inquire after my health. I'd received no reply to the two letters of apology my father had made me write him. After that, I'd balked at further overtures, wanting desperately to dismiss the whole painful episode from my mind.

Now it shames me to admit that I hadn't tried contacting Grandfather again until my father died. When I'd called Grandfather to explain the circumstances and invite him to the funeral, all I'd got for my pains was a gruff refusal. He'd informed me he was too old to travel and dropped the receiver like a hot brick. Dad had been my grandfather's only child.

"What did Grandfather say about me?" I asked cautiously.

After motioning me to a seat, Kandefer retreated to the leather swivel chair behind his desk. "Ah, let me see. He said you were a successful newscaster in Detroit. He was very proud of you. I particularly remember his saying that you were the most successful of his offspring, and by far the easiest on the eyes. With that I must say I agree."

I managed to acknowledge the lawyer's compliment, but just barely. Hearing that Grandfather had bragged about me came as a stunner. While I coped with it, Kandefer rummaged through a stack of papers. "Are you staying at your grandfather's house now?"

"Yes, I spent last night at the castle."

"The castle?"

"That's what the islanders call it."

"I can see why. It's a magnificent old place." He shook his head. "Water on three sides, a view of the harbor just below."

"The Conroy who acquired the land and built the house back in the last century was a retired naval officer. Since then, five generations of Conroys have lived there—fishermen, failed entrepreneurs, you name it."

"Your grandfather was a doctor, wasn't he?"

"Yes." I knew from my father's stories that the first Conroy had been a man of means. Of his descendants, Nate had been the only "success." In his youth, he'd served in World War I and then acquired a medical degree. He went back to the island and established a practice. Close to a half century ago, soon after my grandmother died, he'd stopped practicing. He'd devoted himself to local history, to making a nuisance of himself at town meetings and to disapproving of his son.

After leaving the island for the state university, my father had never returned.

Kandefer glanced at me over the top of his glasses and then handed me a copy of Grandfather's will. "Excepting a small bequest to the historical society and a token to Mr. Egan Halpern, you are his sole heir."

While Kandefer went on about the property, I stared at the document clutched in my hands. My eyes swam and my heart thudded. I hadn't dared to hope for anything like this. Most of his life, my grandfather had seemed to disdain me. Now, in death, he'd thrown me a lifeline. And he'd thrown it when I needed it most desperately.

"With the stipulation that in the event you should decide to sell the property, it may only be sold to a party who has resided on the island for at least twenty years," Kandefer was saying.

That got my attention and I looked up. "Twenty years! But very few people who've been on Big Bass that long could afford to buy the castle."

Kandefer *tch-tched*. "Nevertheless, that was your grandfather's provision, and he stated it very clearly here. Now, except for the boxes, that about wraps it up."

"The boxes?"

"Yes. Your grandfather left you and Mr. Egan Halpern each a sealed container. Earlier this morning, I met with Mr. Halpern and transferred his. I have yours right here." Kandefer fished a shoe-box-size black metal container from a drawer and set it down on the desk between us. I laid an exploratory finger on its lid. As my skin came in contact with the clammy metal, I thought of coffins and old bones.

"It's locked."

"Yes. No key, I'm afraid. You'll have to pry it open."

"You said you'd already given Mr. Halpern his. Was it locked, as well?"

"Both boxes were sealed and I have no idea what's inside either. That will be for you and Mr. Halpern to discover. A little mystery." Kandefer smiled wryly.

But I couldn't smile back. The finger I had rested on the dull black metal felt cold, and in sudden reaction I yanked it back. It was almost as if the box held something evil, something from which my flesh instinctively shrank.

Back out on the street, I wedged the box amongst the purchases in my shopping bag and tucked the will in my big leather purse. Grandfather had been proud of me. His house was mine. I, who a few days earlier hadn't known where to turn, now owned valuable property. The shocks of the last hour were too much. My stomach quivered, and as my thoughts spun, I walked blindly.

Some inner pilot guided me back toward the harbor. The screams of gulls and the blare of a foghorn restored me to my present situation and I looked around. Across from a marina was a white-frame sandwich shop. Realizing how badly I needed a cup of coffee, I steered myself in its direction. As I opened the door to walk in, my eye caught a sleek black sloop moored at the dock. The *Nighthawk,* I thought. Egan is around here somewhere.

So, it didn't surprise me when he pushed the door open and strode in. I had just finished a bowl of chowder and was sipping coffee, which managed to be both burned and watery at the same time. While he crossed to my table, I studied him. He wore jeans and a sturdy gray wool crewneck sweater. The black jacket and the box I'd spotted him with earlier were nowhere in sight.

Overhead, the fluorescent lights brought out the gray in his black curls and emphasized the harsh lines that now carved his face. None of that made him any less attractive. He was still the kind of man that women stare at, witness the young waitress who eagerly welcomed him.

"We meet again." He stood looking down at me with hooded eyes.

"So we do."

"Mind if I sit down?"

"Not at all, though I was just about to pay my bill." I glanced at my watch. "Next ferry should be leaving in about twenty minutes."

Egan's hand stilled on the chair he'd been about to pull out. "You're returning to the island?"

"Yes. Where else?" I said lightly.

"I thought you might be going back to where you came from, back to Detroit."

I shook my head, realizing as I said the words just how true they were. "Detroit isn't my home anymore. After today, my home is on Big Bass."

Egan lifted an eyebrow. "Kandefer mentioned he was meeting with you this morning. Does that mean Nate left you his property?"

"Yes, he did. That and a black box." I glanced at the shopping bag on the floor beside my feet and so did Egan. I thought I saw his mouth tighten and then relax. He smiled. Real amusement gleamed between his lashes. "Well, well," he drawled, "guess I'm the Big Bass welcoming committee." He rubbed his jaw. "I have a proposal. Since you're ready to get back home, and so am I, why not come with me on the *Nighthawk?*" He cocked a thumb in the direction of his boat, which could be seen through the fly-specked window.

"I don't know."

"Why not? Save you the price of a ferry ticket, and as I recall, you used to like sailing."

I felt myself blush.

Egan saw and cocked his head. "Are you afraid to be alone on a sailboat with me, Katy?"

"Of course not. Why should I be?"

He didn't answer that. Just waited. We both knew what had happened between us on his sailboat when we were kids.

Abruptly, I stood and gathered up my purse and shopping bag. "Of course I'll come," I said. "Just lead the way."

ABOARD THE *NIGHTHAWK*, Egan started the inboard engine and then began casting off lines. When I offered to help, he let his gaze play over my skirt and Italian suede boots and laughed. "You just sit there and look like a *Vogue* model. I'm used to handling the *Nighthawk* on my own."

Though he was right about my not being dressed for crewing, I resented the remark about looking like a model. I'm tall and blond, and when I anchored the news in Detroit, people described me as a young Candice Bergen. But descriptions like that never gave me much pleasure. Since kindergarten, when I was taunted as teacher's pet, people have insinuated that what success I've had has been due to my looks. In my opinion, my appearance has been more of a hindrance than a help.

Once we were out of the harbor, Egan let me take the tiller while he hauled up the jib and mainsail. "You've got a beautiful boat," I complimented when he came back, retrieved the tiller from me and cut the engine. After its last sputter, the only sound was the snap of the wind against the sails and the rush of the water as the hull knifed through it.

"Thanks."

"Did you design and build it yourself?"

"I did."

"It doesn't surprise me that you've become a success-ful boat builder. What ever happened to the *Wind Lass?*"

Egan gave the winch a turn to adjust the angle of the mainsail. "You remember that old wreck?"

A woman doesn't forget where she received her first important kiss or who gave it to her. I'd never forget the *Wind Lass.* Aloud, I said, "It wasn't a wreck."

"Sure was. Piece of junk I rescued from the worms for pennies and spent two years gluing and nailing before she'd even stay afloat. It was several years after you left the island before I could afford any better."

"I hear you've done very well for yourself."

"Who told you that?"

"Flo Hadditer. I ran into her on the ferry coming over."

"Just what did she say?"

"Only that your business is doing very well and that you're an island success story."

"Well, I don't sleep in a shack anymore. These days, the Halperns live on the right side of the bay. In fact, you may know my house. It's the Macaster place."

I knew it well, a fine old Georgian-style frame house overlooking the water. On the way to the ferry this morning, I'd noticed that it had been beautifully re-stored, painted a pale yellow with white trim, its lawn a velvety well-groomed green. If Egan could afford the Macaster place, he'd done very well indeed. Of course, he'd told me where he lived because he wanted me to know that about him.

"I hear you're quite the success story yourself," he said. "Newscaster in Detroit, isn't it?"

"I used to anchor the six o'clock news."

"Used to? Does that mean you've gone on to bigger and better things?"

"No. In fact, at the moment I'm unemployed."

He gazed at me speculatively. "Sounds as if there's a story behind that."

"There is."

"But it's not one you're inclined to tell?"

"Not at the moment. What about you? I met your son yesterday." Briefly, I described the circumstances of our encounter. "He's a lot like you," I concluded. "How many children do you and your wife have now?"

"There's only Rex," Egan said stiffly. "His mother died a few years back."

The news shocked me. "Oh, Egan, I'm sorry. I had no idea."

"After Nate's funeral, I saw you talking to Betty Mc-Kenny. She's always been talented at passing on news, so I'm surprised she didn't tell you."

"We only spoke briefly. I haven't seen her since."

"Too busy collecting your inheritance?" he murmured as he adjusted the downhaul. The shifty wind behind us had been gaining strength, and now we were having to raise our voices to hear over it.

"Yes, as a matter of fact."

"Since you're out of work, you must be pretty pleased that Nate left you his place."

"Surprised and very grateful."

Egan fixed his gaze on the angle of the sail. "My antenna picks up stations in Detroit. I saw your news show a couple of times. Seemed to me you did a pretty decent job. It oughtn't to take you long to find the same kind of work someplace else."

"Thanks for the vote of confidence, but broadcast positions are tough to nail these days." Even tougher when word had gone out on the grapevine that you're a troublemaker, I thought to myself. I knew it wouldn't be easy to find employment in my chosen profession any-time soon.

"You really plan on staying on the island, living in the castle?"

"It's my home now. I own it."

He shot me a look of disbelief. "A woman like you could never be content living in an isolated place like Big Bass."

"Just what do you mean, 'a woman like me'?"

Egan's smile was wry. "Sophisticated, used to city lights, the limelight, the high life. A month stuck on Big Bass and you'll be crazy with boredom."

Though I'm hardly the varnished butterfly Egan de-scribed, I was actually a little nervous about the island's isolation. Life there was going to be a lot different from what I'd been accustomed to. "Maybe," I said cau-tiously, "maybe not. Since I'm out of work, I don't re-ally have much choice."

"You could sell out. The castle sits on a prime piece of land. Its price ought to give you a pretty good stake."

"A provision in Grandfather's will makes it hard to sell for top dollar."

"What provision is that?"

"I'm not supposed to sell the castle to anyone who hasn't been a permanent, full-time resident of the island for at least twenty years."

For a moment, Egan looked thunderstruck. Then, perhaps to give himself time to think, he began making more adjustments in the sails.

We were wing and wing now, taking full advantage of the following wind. But the breeze was unreliable, rak-ing cat's-paws on the slate-gray water as it spat in sudden puffs and gusts. I had long ago pushed my collar up around my throat. Now I wrapped my arms across my chest. I was shaking, I realized. Was it from the damp chill slicing through my clothing? Or was it from the tension of being alone like this with Egan and of reviving feelings and animosities that I had thought dead and buried?

With his hand on the tiller, Egan settled back across from me in the cockpit. The wind had whipped up his curls and his eyelashes were clumped together in spikes from the spray flung up as we plowed along.

"Sorry for the bumpy ride," he said.

"That's okay."

He glanced at the shopping bag next to me which, up until that moment, he had ignored—or pretended to. "Your black box looks identical to mine."

"Does it? Where is yours?" The boxes had been in the back of my mind all during this trip. Perhaps they had been in the back of Egan's, as well. Or perhaps, they'd been in the forefront. Maybe they were the real reason that he'd invited me aboard his boat. And now we were as alone on the *Nighthawk* as any two people could be—only empty gray water heaving around us.

"My box is down below, tucked away safe and sound."

"Have you opened it yet?"

"Not yet. You?"

I shook my head and felt the back of my neck prickle. Just how important did Egan think these boxes were, I wondered. "Not yet."

He sat forward, watching me closely. "I have a proposition for you, Katy."

"Oh?" Interior warning signals jangled.

"I'll take the castle off your hands, and give you a decent price, too." He named a figure that sounded fair, though I couldn't be sure since I didn't know the island's real estate market.

"That's a lot of money."

"Yes, it is, and if you should decide to accept, I have only one requirement."

"What requirement is that?"

"My offer is for the house and everything in it, including the black box just as it is now. Don't tamper with it. Give it to me when you sign over the deed to the castle. Then you can walk away with a big wad of money in your pocket and no ties to the past."

I stared into Egan's eyes and felt more chilled than I could ever be made to feel by the cutting wind that lifted my hair. Now I had no doubt why he'd invited me aboard the *Nighthawk*. The question echoing in my mind was why had I been foolish enough to accept?

"What makes you think I don't want ties to the past?"

The lines of his face stilled and hardened. "Your behavior for the last fourteen years makes that abundantly clear, wouldn't you say? Your grandfather had to die before you troubled to show your face around here again. If I hadn't happened to see you commentating the news one night, I'd have thought you'd dropped off the face of the earth."

"Grandfather considered me a nuisance. He let me know he didn't want me coming back to trouble him. And after what happened between you and me, did you really think I'd be phoning or sending cards?"

"No, Katy, I didn't," Egan replied harshly. "After what happened, I figured you'd never want to see me or this island again. My offer makes that easy for you. So how about it?"

I could tell that he expected me to accept his proposition. And part of me wanted to. In so many ways, it would make things easy. But another part of me rose up in rebellion. Generations of Conroys had lived in the castle, and now it was mine. With Grandfather's passing, I had no living relatives left—only this heritage. The castle was the first home I'd ever owned, and I wasn't ready to part with it yet. But something else was eating at me.

"Just what's in these boxes that's so important to you?" How badly did he want mine, I wondered. Badly enough to take it by force? There had always been a ruthless streak in Egan. That was part of what had attracted me to him. But there had been times when his wildness frightened me.

Egan blinked. "As I told you, I haven't opened mine yet. For all I know, it's empty and so is yours."

"But you don't think so, do you? And obviously Grandfather considered them important, or he wouldn't have left them to us this way. Maybe it's not the castle you really want. Maybe it's just the boxes you're after."

That was just a wild accusation, but it appeared to have flicked Egan on the raw. His eyes slitted. "That's crazy. Of course I want the castle."

"Why? You already own one of the biggest houses on the island. What do you need another one for?"

"The castle sits on a prime piece of property."

"So, it's the land you're after?"

"Among other things."

My thoughts fretted like fire horses hearing the clang of a bell. "Things like the satisfaction of tossing all my family's possessions on the junk heap, things like being able to brag that you've dispossessed the last of the Conroys and now own the most prestigious piece of property on the island? If you could do that, you'd certainly have your revenge, wouldn't you?"

"What makes you think I want revenge, Katy?"

"The expression I saw in your eyes when I said good-bye fourteen years ago."

"You have a long memory."

"I think we both have long memories."

Despite the wind that was howling around us, a faint flush crept into Egan's lean cheeks. "All right, Katy, generations of Conroys have turned up their noses at generations of Halperns. Your grandfather and I became friends, but there was a time when he called my mother and me trash. I won't deny I'd get pleasure out of seeing you turn the keys of his castle over to me, but that's not why I'm willing to shell out hard cash for it. It really is the land I want."

I began to understand. "If you don't intend on living in the castle, are you planning to tear it down?"

When he didn't answer, I surged up and stood rocking on the balls of my feet to keep my balance on the tossing boat while I glared down at him. "That's it, isn't it? You want to tear it down and build something else there."

"It's not as if the castle is a national treasure. The time is right for some new development on the harbor," he replied tightly.

"What development? A hotel, a shopping center, condos?" I pictured my family home bulldozed and replaced by some glass-and-concrete tourist trap, and indignation flooded me. "How dare you?" I exclaimed, so angry, I wanted to scratch his eyes out. I took a step toward him, half meaning to do exactly that, when the wind dropped abruptly.

"Sit down, Katy. It's going to shift."

Even as the words came out of his mouth, the wind snapped around to the other side of the sail. The boat jibed and the boom came crashing across the cockpit. I ducked, but not soon enough. A stinging blow to my head sent me flying sideways. My arms flailed and I lost all sense of balance. *I'm going into the water,* I thought as I toppled backward. I was half off the boat, my feet too far off the floorboards to gain purchase, when Egan's hand clamped my arm.

He leaned over me and stared down into my face, and as I stared back, I saw that his eyes were the same deadly shade of blue as blade steel. His grip was all that stood between me and the cold gray water, which lashed at my hair and spattered icy drops on my neck.

Through my sick dizziness and the pain in my head, I knew I was helpless and in deadly danger. What if Egan let go of me? What if I fell into the lake? I was not a particularly strong swimmer. It wouldn't take long for me to drown.

"Egan, don't!" I tried to cry, but the sound stuck in my throat. All I could do was stare into his eyes until my very soul seemed to drown in the lightless depths of his pupils. I felt his hand loosen slightly, his fingers shift. I knew he was going to let me fall.

Then I heard the sharp blast of the ferry's airhorn. Egan glanced to his left and then back down at me. With one swift tug, he yanked me upright and back onto the seat of the cockpit. "Sit there while I put the sails to rights," he commanded. "Then we'll see to your head."

I crouched in the cockpit, shivering, dizzy. Finally, I looked up at Egan. He had the boat back under control now. The sails were tight against the wind, and in the distance I could see the dark line of Big Bass. After giving a winch a half turn, he looked at me over his shoulder. "All right?"

"No." I was shivering so badly I could barely get the word out.

"Head hurt?"

"Yes, but that's not what's really bothering me. You almost let me fall in, didn't you, Egan? And if I had fallen in, I would have drowned."

Though the wind continued blowing around our ears, we seemed in that moment to be caught in a bell jar of dead silence. I saw Egan's throat work. "You're mistaken. I would never let you drown, Katy," he said with deadly quiet. "That would be a waste of a beautiful woman, and I don't believe in waste."

Suddenly, a chill ran up my spine, and for the first time, a suspicion that had been rattling around in the back of my mind came to the forefront. What if Grandfather's death hadn't been accidental? What if he'd been pushed down those stairs—maybe even by someone he'd come to trust?

Chapter Three

"Nothing fancy," Betty said. "Just good old spaghetti and meatballs in sauce out of a jar. But I'd love to have you come talk over old times."

Clutching the receiver to my ear, I grinned. "Sounds great. What shall I bring?"

"Just bring yourself."

Depite my old girlfriend's kindly injunction, I stopped at the village market and picked up a bottle of the island-grown burgundy. When I showed up at Betty's door that evening, I carried the wine in one hand and balanced a chocolate cake in the other.

"Aren't you sweet!" After setting the cake on a table, Betty threw her arms around my neck and gave me a hug.

"Not really," I said. "I got back from Detroit with a carload of my stuff Wednesday. The last couple of days, I've been rattling around the castle unpacking and trying to figure out what to do. It's been lonely."

"Spooky, too, I bet."

"Well, yes, now that you mention it."

Betty rolled her eyes. "There's just something so creepy about that house. Glad I'm not staying alone in it."

"Well, I own it now, so I don't really have much choice. Anyhow, I'm really grateful for the invite out."

Betty, her grandfather, her two adolescent sons and their fifteen-year-old cousin, Mark, lived in a small cottage off a graveled road on the north end of the island. The property had been in her family for three generations and showed its age. Its porch sagged and its narrow clapboards, scoured by the brutal winter wind that came whistling off the lake, were badly in need of a fresh coat of paint.

"We moved back here after Bob took off," she said, naming her delinquent husband with a bitter grimace.

"Well, your grandfather probably feels more at home here," I offered.

"Think so?"

We both looked over at the old man slumped in a wheelchair in a corner of the homey little living room. Bill Wiblin was almost as old as my grandfather had been. Age, however, was just about the only thing Bill had in common with spry, cantankerous Nate. In his early twenties, Bill's life had been blighted by an accident. He'd lived out most of his years in a comatose state.

I remembered Betty's grandfather from my earlier stay on the island. Maybe his white hair hadn't been quite so thin then. Otherwise, he seemed unchanged by the passage of well over a decade.

We ate dinner around a Formica table in the kitchen. While I cleaned up the dishes, Betty put the old man to bed. After the boys had spilled back into the living room to watch television, and Betty had returned from her chore, I told her how much I respected her toughness.

"It can't be easy, raising three boys all on your own and nursing your grandfather. You should get a medal."

"I'd settle for a big fat check." Betty dropped into one of the metal chairs surrounding the Formica table. "Nobody on this island is about to write one, though. Mom sure didn't get any rewards for being a saint. I used to watch my poor mother take care of Gramps and wonder how she did it. Now I know. Ironic, isn't it, that he's outlived both her and his son?" She shook her head. "Well, if Gramps lives so long he has to rely on Mark, Rich or Rusty to bathe and feed him, he's going to be out of luck. In the responsibility department, my two take after their dad. And Mark—" She rolled her eyes. "He's just as shiftless as my older brother was."

"What happened to him and his wife?"

"Car accident. Nobody else left to take care of Mark, so I got elected."

We both fell silent, listening to the low roar of the television and the boys giggling in the other room.

"Since I can't offer a big fat check, will you settle for another glass of wine?" I asked. Betty nodded and grinned tiredly. "You know," she said as I refilled her glass, "during dinner we yakked about the past. What about the future? What's your scheme for the castle, now that you've inherited it?"

I plopped into a chair catty-corner from her and stretched out my legs. "To be honest, I haven't found the answer to that question. In the meantime, though, I have plenty to keep me busy."

"I bet. Dusting that old museum of Nate's would keep an army busy."

"I intend to do a lot more than just dust the place."

"Like what?" Betty sat up, her eyes starting to spark with interest.

"First, the castle needs a thorough cleaning."

"You'll be pawing through piles of junk for weeks."

"Yes, and getting rid of most of it."

"Before you cart your throwaways over to the dump, give me a chance to look them over, will you?"

"Sure."

Betty laughed. "Oh, it's not because I have any empty rooms to fill up here. I've been thinking about opening an antique shop."

"Really?"

"There are a couple on the island now, and they do darn well during tourist season. You know the old saying—one man's trash is another man's—"

Mark stuck his square blond head around the corner. "Gramps is making a racket in his room."

"Lordy," Betty groaned. "I'd better go see what's up. Stay put. I'll be right back."

"What's wrong?" I asked when she returned a few minutes later.

"Nightmare. Surprising, isn't it? To look at his blank face, you'd think nothing was going on in that poor old head of his. Yet Gramps has terrible nightmares. It's as if he's reliving something awful."

"Maybe his accident?" I asked.

"I suppose that's it."

I fingered the stem of my wineglass. "What kind of accident did your grandfather have to make him the way he is?"

Betty took a long sip. "You mean you never heard the story?"

"No, I never did. I was only on the island a few weeks, remember? And except for you and Egan, I didn't associate much with the other island kids."

"I guess it was because you and Egan were so thick that you never heard."

"Heard what? What does your grandfather's accident have to do with Egan?"

"Not with Egan himself, but with his family. His grandfather, Rafe, to be exact. You must know that Egan Halpern comes from a long line of no-accounts."

"I know his people were poor, and that he's had a lot of prejudice to overcome here on the island," I replied stiffly. My grandfather had once described Egan and his relatives to me as trash. I'd glimpsed his mother only once. She'd been a pale-faced, poorly dressed woman. Though I'd never visited their house, I'd heard it was something close to a shack.

"Oh, it wasn't just their being poor," Betty replied. She slipped off her sneakers and put her feet up on a chair. "All the Halpern women were loose, and all the men were drunks and bums."

"That's a little strong, isn't it?"

"Not if half the stories I've heard are true. It looked as if Egan was following in the tradition when he married Debbie. You've got to remember what her reputation was on the island."

I remembered all right. When Egan was a teenager, Debbie Wiley had been a luscious twenty-one-year-old temptress. It wasn't until the end of my relationship with Egan that I learned Debbie had been his steady up until just a few weeks before he met me.

Aloud, I said, "She was a beauty."

"Well, she certainly filled out her bra."

I took a playful swat at Betty's knee. "With that black wavy hair and those wicked green eyes, she was gorgeous."

"No more gorgeous than you. If Egan hadn't already broken up with her, he would have dropped her like a hot potato when you came along."

"Tell me something, Betty. Were they happy together after they married?"

"I don't think so. But who's to say? They kept to themselves and you know what a closemouthed son-of-a-gun Egan can be. To tell the truth, during those years I was having too many problems with my own love life to pay much attention to his and Debbie's."

Hungry for more details about Egan, I wanted to ask why and how Debbie had died. I wanted to know how Egan had coped with her death. Had he mourned her? Was he still mourning her? But part of me found the subject too painful to probe.

"Getting back to my story," Betty said as she set down her empty glass, "according to island gossip, of all the no-good Halperns, Rafe Halpern, Egan's grandfather, was the standout."

"Oh, really? What was so terrible about him?"

"Let's see." Betty began counting off on her fingers. "He was wild with a capital *W.* Always getting into trouble. A real ladies' man and very handsome. People who remember him say Egan inherited his looks. So Rafe must have been one heck of a looker. Anyhow, not only did a lot of women make fools of themselves over him, men liked him, too. That's where Gramps comes in."

"Your grandfather was friends with Rafe?"

"They were drinking buddies. Actually, at that time I think Gramps was considered a reprobate himself. Anyhow, one morning in 1927, they found Gramps lying on a dock, half-dead from a gunshot wound. Rafe had disappeared from the island."

"Your grandfather never recovered from his injuries?"

"We Wiblins are too tough for our own good, I guess. He lived when no one expected him to, but just barely."

"What about Rafe Halpern? Did he ever turn up?"

"No, never." Betty drained her glass and set it on the table. "Rafe was never heard from again. And a good thing. Because if he had come back, my grandmother or my mother would have taken after him with a gun and shot him, they both hated him so much."

Not long after that, I thanked Betty for the spaghetti dinner and the hospitality. We hugged and promised to get together again soon.

"Remember to give me a buzz when you start shoveling out junk."

"Oh, I will."

"Sure I can't give you a ride back?" she asked.

"Oh, no. It's a pretty evening. After all those years of big-city living, I really appreciate the scale of this island. Almost everything is within walking distance."

As I strolled home, I mulled over what I'd learned about Bill Wiblin's injury. I felt so sorry for the poor old man who'd had his life devastated at such a young age. He and Rafe Halpern would both have been barely in their twenties when it happened. Not much more than kids.

The night was pleasantly windless, and I felt comfortable in the wool blazer I wore with my jeans. The moon and stars shone like bright silver in the cloudless sky. Ambling along the tree-lined country road that led back to town, I tried picturing what the island would have been like in the late twenties. It would have been a lot different from the prettied-up tourist retreat of today. Fishing would have been a much more important part of the local economy. Then, too, with Canada so close during that Prohibition era, I suspected there would have been bootlegging.

It wasn't hard to imagine how two wild young men, who'd had too much bootleg liquor, might quarrel. Had Rafe shot Bill and then left him for dead? Obviously that's what Betty and the other islanders thought. Given that Rafe had disappeared the same night, it certainly looked as if that was the case.

What had become of Rafe? Had he run away leaving a pregnant young wife who'd been Egan's grandmother? Or had he been killed, too? Was his body buried on the island or lying at the bottom of the lake?

How awful for Egan to grow up with a violent family history that was the talk of the island and to have to deal with suspicions and resentments created before he was even born. As a child, he and his family had been snickered at and scorned because of things done decades earlier. Of course, Egan was too stiff-necked to let any of his hurts show. But I knew they were there and that they ran deep.

By now I'd reached town. As I crossed the park, I could hear bursts of music from the Canopy. The popular tavern had been built to look like a circus tent with a red-and-white-striped roof. It fit in well with its posh new neighbors. Unlike the newcomer businesses that now lined Main Street, the Canopy had been a Big Bass landmark for decades.

I remembered it well from that summer so long ago. And I remembered well how Debbie Wiley had presided over its bar. Her swaying hips and confident smile had tantalized all the men, local and tourist variety, who hung out there swapping sports lore and draining pitchers of beer. To me, she had seemed so mature, so wickedly sure of herself.

I headed across the park that fronted the harbor. As I approached the seawall, I gazed out over the water. The moon had embossed it with silver tracks. Silhouetted against its luminous disk, I saw the black profile of a sailboat with a lean hull and sails softly bellied in the light night air. It might have been a ghostly pirate ship, so romantically unreal it looked. But instinct told me whose boat it was.

I walked along the seawall toward home. As I lagged along, I kept an eye on the craft, mentally charting its progress and waiting to see if it came in where I thought it would.

I arrived at the edge of the Macaster property just as the *Nighthawk* glided to the dock. If I'd hurried on past, Egan might not have seen me, busy as he and his son were tying off lines. As it was, Egan didn't notice me standing rooted to the spot until almost five minutes later.

"Katy," he exclaimed. Lightly, he jumped from the deck to the wooden dock. "Is that you standing in the middle of my yard?"

Rex gave me a startled look and almost dropped the duffel bag his father had just passed to him.

"It's me, all right. I hope you don't mind my trespassing on your property."

"Well, now, that all depends on the trespasser, doesn't it?"

Through the moon-streaked shadows, Egan's deep voice floated up to me. Its husky note sent a shiver down my back. I stuffed my hands in my jeans pockets and told myself that if I planned to live on Big Bass, I had to make peace with Egan and our past. Why not start now?

"I saw the *Nighthawk* coming in and couldn't resist watching you dock it," I said. "You and your son really have the operation coordinated. The two of you make a very handy crew."

Egan dropped a prideful arm around his son's shoulders. Rex, with his well-proportioned build and handsome dark head, looked like a miniature version of his father. For the briefest flash, it occurred to me that if Egan and I had succeeded in getting married that night we ran away together, we might have had a boy like Rex. Rex might have been my son.

Rex looked at his father worshipfully. "My dad and I sail even in bad storms," he declared proudly. "The *Nighthawk* is the best boat on the lake and we're the best sailors." He strutted forward to get a better look at me. "You're Miss Conroy. I talked to you a few days back, remember?"

"Sure do. You said something about helping me cart junk to the dump. Well, I could use a hand this weekend. How about it?"

"Sure. You mean over at the castle?" When I nodded, he asked, "What kind of stuff? Furniture or just odd stuff?"

"I've only started cleaning, so I can't say for certain. Nothing we can't manage together, though."

"Well, I charge four dollars a trip."

"Hey, when you first asked for the job, you told me three."

Rex grinned impishly. "Inflation."

Egan's hand came down on his son's shoulder again. This time, it was more heavy than prideful. "A deal is a deal, son. If you told Ms. Conroy you'd help her out for three dollars a trip, then that's it. Got me?"

"Sure, Dad. I was just kidding, anyway. When do you want me there?" Rex asked in a more subdued tone.

"Nine in the morning too early?"

"That'll be fine," Egan answered. Turning to the boy, he said sternly, "Now it's time for you to get in and do your homework. Am I right?"

"Yeah, I guess."

We watched Rex cross the lawn and climb the steps to the house. "He reminds me of you," I murmured.

"Why? Because he's so cocky?"

I shot Egan a sideways glance. "He does seem to have inherited your swagger. But there's more. He's smart and enterprising, a born survivor. So, obviously, are you."

"Why, thank you, ma'am. I take that as a real compliment, both to me and my son." He frowned. "Actually, a lot of that attitude of his is put on for show. Rex doesn't always get along with the other island kids."

"Why? He's smart and good-looking. I'd have thought he'd be a natural leader."

Egan snorted. "You may own the biggest house on the island now, Katy, but you're still an outsider. You don't understand what it's like to grow up here. Big Bass isn't a city full of people who don't know one another. Families have lived here for generations. They know everything about one another, including whose father was a drunk and whose mother cleaned houses and took in other people's laundry."

I knew he referred to the Halperns. "Then everybody must appreciate how hard you had to fight for your success. You must be greatly admired."

"Maybe there's some admiration, but there's also resentment. Here on Big Bass, you don't live down the people whose name you carry. When I was a kid, I learned that. Now Rex is learning it, too."

As I gazed up at Egan, I thought of the story I'd heard at Betty's. That, too, was part of his history.

"Does your mother live with you?" I asked.

"She wanted her own place, so I bought Tall Oaks cottage for her. Rex and I take a meal with her there at least once a week."

"Feeling as you do about island prejudice, I'm surprised you haven't moved to the mainland. Is your mother the reason?"

Egan's dark eyebrows ruffled. "Part of the reason, I suppose. Mother's too old and set in her ways to uproot, and I couldn't leave her here with no family. But it's not just that. Big Bass is my home. I was born here. With all its faults, the island's in my blood and I won't be pushed out."

I gazed at the stubborn set of Egan's jaw. What he'd said about the weight of history on this tiny enclosed world disturbed me. Egan and I had a history. For the moment, we were politely ignoring it, but we could never forget it. Then there was the history of different times and people. Echoes of other lives saturated the island's atmosphere and continued to influence it weirdly. I'd felt this at the castle and I'd felt it while I talked to Betty. Suddenly, a heavy sense of foreboding weighed on me.

"What have you been doing with yourself these past few days?" Egan asked. As he lounged no more than a foot away, I felt his eyes graze over me. He'd jammed his left hand into the pocket of his jeans. Moonlight filtering down through a cloud carved his face into sharp angles. He smelled of wind and the lake. As I caught his masculine scent on the night air, it stirred powerful memories. Against my will, my heart quickened.

"Other than closing up my apartment in Detroit, I've just been poking around in the castle. Believe me, there's plenty to do there."

"No doubt. In the course of this exploring, did you open your black box?"

He asked the question casually, too casually. I had been distracted, fighting back a desire to reach out to him and say something foolish. Now, every sense I possessed drew back at attention. "No, I haven't."

"Why not? You've had the time. Aren't you curious?"

"I'm curious, all right. But whenever I go near the thing, I get a bad feeling. I haven't been able to bring myself to pry it open."

"A bad feeling?" Egan laughed. "I didn't know you were the superstitious type, Katy."

"You don't know me very well, do you, Egan?"

"I'd say we got pretty well acquainted when we were kids."

"Not really. If you think about it, we never really talked much."

"There's more than one form of communication."

As I met Egan's eyes, I felt myself flush. "Listen, Egan, why do we keep beating around the bush like this? Why don't we just say it and get it over with? You blame me because I talked you into eloping with me and then chickened out when my father caught us."

"You shouldn't have lied to me about your age, Katy."

"You're right, I shouldn't have. I was a stupid sixteen-year-old with a crush on the island hunk, and I behaved like an idiot. Those days are over. Can't we put them behind us and start fresh? We're neighbors now. Can't we be just that—friends and neighbors?"

As we regarded each other, my question hung between us. He reached out and touched my chin with his forefinger. "Standing there with the moon turning your hair to silver and the breeze blowing it around your face, you look exactly as you did then. And then I thought you were an angel. No, Katy, we can never be friends. Friends move toward each other from neutral ground, and we can never do that. As for the neighbor bit, I don't expect that to last long. You'll never stay on Big Bass.''

I yanked back from his touch. Holding myself rigid while I tried to quell the trembling that had started in my legs, I asked, ''What about your box? Have you opened it?''

''Yes, I have.''

''Well, are you going to tell me what you found inside?''

He smiled tightly. ''I learned a lesson from that teenage angel you were, Katy. She lied to me, then kicked me when I was down and turned her back. Never trust an angel. Maybe I'll tell you my secrets, but only after you've told me yours.''

''What's that supposed to mean?''

The taunting little half smile still lifting the corners of his mouth, he leaned toward me. ''Would you like help, Katy?''

''Help?'' I couldn't think what he had in mind, but it had to be something very specific. The way he'd fixed his eyes on my face, I couldn't miss the wicked glint in them.

''Would you like me to help you open the box tonight? I've got work to do. But for old time's sake, I'm willing to postpone it and come over to your place right now.''

''No, thanks.''

One black eyebrow quirked. ''Are you certain?''

''Positive. Nate left that box to me. I'll open it in my own good time. Or, maybe never.'' I added defiantly.

''Never? Then maybe you should reconsider my offer. It still stands, you know. I'm still willing to buy the castle without even inspecting it first.''

I didn't answer. Instead, I walked away. As I marched off, I half expected to hear Egan's laughter following me. But I heard nothing at all.

Chapter Four

Maybe it wasn't *just* the castle that made sleep problematic for me, but the old house's cavernous emptiness and nocturnal creaks and groans certainly didn't help. It would be another restless night.

For more than a decade, I'd managed to push my memories of Egan and our time together into a dark corner. Coming back and seeing him again dragged those memories into the light. Tonight, standing with him in the moonlight, I'd relived the hunger I'd once felt for him.

All that was long ago, I told myself. It was just teenage hormones, *and you're not a teenager anymore, Katy Conroy.* No, I was a full-grown woman. And I was still having a heck of a time getting to sleep.

Before I finally dropped off, I wondered if I'd dream about Egan. Half of me wanted to. For despite our present tensions, I knew that if I dreamed of the time when we were kids, the dream would be sweetly exciting. But it wasn't to be. The nightmare that came to me had nothing to do with Egan. It featured my ex-fiancé's tight-lipped face as he requested my resignation. The nightmare was about how I'd lost my job and about how my whole life had shattered around my shoulders like a fallen mirror.

I woke up from the bad dream, shaken. My heart pumped with anger and outrage, my brain churned. The wind off the lake had come up more during the night. Fiercely, it raged against the east side of the house where my room was situated. The windows rattled as if seized by an intruder's rough hand, and fingers of frigid air reached through the many cracks and crevices of the old structure.

Suddenly, I had the feeling I was being watched. I jerked up in bed, my gaze darting around the room's dark corners. "Is someone there?" I whispered.

Only the house's agonized moans answered. I rubbed my cold arms through the cotton sleeves of my nightgown. That morning, I'd unearthed all the wool blankets and taken them downstairs to be cleaned. Now I wanted one. But if someone was hiding in the house watching me, waiting for me... "That's goofy, Katy," I told myself sternly. "No one's here but you and your imagination."

After belting my robe, I padded down the hall to the head of the stairs.

Patches of moonlight lit my way to the ground floor and Grandfather's study. I'd stacked the blankets on an old Empire-style couch. Instead of heading for them, I walked across the ragged Oriental rug and pulled out the bottom drawer of Grandfather's big old desk. It was a well of darkness, but I knew what lay at the bottom. The mysterious black metal box that Egan had tried to bargain me out of house and home for.

The day I'd returned from Egan's boat, I'd stuffed the box into this drawer and hadn't looked at it since. Now, almost as if Grandfather had whispered an order into my ear, I knew the time had come for me to open it. Even so, I had trouble bringing myself to reach in and touch it. For long minutes, I crouched there, staring at the thing and listening to the horrid squall of the wind.

The old-fashioned lamp atop the desk didn't shed much light. If anything, the wavering threads of illumination seeping through its dense, leaded glass shade added to the spooky feeling I was getting. What did I mean "was getting?" I'd been feeling spooky ever since I'd come to the island.

Grimacing at my own foolishness, I reached in, slid my hand under the box and lifted it onto the desk. There it sat for several minutes more. How was I going to get the thing open? While I gazed down at it, a sudden gust raked something across the window facing the desk, most probably a branch of the cherry tree in the garden.

I jumped a foot. Hand pressed to my heart, I peered out. The reflection of the light against the windowpane made the glass into a smooth, black surface. What if it wasn't the tree? Again, I had the feeling I wasn't alone. Could somebody be out there looking in at me? No, of course not. No sane person would lurk around the castle in a wind like this at three in the morning. For that matter, why was I up trying to figure out how to open a tin box?

Instead of answering myself, I went searching for something to break its lock. When I returned to the study, I had a small ax Grandfather had used for pruning trees and chopping up firewood.

Rather tentatively, I began whacking at the hasp. As if it were sneering at me, it resisted all my efforts. There seemed something almost personal and insulting in the way it ignored me. My blows grew so angry and frustrated that I could feel the reverberations of them in my shoulder sockets. When the lock finally flew apart, I was gasping and sweating. The lid, when I lifted it, was pocked and dented from the mounting frenzy of my attack.

"Gotcha," I muttered as I sat down and peered inside. A wad of old newspaper lay folded on the top. All this fuss for a piece of yellowed newsprint?

Gingerly, I lifted the paper and gazed at what lay scattered beneath on another brittle bed of newsprint. One by one, I lifted the objects out and held them close to the light. There was a small but perfectly formed and unusually beautiful piece of bluish crystal, a twenty-dollar gold piece dated 1926, a spent bullet casing and a key.

None of these things held the slightest meaning for me. The key looked as if it might go with a piece of furniture, though I had no idea which piece. I tried it on the box's broken lock, but it didn't come close to fitting. Setting it aside, I rolled the crystal between my fingers. It was very pretty. Polished, it might make a nice ornament. But I didn't think it likely that Liz Taylor would come banging on my door to demand it for her collection of jewels.

I turned my attention to the newspaper. The brittle page on the top threatened to disintegrate in my hands as I unfolded it. I could barely read the print. The date, however, caught my eye. November 27, 1927. Almost three-quarters of a century ago.

For a moment, I sat gazing blindly, trying to conjure up the past. The newspaper had been printed during Prohibition, during the era of feathered headbands, Rudolph Valentino, bootleggers and mobsters. Faintly, the tinkle of jazz and the *rat-a-tat-tat* of tommy guns echoed in my imagination.

This got a boost when I glanced at the ads for hair oil and unfamiliar but miraculous-sounding beauty products. Amused, I started reading the articles. The headline story was about the opening of the Holland Tunnel. Beneath it was a piece on a gangster named Spike Shawnaway. He was a major bootlegger in the Cleveland area, who'd been killed in a mob shootout. "As Shawnaway lay gasping out his last breath on the dirty pavement, blood trickled from his mouth," the article ended.

Reading these words made a shiver ripple up my spine. It was a strange feeling, sitting alone in this old house, reading about this ancient drama, while I rolled the blue crystal between my fingers. It was as if a time warp lay in the shadows just beyond the circle of lamplight. I had the oddest conviction that all I had to do to be whisked back to the past was get up and step into those shadows. I had an even odder feeling that the gangsters in the newspaper article might be hovering there, waiting to greet me.

I swear I'm not the superstitious type. But what happened next would have given anyone the creeps. A cold breath riffled through the hairs on the back of my neck. As giant goose bumps lifted all over my body, I sprang to my feet and whirled. Nothing. Nothing but night and silence. Then I turned and saw him.

Egan was staring at me through the window. Yet it wasn't the Egan I knew. He looked so pale and strange, it stopped my heart. His expression as he gazed at me was filled with spite. It was as if he were his own evil twin and filled with unspeakable rage.

Terrified by the hostility radiating from him, I screamed and leaped back. I rushed to the side of a bookcase and switched on the overhead fixture. As light flooded the room, I spun to confront Egan. He was gone.

I stood there, shaken. My breath rasped and my heart hammered at my ribs. What had just happened? Was my imagination running completely wild? Had I really seen Egan looking at me as if he wanted to strangle me?

Of course I had. Spooked, I might be, but I wasn't crazy. Anger slammed through me. Just where did Egan Halpern get off hanging around my property in the middle of the night? What right did he have spying on me and trying to scare me? Well, I'd show him I didn't scare so easily.

I went to the closet in the hall, threw on a raincoat and slipped my feet into a pair of old tennis shoes. Farther down the hall, I grabbed a flashlight out of a drawer. Outside, I stood on the edge of the porch. My hair whipped around my face, half blinding me as I peered around the corner toward the study window and squinted into the darkness.

"Egan?" I shouted above the wind.

No answer but the crack and scrape of a branch against the gutter.

"Egan, are you out there? Listen, Egan, this is ridiculous. I know you're there. I saw you. Stop playing games with me. We're grown people now, adults—not silly kids."

A leaf rustled across the toe of my foot. Choking back a frightened squeak, I switched on the flashlight and stepped off the porch. As I walked back along the side of the house, my beam played on the grass. I saw no sign of Egan.

Finally, I stood at the window where he'd looked in at me. Minutely, I played the flash over the damp earth where he must have stood. There were no footprints.

As I acknowledged this, a sinking tightness gripped my insides. Had I hallucinated Egan's face? If not, why was he spying on me and staring at me with such hatred? In my other recent encounters with Egan, there'd been muted hostility and sexual tension. But there'd been nothing like the spite I'd seen on his face in the window. And if he'd really been standing outside the study looking in, whose breath had I felt on the back of my neck? Maybe this whole thing was just some sort of nightmare.

But I wasn't asleep. No, I was wide-awake and trembling with panic.

There's one thing I've learned. If you've got a problem, take action. If you've got a question, get it answered. I resolved to do just that.

THE FOLLOWING MORNING I caught sight of Egan in the village. He was striding toward the bait shop, his long legs eating up the dusty stretch of road fronting the marina. The sun was out. It glinted on his black hair while the light breeze of the lake played with it, caressing its tendrils like an affectionate woman.

Shifting my bag of groceries to my other arm, I hurried across the street and cut a diagonal path through the park. I caught up with him on the corner. "Egan, hey, wait up!"

He spotted me and stopped. He wore a quizzical half smile on his lips as I trotted up. He also wore sunglasses, so I couldn't see the expression in his eyes.

"You look as if you've been running a marathon," he said. "What are you so hot and bothered about?"

"Egan, I think it's time we talked."

His right eyebrow quirked. "You do? What about?"

"About what happened last night."

He gave a careless little shrug. "It's okay, Katy. I don't mind you trespassing on my property to get to yours."

I stared at him, baffled. Then I remembered how I'd run into him coming back from a night sail with his son. "I'm not talking about that. I'm talking about what happened later."

Both eyebrows went up. "What happened later?"

"As if you didn't know. Stop treating me like an idiot, Egan."

"Katy, I'll be treating you like a mental case, if you don't use plain English to explain what's bugging you. Now, what's this all about?"

His air of baffled condescension infuriated me. This was going too far. "Why were you prowling around my property at three in the morning? Why did you look in at me through the window with that horrible expression on your face? Were you trying to get me to sell the castle to you by scaring me? Because if you were, it's not going to work. I'm a big girl now, and I don't scare so easily. Try pulling a stunt like that again, and I'll report you to the police as a Peeping Tom."

"Well, that will certainly break the monotony of Ralph Creech's day," Egan snapped, referring to Big Bass's aging, beer-bellied sheriff. "I think I know what his reaction will be, though. Ralph knows I'm no peeper, but he doesn't know much about you. Start making wild accusations like that, and he'll call over to the mainland for a team of men in white coats to cart you away."

Trembling with rage, I opened my mouth to reply. My grocery bag slipped out of my arm and crashed to the sidewalk. Bread, bananas, canned soup, pasta and a small bag of sugar scattered over the sidewalk.

"These'll be bruised now," Egan said, scooping up the bananas and handing them to me. "You seem to be losing it in more ways than one, don't you, Katy?"

I was speechless. I snatched the bananas and stuffed them into the bag. "Egan," I said through my teeth. "I'm serious. Last night, sometime between two and three in the morning, I opened Grandfather's tin box."

"Oh? At two o'clock in the morning? So, what did you find inside?"

"None of your business. What I want to know from you is why, when I looked up, you were on the other side of the study window, glaring at me as if you'd like to kill me."

Egan eyed me without expression. "Between two and three in the morning last night, I wasn't even on the island."

"Of course you were. I spoke to you."

"That was around nine p.m. A little before midnight, I got a call from my cousin on Smallmouth," he said, referring to one of the smaller islands that lie east of Big Bass. "At two in the morning, I was helping him catch his trawler. It cut loose in the gale, and he was afraid he was going to lose it."

"Why should I believe you?"

"Why should you? Frankly, I don't give a damn whether you believe me or not. The idea that I'd go sneaking around your property in the dead of night to catch a glimpse of you in your nightgown is ridiculous. If you'll think back, Katy, I've seen you in considerably less than a nightgown. So why would I bother?"

While I tried to gather my stuttering thoughts for an angry reply, Roland Broyles, the proprietor of the bait shop, stuck his head out the door. "Something wrong out here?"

Egan glanced at him and then grinned wickedly at me. "Rolly, tell this lady where we were last night and what we were doing."

The white-haired man gazed at Egan and me in surprise. "Why, we were helping your cousin over on Smallmouth. You needed a shallow draft to get that old trawler of his off a sandbar, so you rented mine. But I'm the only one knows the secret to making her cranky motor run." He shook his head. "That was some adventure we had, from midnight 'til nearly five in the morning. No wonder my tail is dragging."

The silence probably lasted no more than a half minute. To me, it seemed much longer. I wanted to shout that what Broyles said couldn't be true. Egan hadn't been in the middle of the lake rescuing boats. He'd been in my backyard. But I couldn't very well call Roland a liar and continue living on Big Bass and shopping in town.

I kept my frustrated denials between my teeth. "Thank you," I said to Egan as I grabbed my groceries and turned on my heel and walked away, well aware that both men were staring after me as if I were the madwoman of Lake Erie.

Nevertheless, I would have been able to retreat with dignity, if my sorely tried paper sack hadn't burst at that point. Once again, it dumped its contents on the sidewalk just a few yards from Broyles's door.

"Damn!" I exclaimed. As I crouched down, I heard footsteps behind me.

"You're not having a good afternoon, are you?"

"You might say that." I didn't look at Egan, though I knew he had crouched down next to me. Out of the corner of my eye I could see the bulge of his muscular thigh straining against his faded jeans.

"Let me help you."

"I don't need your help." I grabbed uselessly at a can of tomatoes, which went rolling beyond my grasp.

"Of course you do. Don't be so stiff-necked, Katy. Your paper sack is a lost cause. Here, use this one." He offered me a plastic bag from Broyles's store.

Grudgingly, I took it. "Thanks."

"Now see, that didn't hurt, did it?"

"What?" As I stuffed the plastic bag with my mangled and dented groceries, I shot Egan a suspicious look.

"Being civil to me. It didn't cause you any serious pain, did it?" His white teeth flashed, and part of my brain observed that Egan's grin was just as devastating now as it had been years back.

"Nothing I can't handle."

"Good, then maybe you'll try it more often. With the two of us constantly running into each other on the island, things will go a lot more smoothly if you're polite."

"You really care whether or not I'm polite?" I asked curiously.

"Sure." He picked up my bulging bag of repacked groceries and straightened. "Seems like every time we see each other, we get into an argument. Why is that?"

"Maybe we don't trust each other."

"It's obvious you don't trust me. But you're an intelligent woman. You don't really believe I was making faces at you through your window last night, do you?"

I wanted to tell him no, but how could I? "I saw you."

"You didn't see me, Katy. You saw the reflection of the moon or a distortion of your own face. The castle is famous for spooking people. Old Nate lost a string of housekeepers, who insisted it was haunted. It's amazing what an overactive imagination will do to you in a place like that." Ignoring my silent refusal to agree, he glanced inside the shopping bag he still held. "These bananas are really goners now. I hope you weren't planning on having them for lunch."

"Well, yes. Part of my lunch, anyway."

"I have a better idea. I ran into Wat Benchley down at the ferry. He tells me you've put your car up for sale, and that it's a mighty fancy piece of metal."

I nodded suspiciously. "It's a three-year-old RX-7. I've left it with a dealer in Sandusky, who said he'd sell it for me on commission."

"Well, now, I've always wanted to drive a sports car. What are you asking for it?"

Egan whistled when he heard the price. "Not exactly giving it away, are you?"

"I can't afford to give it away. I'm selling it because I need the money. Anyway, it's worth that much."

Egan shot me that ruinous grin again. "Don't get all ruffled up. I'm not objecting to the price. If the car's in good condition, it's fair. Tell you what. Ferry's going to leave in ten minutes. Why don't we get aboard, have lunch in Sandusky and take a look at this automotive wonder you're peddling?"

I could hardly believe my ears. "You really think you might be interested in buying?"

"I wouldn't make this proposal if I weren't."

As I searched his face, I felt memories tug at my heart. Looking at him standing there so tall and handsome and vividly male, I couldn't believe what I'd seen through my window was real, either. Egan was right. It didn't make sense to think he'd pull such a crazy stunt. I felt myself responding like a withered sponge to water to the teasing smile lighting Egan's eyes, and I couldn't do a thing about it. Despite the angry emotion still humming between us, I couldn't bear the thought of turning away from him. I wanted to be with him.

"All right. If you're really interested in the car, you're on."

After a silent ten-minute drive in Egan's pickup, we managed to scramble aboard the ferry just in time. Sitting on the top deck with the spring wind blowing through our hair, we started to talk.

"What's it like being back on the island after all these years?" Egan asked.

"Strange, disturbing in a way. Everything's changed so much."

"We've prettied ourselves up, added a few coats of paint and some new buildings. But underneath it all, Big Bass is still the same. That's because the people are still the same. People don't really change. They just get older."

I felt my cheeks flush. If Egan really believed that, he must think my attraction to him hadn't altered, either.

As if he were catching my thought, he turned to me and said, "Of course, that doesn't apply to feelings. Feelings change all the time. That's one thing it's always a mistake to count on."

Instead of answering, I gazed out over the lake. With the sun shooting gold and azure sparks off its crushed-silk surface, it was the same shade of translucent indigo as Egan's eyes. He was wrong, I thought. When it came to Egan Halpern, the years hadn't really changed my feelings all that much.

We lingered over lunch in Sandusky and talked some more. I asked Egan how he and my grandfather had become friendly.

"I wouldn't describe us as friendly, exactly. We shared a mutual interest in local history."

"Yes, but you must have started talking to each other somehow. Did you approach him first?"

"No, actually it was the other way around. He said he'd heard I was interested in island history and asked if I'd like to see some of his memorabilia. I said sure, and that's how it started."

I had a hard time picturing this. Why would Grandfather have made overtures with someone from a family I knew he'd looked down on? Mystified, I asked Egan how he'd become such a history buff in the first place.

"Originally, I just wanted to understand the island better and learn more about my own family," he answered. "But after I started reading, my interests widened and I couldn't stop. The War of 1812 is really fascinating."

"Maybe you should have majored in history."

"Maybe I would have, if I'd had the chance to go to college."

Again, I felt my cheeks redden. Of course, Egan couldn't have gone to college. I'd learned from Betty that he'd married a pregnant Debbie before he was out of his teens. Debbie had lost that child and had Rex later.

Seeing my embarrassed expression, and interpreting it correctly, he shrugged. "It's turned out all right. There's a lot to be said for educating yourself. Maybe it sounds like bragging, but I honestly believe I'm as well read as most men my age with a bachelor's degree."

Remembering some of the professional types I'd dated, I didn't doubt that for a minute.

"What about you, Katy," Egan said. "What do you like to read?"

"You mean who are my favorite authors, or do I prefer books on current affairs to poetry and fiction?"

"All of it. I want to find out about you."

Though part of me was skeptical of this sudden interest, I was too flattered not to open up like a water lily in a patch of sun. Wary though I was of Egan, he still had the power to charm me at will. I liked looking at him, listening to him. Even the way he squinted out over the water, narrowing his eyes to sapphire slits as he sipped a beer, enchanted me. I could have sat talking to him all day. *Oh Lord,* I thought, *I'm too smart to fall for him all over again, aren't I?*

By the time we proceeded to the lot where my bottle-green RX-7 sat parked, it was almost three in the afternoon, and I was having to fight hard not to look for excuses to touch Egan's hand or brush an arm casually against his shoulder. Distrustful though I was of his motives in buying my car, I was still pathetically hungry for some physical contact with him.

Egan whistled when he saw the car. He was even more enthusiastic after he drove it. "It's a beauty," he exclaimed an hour later after he pulled back onto the lot. "The shift seems a little sticky. Otherwise, it drives like a dream. And it's got all the extras, too. You didn't spare any expense."

"No, I didn't," I admitted ruefully. The RX-7 had been my greatest extravagance and I'd lived to regret it. "At the time, my career was going great. I'd just received a fat raise, and I was in the mood to indulge myself. When I saw it in the showroom, I fell in love with it."

"It's that kind of automobile," Egan agreed. "Sure you want to part with it now?"

"If I'm going to go on paying for sacks of groceries like the one I spread all over the sidewalk this morning, I have to sell the car."

Soberly, Egan studied me. "You're serious, aren't you?"

"Believe me, what I'm saying is no laughing matter."

"You don't have to answer, but I can't help being curious. How did it come to that, Katy?"

"I told you, I lost my job."

"But your family had money. Wasn't your father a very successful banker?"

"He was when I was a kid. Just before he died, Dad got wiped out in a real estate deal that went sour. What he left barely paid for his funeral expenses. When I lost my job, I had a fairly substantial savings account. But I've been unemployed for almost six months. It's unbelievable what car payments, rent and food can do to a savings account in six months. When I came to the island for Grandfather's funeral, I was just about wiped out. I can't afford to own a car like this anymore."

"Then consider it sold," Egan said.

I blinked. "Aren't you going to bargain with me, try to get the price down?" Again, I wondered about his motives.

"No. I'm satisfied you wouldn't cheat me. You wouldn't, would you?"

"No, of course not."

"Then that's good enough for me." He extended his hand. I took it, and as his warm, strong fingers closed around mine, I smiled up into his eyes and felt time slip away. For that instant, I was the same naive, love-struck young girl I'd been more than a decade earlier.

The mood lasted until we got back to the island. Egan returned to work, and I walked back to the castle. Was I crazy, I asked myself as I opened the screen door and stepped into the kitchen. I reached into my pocket and took out the fat check Egan had written for me. Distractedly, I set it aside and unpacked my supplies. All the while, I kept mulling over the day and my conversations with Egan. He had been a wonderful companion. He'd seemed truly interested in what I had to say, and when he'd talked about himself, he'd said things that made me like him and want to know more.

I peeled a banana. Egan had been right—it was bruised. I ate it anyway, then walked back to Grandfather's study and took the tin box out of the desk drawer where I'd stowed it.

While I'd been with Egan this afternoon, I'd accepted his word. I'd even begun to accept his explanation that I'd imagined seeing him through my window last night. But now that I was back in the house and alone, I wasn't so sure. Was I letting him get under my skin again? Admittedly, I had a weakness for the man. Was I falling for his charm against my better judgment?

Left without an answer, I opened the box and looked down at the baffling objects it held. Then, I lifted out the blue crystal. "No," I murmured as I rolled it between my fingers, feeling its smooth surfaces and the slick edges of its facets. I had not imagined Egan at my window. I had seen him. I just didn't know how or why.

I must have sat there for over an hour examining the items in the box and reading every inch of the sheets of newspaper in the box. Only the article on Spike Shawnaway seemed significant. But what was its meaning? What connection could it have with the crystal or the gold coin? If Grandfather wanted me to know something, why hadn't he just told me? Why had he left me this peculiar puzzle? Was it some sort of beyond-the-grave joke? I picked up the key. Perhaps it unlocked something that contained further clues.

I spent the next hour trying it on all the doors in the house and every blanket chest and desk drawer with a keyhole. It didn't fit any of them. But it must fit something, I told myself. Somewhere, somehow, this key was meant to unlock a secret.

Chapter Five

That weekend, Rex showed up at my door. "Nine on the dot," I said when I opened up. "You're very punctual."

"My dad rousted me out of bed in plenty of time. He's got a thing for meeting your obligations and living up to your word and stuff. He's always lecturing me on that."

"Well, I appreciate his good intentions. There's plenty of work here, and I'm anxious to get on with it. Come on in."

As Rex strolled past me, I admired his good-natured cockiness. He was dressed in the latest fashion—Air Jordan sneakers, torn jeans, shapeless sweatshirt. A bright red baseball cap perched backward on his curly black hair, which had the shine of a crow's wing in the morning sun. In a few years, he would be as devastating to the opposite sex as his father had been—and still was.

"Have you been in the house before?" I asked. Rex had stopped short in the living room. With a bemused air, he looked around.

"A couple of times I came with my dad when he was doing stuff for the historical society with old man Co—with your grandfather. It looks different—cleaner and not so messy."

"Well, I hope so. That's most of what I've been doing lately—polishing, dusting, throwing away junk. There's still plenty to do, though, as you can see from those boxes. They're full of old, moth-eaten blankets. You can start by taking those to the dump."

Rex, for all his cheekiness, proved a willing worker. He was also a talkative one, full of questions. "My dad told me about the car he bought from you," he remarked as he helped me with a box of moldy knickknacks. "He's keeping it on the mainland to use when he goes on business trips. I can't wait to see it."

"I hope you and your father will get as much pleasure out of it as I did."

"What will you do when you want to go someplace now?"

"Well, I don't need a car here on the island. Big Bass is small enough so I can ride a bike just about any place I want to go. I guess if I need to get someplace on the mainland I'll have to take a bus or rent a car."

"A lot of people around here do that—rent cars when they go away, I mean. It's nice living on an island where you don't need a car, don't you think?"

I looked up from the pile of old newspapers I was bundling and shot Rex a surprised glance. He was watching me with a hopeful expression on his face, as if he were an encyclopedia salesman zeroing in on a likely customer. "Sure, it's nice," I agreed. "Nice and cheap. Right now I'm all for that."

"I heard you used to be on TV," he remarked some time later. He'd parked his pedicab, having just arrived from his second run to the dump.

"That's right. That stack of old magazines is next. Oh, and see that pile of cloth-covered electrical cords? Those can also go, along with the faded pillows and the stained towels and doilies.''

"What a bunch of junk.''

"They say one man's trash is another man's treasure, but I don't think anybody is going to want this Christmas wreath. It looks as if bats have been nesting in it.''

With a scornful flare of his nostrils, Rex stuffed the wreath in with another box of throwaways. "Did you like being on TV?''

"I liked it fine.''

"Then how come you're not doing it anymore?''

"That's a long story, Rex.''

Rex grinned. "I know what that means. My dad says that when there's something he doesn't want to talk about.''

"Does that happen often?'' I knew I had no business asking, but I was curious about Egan as a father. From what I'd seen so far, I had to give him high marks.

"Nah. My dad and me, we talk about most everything. He's always giving me advice.''

"Oh? About what?''

"All kinds of stuff—like sailing stuff, and how to deal with guys who make trouble for you. Guys like Mark Wiblin.'' As he spoke Betty's nephew's name, his expression darkened.

"I gather Mark Wiblin isn't a friend of yours?''

"He's always ragging on me, trying to put me down and saying stuff about my family. I used to get in fights with him and his gang all the time. But my dad taught me to ignore stuff like that. Dad says it's who I am that counts, not what my relatives did a hundred years ago.''

"Your father is right. I hope you listen to him.''

"I do—at least most of the time, I do." Rex shouldered a moth-eaten stuffed owl destined for the dump. "My dad's my best friend."

As I watched Rex stride out to his pedicab, I thought about what he'd just revealed. It stunned me that despite Egan's success, island kids still taunted his son for being a Halpern. Maybe not all of Egan's bitterness was unjustified.

A couple of hours later, I'd sat Rex down to a bologna sandwich and a glass of milk when Egan came to the house.

"Something smells good," he said when I opened the back door.

"I'm just about to take chocolate chip cookies out of the oven. Want some?"

"I've never turned down a homemade chocolate chip cookie." As he walked into the kitchen, he said to his son, "I see you're making yourself right at home."

Rex chewed and swallowed. "I didn't ask her to give me lunch. She had it ready when I got back from my last trip to the dump."

"Hey, no need to get all defensive. If a pretty lady like this offered me lunch, I wouldn't turn her down, either."

I looked from father to son and back, once again impressed by their resemblance. Egan caught my eye. As a slow smile lifted his mouth, I felt my heartbeat quicken. The pale, angry face at the window seemed like nothing more than a bad dream. Was I fooling myself, wanting so desperately not to believe that the vibrantly attractive man standing in the middle of my kitchen could do something so despicable, so downright crazy?

Desire gave in to logic. "I've got plenty more bread and bologna, if you'd like a sandwich." I said. "But it's not going to come free."

Rex gave a little whoop and crammed the rest of his sandwich into his mouth. Ignoring his son's jeer, Egan cocked his eyebrow and looked me up and down. "What's the price of bologna around here?"

"Some of that muscle I see bulging in your manly shoulders. I've got a couple of pieces of furniture I'd like moved. Rex and I can't do it alone, but with a big strong brute like you at our side, it should be a snap."

"Brute, is it?" Egan chuckled and eyed me roguishly. "Okay, milady, this brute is at your service. But first, the sandwich, at least a half dozen of those cookies I smell and a cup of strong, hot coffee."

"You've got a deal."

The kitchen became a haven, fragrant with the aromas of warm baking and fresh-brewed coffee. We lingered around the old painted-ash table, eating and sipping. Egan described his latest design project, a racy yawl for a wealthy CEO in Grosse Pointe. Rex bragged about all the trash he'd carted off for me.

"I hope you're not throwing out anything valuable, Katy," Egan said. "There could be some valuable stuff here."

"I'm being very careful. I don't think I've tossed out anything valuable so far. Betty is going to come over next week and check out what's left. She's opening an antique store."

"Yes, I heard that. I hope it works out for her. She hasn't exactly been a lucky lady."

"No, she hasn't." Across the table, Egan and I looked at each other. As our eyes locked, time seemed to split into a spectrum. Past and present streamed around us as if they were different aspects of the same flow. I felt the echoes of our youth like a distant, bittersweet song. Neither of us had been lucky in love, I thought. A yearning caught at my throat, and my gaze dropped.

Egan cleared his throat before speaking again. His voice sounded thick. "Well, you've kept your part of our bargain. Now it's time for me to keep mine. Where is this furniture you want moved?"

"It's a big old cabinet in the hall," Rex piped up after jamming a final cookie into his mouth. "She wants it in the kitchen."

"Let's go have a look."

The piece was a cherry corner cabinet, wedged in a dark alcove beneath the staircase. "It's really a fine old cabinet," I said. "I emptied all the china out of it yesterday. I thought I'd like to clean it up and set it where it could be appreciated. There's really not enough shelf space in that old-fashioned kitchen."

Egan ran a finger along a beveled molding on the top of the piece in question. "Judging from all this dust, it hasn't been moved in half a century."

"Man, nothing in this house has been moved in half a century," Rex declared.

"Well, it's not quite that bad. But close," I conceded.

Egan put his shoulder to one side of the cabinet, and Rex and I helped steady it on the other end. Slowly, we inched it out of its corner. We had moved it perhaps half a foot, when a loud crash startled us.

"Something fell down back there, something real heavy."

"I think we know that, son." The cabinet had stood undusted for so long that when Egan wiped a hand across his forehead, he left a streak of soot. "Whatever fell must have been lying on top against the wall. I'll move the cabinet out a few more inches.''

Five minutes later, I was able to peer behind the massive piece of furniture and make out the object lying admid the undisturbed dust and grit of decades. ''My God, it's an old gun.''

''No kidding,'' Rex yelped.

Without a word, Egan came around to my side, pushed me politely, but firmly, out of the way and reached a long arm into the opening.

''It's a six-shooter,'' Rex declared when the weapon came out into the light.

''It's an old revolver,'' Egan agreed.

''For heaven's sake, what's a thing like that doing hidden away in the hall?'' As I stared at the gun, I crossed my arms over my chest. Dull black and heavy-looking, it gave me a strange feeling. I didn't like knowing it had been hidden there. Who had hidden it, and why?

''Can I hold it, Dad?''

''Not until I make sure it isn't loaded.'' As he spoke, Egan spun the cylinder. ''I'm no expert on guns, but this looks to me like World War I vintage.''

''Then it's an antique?''

''Yes, I suspect it is.'' Egan's gaze never left the revolver. Obviously, it fascinated him. There was a calculating expression on his face. Did the firearm mean something special to him? Indeed, it seemed to have the same effect on Rex. He was staring at it as if it were the Holy Grail itself.

''It must have been Grandfather's gun.''

''I suppose it must have.'' Egan aimed the gun at the empty hallway and sighted along it. As I watched him handle the weapon, I felt disturbed in ways I couldn't put into words. Suddenly, Egan looked like a stranger, a very menacing stranger. A ripple of fear coursed through my body.

"Why on earth would Grandfather hide it up there?" I muttered.

"I don't know, but apparently he had a reason." Egan's eyes never left the gun, which he held as if he intended to fire. "Katy, would you mind if I took it home with me?"

I stood there scowling at the thing in Egan's hand and hugging myself. "Frankly, yes, I would."

If I had expected Egan to hand the gun over meekly, I was mistaken. He lowered it and stood there studying me. The look in his eye suggested he was speculating whether or not to honor my refusal. "Do you mind telling me why you won't let me take it? I don't plan to steal the gun, Katy. I will return it."

"It belonged to my grandfather and now it belongs to me. I'd rather it didn't leave this house until I've decided what to do with it."

For long seconds, we eyed each other in a silent tug of wills. All the earlier good feelings of the kitchen dissolved like a mirage. I had felt so good sitting at the kitchen table with Rex and Egan. Now I felt cold and sick. Without turning my head, I sensed Rex staring at Egan and me. He, too, must have felt the wordless struggle going on between us.

"Very well," Egan said tightly. As he handed me the gun, his eyes were icy. He turned his back on me and put his shoulder against the cabinet. "Let's get this moved, son. We have to be on our way."

THAT NIGHT, I had a frightening dream. I was walking along a pebble beach. In the distance, I could see Egan sitting on a rock. His back was to me, and he wore an outfit that struck me as odd—denim overalls and a faded plaid shirt. I called his name and ran toward him. It seemed important that I get him to turn around and look at me. I wanted him to take me into his arms and comfort me. But as I drew closer, a feeling of dread possessed me and I slowed down. "Egan," I whispered, "is that you?"

Slowly, he turned and I screamed. It wasn't Egan's face under that mop of black curls. It was a skeleton head.

I woke up early the next morning, put on my robe and went downstairs to fix my breakfast. But as I walked past Grandfather's study, I made a quick detour. I'd stuck the revolver in the desk drawer along with the metal box, intending to see if the bullet from the box fit the gun. Impulsively, I opened it to have a look. My lips parted in a gasp. The gun was gone and so was the box.

"THERE'S SOMETHING bothering you, isn't there? Has that old house been giving you trouble?"

Gazing at me wide-eyed, Betty pushed a windblown tendril back from her freckled forehead. We were aboard the ferry to the mainland. Betty and I had bumped into each other at the dock, both intent on doing errands in Sandusky. We had a warm, sunny day. Except for the foam churned up by the ferry's engines, the water was bright blue.

"You weren't out late last night, by any chance, were you?"

"As a matter of fact, I was," she replied. "There was a meeting of the library committee, and it didn't let out until after midnight."

"On your way home, did you pass my house?"

When Betty nodded, I couldn't resist asking, "Did you see anybody sneaking around?"

"Sneaking around?" She looked puzzled. "Why are you asking? Did something happen last night?"

Though I hadn't intended to tell anybody about the disappearance of the box and the gun, I found myself spilling the whole story along with my suspicions.

Betty's eyes became saucer-wide. "Now, let me see if I've got this straight, Katy. You think that some time last night, while you were asleep, Egan Halpern sneaked into your house? You think he did this to pinch a tin box and an old gun?"

"I know it sounds loony, Betty."

"It does. But hey, these days half the world sounds loony."

"If this happened to you, what would you think? Egan wanted the box. To get his hands on it, he even offered to buy my house. When I opened the box, I caught him looking at me through the window."

Betty raised her eyebrows at this. "Are you sure? That doesn't sound like Egan. I mean, I'm no big fan of his. He can be arrogant and overbearing. But I've never known him to be sneaky."

"I'm sure," I said tightly. If I'd entertained doubts before, I was certain of what I'd seen now. "When he and I found the gun behind that cabinet, he was fascinated by it. He asked me if he could have it and when I refused, he was miffed. That very night it disappears. What else can I think? Egan was the only one who even knew I had the thing."

Betty snickered. "Dream on. You wouldn't be so naive if you'd lived in these parts a little longer. Katy, by nightfall everyone on the island knew you'd found that gun."

"You think Egan went around telling people?"

"It's likely he mentioned it. I know for sure Rex did. When Mark came home, he was full of it."

Deflated, I sat back on the bench. One of the hordes of gulls following the ferry dived past my ear, shrieking. It had never occurred to me that anyone but Rex and Egan knew about the old revolver.

"Why would anyone go to the trouble of stealing that thing in the first place?" Betty said.

"I don't know. And I don't know why my grandfather would have hidden it like that. But I intend to find out."

"Well, good luck."

During the rest of the boat trip, Betty chattered. She was headed for an auction in hopes of picking up some bargain store fittings for the antique shop she had in the works. "You're welcome to come along," she offered.

"Betty, the last thing I need is somebody else's old furniture. No, I have some plans of my own for this afternoon."

"Like what?" We were nearing shore, so she had to shout over the ferry's tooting horn.

"Well, for one thing, I'm going to have this made into a piece of jewelry." I dug in my purse and produced a wad of tissue. When I unfolded it, Grandfather's blue crystal glinted in the spring sun. Luckily, the crystal hadn't been inside the box when it was stolen.

"Oh, how pretty." Betty lifted the shaft of quartz and held it to the light. "What an unusual color. Is it island crystal?"

"I have no idea. I know there's a crystal cave on the island."

"Yes, Zeke Banroth's place. It caters to tourists. Don't recall ever seeing this color there." Betty handed the crystal back. "Let me know if you come across any more of this stuff. I bet I could sell it. In fact, I wouldn't mind a piece like this for myself."

A few minutes later, Betty and I parted at the dock. My first stop was a jeweler's on Main Street. I dropped the crystal off there so it could be fitted with a ring for a neck chain. I don't know why I wanted to wear it. I only know the impulse was very strong. Ever since I'd held the crystal in my hand and rubbed my forefinger over its pale blue facets, I'd felt a sense of connection with it.

Outside the jeweler's, I caught a cab to the library and started my research project. Sandusky doesn't have the biggest library in the world. Fortunately, it does boast a complete back record of area newspapers preserved on microfilm.

After settling in at a carrel with three years' worth of microfilm dating between 1925 and 1928, I began to search for the name Spike Shawnaway. White print flashed onto the black screen. Reading it, I quickly fell down Alice in Wonderland's rabbit hole and into a different place.

The newspapers, with their funny ads and sensational headlines, were like a time machine. "Valentino is Dead," "Byrd and Bennett fly over North Pole," "Lucky Lindy Hops over the Atlantic," "Al Capone Makes Fortune in Rackets." They conducted me to an era of gangsters and speakeasies, of fast money and fast boats. Guarded by machine guns, those speedboats had run between Canada and the States, loaded with barrels of bootleg liquor.

The newspaper articles soon taught me that Spike Shawnaway had been a major player in this Jazz Age melodrama. He was a colorful Prohibition gangster, who'd raked in piles of money from bootlegging, prostitution and, apparently, robbery. "Shawnaway Denies

Involvement in Government Gold Heist," one headline blared. "A Million in Gold Lifted off Armored Truck—Government Suspects Shawnaway," another trumpeted.

That caught my attention. I read the article once, then reread it. In 1927, a band of masked hoodlums waylaid an armored truck. The truck was en route to a federal reserve bank, loaded with gold coins. A million dollars in gold would have been equivalent to many times that amount now. Had the loot ever been recovered, I wondered. I thought of the single gold coin in Grandfather's tin box. The date on it had been 1926. Could the coin have come from this heist? If so, what was my grandfather doing with it? And why had he wanted me to have it?

It was late in the afternoon when I finally returned the rolls of microfilm to the shelves. I'd read several accounts of how Spike Shawnaway met his end, gunned down in a parking lot by a rival gang. However, though I had gone through every inch of microfilm up until 1928, I'd found no report of the million in gold ever being recovered. So far as I could tell, the secret of its whereabouts had died with him.

Pondering this, I walked out into the late-afternoon sunlight. The breeze blew a strand of hair across my eyes. As I glanced up to brush it back, I caught sight of a tall, lean, dark-haired man rounding the corner. Egan? I couldn't be sure, but it gave me an unsettling feeling to think he might have come over to Sandusky on the same day I'd chosen to come.

If so, it was an odd coincidence—even odder that he should be walking down this street at this particular time. For all I knew, he'd been in the library. He could even have been watching me. Sitting hunched over that viewer looking at microfilm, I'd been oblivious. Genghis Khan himself could have stood breathing down my neck and I wouldn't have noticed.

Deep in thought, I headed toward the main part of town. Was I being paranoid to think Egan might have followed me? Maybe so, but he was caught up in all this somehow. Even if he hadn't stolen my box, he had its mate. Did it contain more pieces of this puzzle? And if it did, why had Grandfather wanted him to have them?

Chewing this over, I started to cross the street. As I walked past the line of parked cars, a roaring engine split the quiet afternoon. Startled, I looked up in time to see a red blur barreling toward me. As I screamed and jumped back, metal slammed into my body. The impact hurled me to the pavement. I tasted blood.

"Miss, miss! Are you all right?"

"Uh?" I stared up into a man's worried face. Behind his glasses, his eyes seemed too big.

"What happened? Did you faint? Is anything broken?"

"Uh?" My tongue was a thick wad. I saw him through a haze of shock and couldn't find the words to speak.

"Here, let me help you up. You need medical attention. I'll drive you to the hospital."

I'm not sure what happened after that. Reality didn't snap back into focus until I was in the emergency room.

"A few scrapes and bruises and a mild concussion," the doctor said. "You're very lucky."

"I don't feel lucky."

"Not everyone can tangle with the front end of an automobile and walk away with such light injuries. I don't suppose you saw who the hit-and-run driver was?"

"All I saw was a red blur."

"Do you have any idea of the make or model?"

"None."

"Well, that's unfortunate. I'll have to fill out an accident report. But I don't suppose the police will be able to do much with so little to go on."

"No, I don't suppose they will."

"Probably just a teenager tanked up on too much beer."

"Probably," I mumbled. But a sick feeling inside me didn't agree. That car had come at me deliberately. The driver had known who he was trying to hit. He hadn't planned to just bruise me and scare the living daylights out of me. He'd planned to kill me.

Soon after, the doctor released me. Following a useless interview with the police, I caught the ferry for home. As the boat plowed through the water, I brooded about what I was going home to. I'd been trying to believe that I'd found a place I could make my own on Big Bass. But why go on kidding myself? The castle felt more like a haunted house than a safe haven. It sulked over its spit of land like a huge, gloomy crow. What was it guarding? What secrets did it hoard?

As I listened to the creaks and groans the castle made that night, I felt it was trying to tell me something. It was trying to warn me. Grandfather's house doesn't want me for its mistress, I thought. Probably, it resents all the cleaning and throwing away I've been doing. It wants me to go away and leave it alone with its ghosts. Why don't I? Why don't I just give Egan what he wants, sell the castle to him and leave? When I finally went to sleep, I had decided to do exactly that.

IN THE KITCHEN the next morning, I changed my mind. As I sipped a cup of hot coffee, I knew I couldn't just give up. I looked around at the heavy iron pots hanging on hooks under the tall painted oak cabinets. My gaze fell to the plank floor polished by the feet of generations of my ancestors.

That first day back on the island, I had thought it ironic that this house had sheltered my grandfather for ninety-odd years and then killed him. What if it hadn't killed him? What if his fatal fall down those cellar stairs hadn't been an accident?

The phone rang. It was Betty. "Katy, thank goodness I got you. I've been worried. I called several times yesterday, but you were never at home."

"I got back from Sandusky late yesterday. As a matter of fact, I had a little accident." As unemotionally as I could manage, I described how I'd been knocked down by a hit-and-run driver.

"Why, Katy, that's terrible. You could have been killed."

"I suppose I could have."

"Did you see who was driving?"

"No, but it was probably just some kid." I didn't mention that I thought I might have seen Egan just a few minutes before the car came at me. That didn't mean it wasn't on my mind. Had I seen Egan? If so, what was he doing in Sandusky? Was there any possibility that he had been the driver of that hit-and-run vehicle? And if there was, why? What motive could he have?

You need the answer to that and a lot of other puzzle pieces, I told myself after I hung up. And I thought I knew where to look for the key. If I was ever to have any peace of mind, I had to solve the riddle Grandfather had left me. But solving it meant getting back the stolen box and finding out what Egan's contained. I could think of only one way to do that.

After midnight, I pulled on black slacks and a black turtleneck sweater. With a small flashlight in a pouch around my waist, I left the house. It was a cool, windless night. Though stars spangled the sky, a ragged patch of cloud darkened the face of the half moon. A perfect night to play cat burglar.

Chapter Six

Staying in the shadows of the trees, I made my way along
the waterfront and headed for the Macaster place. As I
crossed onto Egan's property, I looked around anxious-
ly. A light still showed in one of his downstairs windows.
What was Egan doing up so late?

Had he been behind the wheel of that red car? I reacted to the idea with revulsion. No, I told myself, no!
After all, the car Egan now drove when he was on the
mainland was my RX-7, and it wasn't red. But what if
he'd been in a borrowed car? There were times when I
divined a deep well of anger in Egan. I could almost see
it bubbling and seething just below his surface. What if
he'd seen me and that well of anger had boiled over? Or
perhaps there was another reason that Egan might want
to harm me—a reason I knew nothing of and must discover before it was too late.

I simply couldn't dismiss the suspicions plaguing me.
They hovered around my head like bats from some evil
cave in my psyche. Murder and plots aside, I still thought
it entirely possible that Egan had taken the box and the
gun. I certainly knew he'd wanted them. Tonight, I'd find
out.

Turning back to the water, I picked out the *Night-hawk's* rakish profile. The sloop was tied at Egan's private dock. As I approached it, I heard the gentle slosh of lake water against mossy pilings. The last time I'd heard about the box that matched my missing one, it had been aboard the *Nighthawk*. More than likely, Egan had put it away in his house by now. But he might not have.

Years back, I remember his taking a note I'd written to him out of a sailbag and telling me he never had any privacy at home. Whenever he wanted to keep something away from prying eyes, he left it on his boat. Of course, he must have all the privacy he wanted now. But habits formed in youth die hard. A sailboat could have a hundred hiding holes that only its builder would know of. Egan might have hidden his box aboard, and he might have stowed my box and gun there, too.

The moon slid behind a cloud. Taking advantage of the darkness, I hurried onto the dock. The bottoms of my sneakers, damp from the grass, squeaked faintly on the weathered boards. I kept shooting glances over my shoulder. Though I was sure no one could see me, my nerves were definitely on edge.

I had just pulled the stern line on the *Nighthawk* taut enough so I could jump on deck, when a noise made me freeze. *That was a door slamming shut back at Egan's house,* warned my brain. I dropped the line as if it were electrified, and hurried to the end of the dock. Muscles registering a strong objection, I lowered myself over the edge onto a rickety wooden swimming ladder. Fortunately, the water was low enough so I could climb down several rungs. Even so, I had to hunch almost double to keep my head out of sight. Immediately, cold lake seeped through my canvas shoes and turned my feet into blocks of ice.

The noise was probably nothing, I told myself. *Maybe Egan was putting out the cat or the garbage. I probably didn't have to hide at all.* A couple of minutes later, the dock vibrated. Someone who weighed about two hundred pounds and had a firm tread was walking down the dock. The wooden rail on the swimming ladder cut into my palm. My heart stopped and my breath congealed in my throat. I waited to be discovered. How in the world was I going to explain this?

The footfalls ceased. The silence stretched painfully. Water sloshed against my ankles. Finally, I risked discovery and peered over the edge of the dock to see what was going on.

Egan stood parallel to where the *Nighthawk* was secured. Lucky for me, he was looking back at the house. Though I knew I should duck in case he turned, I couldn't move. The sight of him riveted me.

As my gaze wandered over Egan, it was as if I were seeing him for the first time. Standing there, a dark silhouette outlined by the moon, he seemed more than human. I thought of a defiant captain astride the deck of his tossing vessel, shaking his fist at the storm. I thought of a god, standing with his feet planted wide on the earth, but really belonging to the wind and the sea.

As he stood there silent and still, I marveled at how firmly his head was planted on the strong column of his neck. And what a sturdy platform his broad shoulders made for that fine, strong neck. It seemed he had been physically built to bear the heavy blows life had dealt him. His upper body had such a sculptural solidity. It gave out a tactile impression of strength and endurance.

He wore a light colored shirt and stood arms akimbo, his sleeves loosely rolled to his forearms. His narrow hips, encased in jeans, drew my gaze. With a sudden rush of memory, I recalled how his muscular legs had felt entwined with mine. We had made love only once in our youth, but it had been wild and thrilling. I had kept that memory of our intimacy buried for years. Now it surfaced with such force that it made my throat ache and I felt breathless and hot.

I heard him murmur something and strained to hear the words. But I couldn't make them out. What had he said? There was so much about Egan I couldn't quite fathom.

Struggling to cope with the emotions stirred up inside me, I lost consciousness of the lake water icing my toes and the rough wood of the ladder spearing splinters into the flesh of my palms. All I could think about was how desperately I had once loved Egan. I had responded to him as if he were the matching half of my body and soul. I had yearned for him, and with the heedless impetuosity of my youth and inexperience, I'd been willing to do anything to have him. And I would have sworn that he'd felt the same way about me. *Oh, Egan,* I thought with a pang so sharp and deep it seemed to turn my innards upside down, *how could this have happened to us?*

As if he'd heard my anguished mental cry, Egan pivoted. I dropped back down. As I clung to the ladder, curled like a fetus so my head remained below the level of the dock, I felt him walking toward me. With every footfall, the wooden structure vibrated against my body.

At the very edge, he stopped. His feet were mere inches from my head and my knuckles. It seemed at any moment he would look down and see me. Perhaps he could see me now. Then why wasn't he saying something?

I clung there, my hands cold and numb. My muscles cried for relief, and my feet were chunks of glacier inside my soaked sneakers. The moon came out and struck the

water with a cool, white hand. Finally, I risked an up-
ward glance. I couldn't see anything but the tips of
Egan's shoes. He must be standing there looking at the
lake, perhaps listening to the wind rustle its surface. Why
was he so silent, I wondered. What was he thinking?
Might he be thinking of me? A powerful intuition wrung
from my heightened emotions told me he was.

Footsteps thudded softly back down the length of the
wooden structure. I must have held my cramped position another ten minutes before I dared raise my head
over the edge. When I finally did, Egan was nowhere in
sight. I was relieved, of course. But I also felt strangely
abandoned.

By that time, my muscles were so knotted, I could
barely haul my body back up onto the dock. When I did,
I lay shivering in reaction. Finally, I pulled myself together and got to my feet. All the lights were off in the
house now. Egan must have gone to bed.

Though I had only a splinter of moon for light, it was
enough to pull the *Nighthawk* close to the dock and jump
aboard. I went to the hatch, hoping Egan might have left
it open. No such luck. He'd padlocked it tight.

Now what? Go back home and forget this whole mis-
adventure? Much as I wanted to do that, I couldn't. I had
invested too much energy into this. Back on the dock, I
stood looking at the house. Did Egan have a dog? No, if
he did, it would have barked by now.

I walked up the lawn. Keeping to the shadows, I made
a circuit of the house. Anywhere else on earth, I mused,
spotlights and a burglar alarm would guard a big place
like this. Since the house was on Big Bass, half the windows were probably unlocked. The doors might be, too.

After I'd walked the perimeter of the stone foundation and assured myself that none of the bedroom lights were still on, I tried the back door. Locked.

I sat on the stoop for fifteen or twenty minutes, waiting while the night deepened. Then I went to the corner where I judged Egan would have his office and tried the window. It slid up with a faint squeal. I drew back from the noise as if it had scalded me and glanced apprehensively at the upstairs windows. No light flashed on. No angry baritone voice shouted "Who's there?"

Still, I waited before I approached the window again. When I did, I pushed it up another inch or two. Then I retrieved a picnic bench from the backyard and used it for a mounting block. Heart thudding like a pile driver, I hoisted myself through the window and stood.

When my eyes adjusted, I found I was not in an office, but in a rather sparsely furnished dining room. If Egan had a downstairs office, it must be across the hall. A few minutes later, I located it and played my flashlight around the walls. Unlike Egan's neat and well-ordered boats, his office was cluttered. Stacks of books and papers carpeted every surface. Egan was either untidy beyond belief or extremely busy. I glanced at a printed page lying next to his laser printer. It was about Lake Erie naval history. So he really was writing a book.

I began to hunt. Trying not to make any obvious signs of disturbance, I sifted through papers and ran my hand along shelves. None of the file or desk drawers were locked, so I could open them all. I didn't find Grandfather's metal boxes. Either Egan had taken them upstairs or stowed them on the *Nighthawk*. I couldn't go upstairs, but the boat remained a tempting place to search.

On impulse, I went to the kitchen and directed the beam of my flashlight over the wall next to the door. Sure enough, keys dangled from a small wooden plaque with brass hooks. Back at Sandusky harbor, I had watched Egan unlock the *Nighthawk.* His key ring had been distinctive. Now I recognized its leather tab and lifted it from its hook. Come hell or high water, I wasn't going to give up until I'd found out if my box was on Egan's sailboat.

Outside, I had to stand several minutes with my hand over my heart. Clearly, I wasn't cut out for the life of a cat burglar. I felt light-headed with nerves. Scratch another career option off the short list, I thought. When my breathing had finally slowed enough so I could walk without keeling over, I made my way down the lawn to the dock.

Aboard the *Nighthawk,* I slipped Egan's key into the padlock that sealed the hatch. Smooth as silk, the key turned and the lock fell open. Bingo! I put my head inside the hatch and saw nothing but utter blackness.

Reaching into my pocket, I withdrew my flashlight and switched it on. Instantly, I realized my mistake and stuck it down inside the hatch. Glancing over my shoulder, I waited for some sign that the light had been seen from the house. Nothing.

Again, I flattened my palm against my frantically pounding heart. Then I peered down inside the boat. Unlike Egan's study, the cabin was model-neat. Tweed cushions on the bench seats looked freshly vacuumed. Cups and plates had been stowed on immaculate shelves cleverly designed to keep them from falling out in rough weather. I saw a stack of life preservers arranged neatly on the cabin's sole. To the right, there was a small kitchen table hinged to the wall. It had been left open. Grandfather's box sat on top of it.

For a moment, my heart stopped beating. Then it rat-a-tat-tated so fast, I was afraid it might crash through my rib cage. Conceivably, this might be Egan's box, but in my heart I *knew* it was mine. Egan had stolen it from me. Had he also taken the gun? If so, where was it? And why? *Why?* I felt sick. So sick I almost turned away without exploring further.

But having gone this far, I had to know the whole truth. Gingerly, I climbed down the steps into the cabin. With care, I set the flashlight on the table so it shed a halo of light. For several seconds, I stood gazing down at the box.

It gave me the same eerie feeling I'd received from it the first time I'd seen it. Some sixth sense knew it contained evil and that if I opened it, the evil would reach out and swallow me. This is silly, I reassured myself. I rubbed the palm of my cold hands together, chafing them to get some blood flowing. I couldn't just stand there dithering. I had to pursue this all the way.

Carefully, I lifted the lid. Since I'd expected to find it locked, it surprised me when the lid opened smoothly. What I found inside surprised me even more. It contained an old-fashioned gold watch on a chain, a knife and a great many gold pieces. This wasn't my box. It was Egan's.

At this point, I suppose I should have acknowledged that I'd made a mistake. I should have replaced the lid and scurried home. But the gold fascinated me. I picked a piece up and shone my flash at it. Like mine, it was a twenty-dollar gold piece dated 1926. But I'd had only one gold piece. Egan had so many, they almost covered the bottom of the box.

I spared each of these a quick glance. The watch was the type men wore dangling from their vests before wristwatches became popular. The sturdy jackknife looked to be of about the same vintage. My gaze went back to the heaped coins. I'd never seen so much gold in my life.

I picked up a handful of them. I felt their weight and then let them run through my fingers. The feeling was sensuous, silken, oddly exciting. For the first time in my life, I began to understand the lure of gold. Oh, I had heard the stories, seen the movies. I'd known that through the centuries, men had killed for gold, sold their souls for gold. Before, it had only been an idea I'd never really understood. Now it became a reality I could grasp.

Just how much gold was here, I wondered. I sat down in front of the box and counted the gold pieces. When I finished, I had ten stacks of ten. Two thousand dollars in 1926 gold coins. What were they worth now, I wondered. Quite a bit more than their nominal value, I guessed.

Why had Grandfather left all this money to Egan? What connection did it and the watch and knife have with the objects in my box? Why was the box sitting on the table? Had Egan been looking at it tonight? Had Egan been thinking about it when he walked out on the dock and stood within inches of my hiding place? A bitter taste seeped into my mouth. I'd imagined he was thinking about me, when probably he'd really been thinking about this gold.

While my head buzzed with questions, I put the gold back and replaced the lid. Then I switched off the flashlight and climbed the staircase. My first clue that something was wrong came when I turned to replace the hatch cover.

The deck shuddered and I heard a soft thud. I half turned, when a heavy blow knocked me sideways. Sprawling back on the deck, I looked up to see a faceless shadow coming at me. With a scream, I lashed out at it, kicking and biting. Something struck me on the head so hard my ears rang. An explosion went off behind my eyes. Then the world disappeared.

"OHHH," I heard a distant voice groan. I realized the groans were coming from me. "Ohhhh." A hand smoothed my hair. Then it came to rest on my forehead. Though the palm felt slightly leathery, the touch was gentle.

"Uhhhhh."

"Are you okay, Katy?"

The voice was deep and familiar. As it sank into my consciousness, I opened my eyes.

"Are you okay?"

Egan was leaning over me, his face very close to mine. His eyes were dark. I couldn't be sure whether with worry or anger.

"I hurt all over."

"I know. I'm sorry about that."

"Where am I?" I struggled to sit up. Firmly, Egan held me in place.

"You're in the cabin of the *Nighthawk*. I carried you here after I hit you. I didn't know it was you, Katy."

Hardly hearing his words, I stared up at him in shock. "It was you who attacked me? You were the one who hit me?"

"Not deliberately. I was only trying to stop you. I thought you were a thief."

I lay there gazing at him and reliving that terrifying moment when he'd lunged at me and thrown me to the deck. Every joint in my body ached. I was probably a mass of bruises. But of even more concern this minute was how I was going to explain my presence on Egan's boat.

"I'm a light sleeper," he said. "Something woke me up. I saw a light down here on the dock and got up to investigate. Then I found the dining room window open and a damp footprint just outside it. Rex was still asleep, so I knew it couldn't be his. I figured I had a burglar."

"There are no burglars on Big Bass," I said. As I spoke, I thought, *some undercover type you make, Katy.* I had left Egan's house through the back door and forgotten all about the window in the dining room.

He was shaking his head. "Since we started getting so many tourists over here, Big Bass isn't so quiet. Sometimes college kids will come over, drink themselves silly at the bars and do stupid things. I thought one was trying to steal the *Nighthawk* and take it out for a joyride."

"You were lying in wait for me on the dock," I accused. Remembering the stolen keys, the box, the gold, my mind raced. The moment was surely at hand when Egan would demand an explanation. What was I going to say?

Egan waved an impatient hand. "Okay, I was lying in wait for a thief. By the time you came out of the hatch, I'd worked up quite an angry head of steam. But I'd never have jumped you like that if I'd recognized you. All I could see was a dark figure."

"You couldn't tell I was a woman?"

"Of course not. All I could tell was that you'd been fooling around inside my boat where you had no business, which I'd like you to explain, by the way. But before we get into it, are you all right? Can you move?

After I carried you down here, I checked you over. Nothing seems broken.''

Intently, Egan stared into my eyes. I knew from my hospital experience in Sandusky that he was monitoring for signs of concussion. Half-hypnotized, I stared back at him. His face was so close, I could see the black ring that emphasized the cornflower-blue of his irises. No red veins marred the whites of his eyes. The long sooty lashes that framed them emphasized their clarity.

His ebony curls, on the other hand, stuck up so wildly around his head that he might have been yanking at them. Black stubble peppered his lean cheeks and cleft chin. His lips were thinned as if by strong emotion. What emotion, I wondered. Anger? Fury?

"I feel like a Barbie doll that's been slammed against the wall by an angry kid," I complained. "But I don't think anything's broken." While Egan watched, I tested my arms and legs, curled my fingers and toes.

"Do you want to try to sit up?"

"Yes."

He helped me into an upright position and put a boat cushion behind my head and shoulders. I leaned against it and let out a long, slow breath.

"How are you doing so far?"

"Okay. I'm a little woozy. You hit me on the head."

"I know. But it isn't as if I didn't have a reason. What were you doing on my boat?"

"Egan, please, not now. I have the mother of all headaches."

"I want an explanation, Katy. But in the meantime, these ought to help." He shook two tablets out of a green bottle and filled a glass of water from the tap in the galley sink.

"You have running water on board?"

"All the comforts of home. I'm going to fix you a cup of hot tea now. Do you think you can drink it?"

"Yes. Thanks."

While Egan busied himself at the stove, I swallowed the tablets and sipped from the glass. Then I looked around. An overhead light in the cabin shed a watery glow. I was sitting with my legs out on a bench that turned into a bunk. Across from me and to the right was the *Nighthawk*'s compact galley. The black box still sat on the table where I'd left it. As I spotted it, my mouth went dry.

Egan turned and caught my eye. "Your tea will be ready in a couple of minutes." Deliberately, he leaned against a bulkhead and folded his arms across his chest. In the tight, enclosed space of the cabin, he loomed very large. I felt engulfed by his field of masculine energy.

"Now that we've established I haven't killed you, how about answering my question. What's this all about, Katy?"

"What's what all about?"

"Come on, what are you doing sneaking around my property in the dead of night? You're lucky all you got was a knock on the head. I might have hurt you a lot worse in that scuffle." His eyebrows snapped together. "What the hell were you up to?"

"I haven't stolen anything."

"You had my keys. I found them in your pocket."

I gave him a look. "Just how thorough a tour of my body did you take after you knocked me unconscious?"

"Complete enough to make sure you were still in good shape. I found you were." He flashed me a wolfish grin with a cruel edge. "In fact, for a woman your age, you're in excellent shape."

"My age?"

Egan slammed a fist against the side of the bulkhead. "Let's stop playing games and get to the point, Katy. Why did you break into my house and then into the *Nighthawk?* What did you hope to find? Did it have something to do with what's on the table, by any chance?"

We both turned our attention to the black box. It sat there like a miniature coffin. The cabin's battery-generated light drew a faintly greenish cast from its dull black sheen, as if all the gold piled up inside was subtly leaking through.

"All right," I said. "You got me dead to rights. I confess I was down here because I wanted to see if you had my box."

He looked astonished. "Yours? Why would you think I had yours?"

"Two nights ago, it was stolen along with that gun we found."

Tension in the cabin constricted. Egan's voice, when he finally spoke, was dangerously quiet. "You thought I stole it?"

"The possibility occurred to me."

The shrill whistle of the tea kettle broke into the next taut silence. Without comment, Egan turned to fill a plastic mug. Handing it to me, he said, "Why would you think I'd steal from you? Is it because I'm a Halpern, and no matter what a Halpern does on this island, he's still trash?"

"Egan, no. Of course not."

I wasn't even sure he'd heard my shocked denial. "I'm tired of paying for the sins of my father and grandfathers," he declared bitterly. "I'm not like them, and neither is Rex."

"Egan, that's not the reason. I thought you might have taken it because you seemed to want it so badly, and because you were so fascinated by the gun. You looked angry when I wouldn't give it to you."

"On that flimsy basis, you were willing to come sneaking over here and break into my house and my boat?"

"I know it sounds crazy."

" 'Crazy' is not a strong enough word. 'Criminal' fits, though. I could turn you over to our fine sheriff for this. Maybe I ought to give him a call."

"Oh, Egan, you're not going to do that, are you?" I was horrified. My reputation on the island would really be mud if he did that.

"I won't, for now, but only because I know he doesn't like to be jarred from a sound sleep. Why did you think you'd find your box on the *Nighthawk?*"

"Just a hunch. I remembered how you always kept valuables hidden on your boat."

Egan's eyes narrowed. "You have a good memory."

"Where you're concerned, I suppose I do." I felt myself flush as I said the words.

"That makes two of us, Katy. I remember a lot about you. One thing I specially remember is how trusting you used to be—trusting as a baby. Apparently, that's changed."

"Egan, you can't blame me for thinking you might have taken my box. Only a fool wouldn't be suspicious after some of the things that have happened lately."

"What things? Oh yes—" He rolled his eyes in comprehension. "You mean seeing my face glaring at you through the window?"

"I really did see you, Egan."

"That's impossible," he snapped. "You were hallucinating or having a bad dream. Nor did I take your box and gun." He tapped the metal container beneath his hand. "If you opened this, you know it's not yours."

"I did open it." Nervously, I rotated my mug between my palms. "That's quite a stack of gold Grandfather left you. It must be worth a lot in modern currency."

"Quite a sum. I made some inquiries." Egan's eyes narrowed again. "Oh, I get it. I suppose now you think that when I made an offer on the castle and your unopened box, I was trying to cheat you."

"That hadn't occurred to me."

"The way your mind works, sooner or later it would have, though, right? Okay," he said roughly, "let's get this straight right now. I didn't have ideas of cheating you or anybody. Believe it or not, at the time I made the offer, I hadn't looked inside my box. I had no notion it was full of gold."

I stared up into his angry face. "Even if you had wanted to bilk me, you'd have been disappointed. Grandfather left me only one gold coin."

There was a brief silence while Egan digested that. "Nate was an eccentric old man," he finally responded.

"No stranger than you." I rubbed my cold hands together. "Why haven't you deposited your money in a bank?"

Egan watched me grimly. "You know, I've been asking myself that same question. To tell you the truth, I haven't been able to let go of it. I think the stuff has a spell on it." Suddenly, Egan leaned forward, took my shoulders between his powerful hands, and stared intently into my eyes. "I asked your permission to take the gun," he said gruffly.

"Yes, you did."

His hands tightened almost painfully. "Earlier, I made you a fair offer for the castle."

"I know you did, very fair."

"Yet you accuse me of hanging around your property to harass you and then of breaking into your house and stealing from you. You're like everyone else on this damn island, Katy. Ready, no, anxious to think the worst of me."

Caught in his powerful grip, I stared into his tormented features. "Egan, that's simply not true. Are you forgetting that I was once so in love with you that I was willing to run off and marry you?"

His lips drew back from his teeth. "No," he said with dangerous quietness, "I haven't forgotten that. I haven't forgotten a single thing about that. I remember it all in perfect detail."

I felt a flush rise to my throat. Nervously, I swallowed. "It was a long time ago."

"No, Katy, it was only yesterday. I knew that when I saw you at your grandfather's funeral. The really big emotions in our lives never grow old. They're like jack-in-the-boxes—just when we think we've packed them away, they jump back out at us."

Imprisoned between the vise of his hands, I felt myself start to shake. In that split second, all the years separating Egan and me and what we'd felt for each other were stripped away. Vividly, I remembered the night we made love to each other on his sailboat, the *Wind Lass*.

I'd been a virgin, but Egan hadn't seduced me. I'd been so wildly in love with him that I'd been eager for his kisses and everything else he had to give me. I'd been so crazy about him that I'd lied to him about my age and convinced him I was old enough to be his lover. Afterward, stunned by the power of what had happened between us, I'd lost my nerve and dissolved into anxious tears.

"What's wrong?" Egan had whispered, kissing my ear and my hair. "Did I hurt you? I didn't realize you were still a virgin. Why didn't you tell me?"

I'd only cried harder. Realizing for the first time what a novice I'd been and anxious to reassure me, he'd asked me to marry him. I'd agreed, but only if we eloped. Reluctantly, Egan had given in to me and, like the two naive children we still were, we'd laid our plans.

Tearing myself back to the present, I cried, "Oh, Egan, can't you ever forgive me for what happened when we ran away together? I know how my father humiliated you. I know he made you feel like dirt. But I wasn't responsible for that. I have no idea how Grandfather found out in time to warn him. Please believe me."

"It doesn't matter whether I believe you. You were just a kid. Us getting married would never have worked."

"I wanted it to," I said softly and felt tears spring into my eyes. I tried to look away so he wouldn't see, but with him still holding me imprisoned in his grip, it was impossible to hide.

For a tense moment, there was silence. Then he eased the pressure of his hands and said in a low voice, "I did too. But you may have noticed, Katy, nobody gets what they want. So they have to make do. Katy, I haven't stolen from you. I haven't plotted against you or tried to threaten you. Do you believe me?"

Our gazes locked, and I blinked back the tears. Some part of me seemed to sink into the clear depths of his eyes. "Egan," I whispered.

"Katy." One of his hands lifted from my shoulder and touched my hair. He let a strand of it curl over his finger. "You've changed," he murmured, "but not in ways that are going to help me. Why couldn't you have become dowdy, or fat, or uninteresting? Why did you have to get more beautiful?"

Somewhere deep inside me an invisible dam broke. Currents of feeling I'd kept locked away for years flooded out of control. Every bit of breath and bone and blood that I possessed told me I could trust this man with my life. The voice of caution faded to a tiny murmur.

As if hearing me whisper his name had moved him deeply, Egan's throat worked. Finally releasing me, he got up and paced the short length of the cabin. Then he dropped onto the bench at my side. "Katy, it's time I did some explaining about why I wanted both boxes. Before he died, Nate told me about them. He never mentioned anything about gold, but he hinted they might hold clues about my grandfather's disappearance."

"Your grandfather?"

Egan nodded. "Rafe Halpern is still a bad word on this island."

"I know. Betty told me about him."

"Then you realize that the islanders think he's responsible for what happened to Bill Wiblin. Poor old Bill is a living reproach to us Halperns. For Rex's sake, I'd like to know the truth about Rafe and, if possible, clear his name."

"You thought you'd be able to do that if you had both boxes?"

Egan inclined his head. "These last couple of years, I got to know old Nate pretty well. Games and riddles were his thing. He liked to baffle people and catch them off guard. Once when we were playing checkers, he said he was sorry he'd stopped you and me from running away together."

"He did?" I was amazed, strangely thrilled. So Grandfather *had* forgiven me. If only I'd known that and not stayed away from him until it was too late.

"He wished we'd married and provided him with a houseful of great-grandchildren to play checkers with." Egan paused while I took this in, then added, "To be honest, I wondered if he divided the clues between us out of some addlepated notion of playing matchmaker from the grave. He was a manipulator. I've never cared much for the idea of being manipulated, especially by an ego-maniacal old fox like Nate."

"So you weren't going to play his game. Is that why you were so cold to me when we first met again?"

Never taking his eyes from mine, Egan tipped my face up with one hand. "Was I cold to you?"

"You know you were."

"Then, I suppose that was part of it."

"What was the other part?"

"Can't you guess?" His face came closer, his lips within inches of mine.

Slowly, I shook my head. "I don't have a clue."

A half smile quirked Egan's mouth and his voice lowered just a notch, as I felt one of his arms capture my waist. "Oh, I doubt that, Katy. You always were pretty swift. I think you've got all the clues you need."

"Egan..."

"Let's get it out in the open and stop pretending it isn't there. The minute I saw you again, I knew I wasn't over you the way I'd told myself. I still wanted you, Katy. God help me, I want you now."

"You do?" I leaned toward him.

"You know I do. You've always known. All the time we've been talking, I've itched to touch you—you must have known. Hell, when I was checking you over while

you were unconscious, I was worried sick, afraid I'd hurt
you. But all the while, running my hands over you was
driving me crazy."

I couldn't hide my smile, and Egan saw it. "You like
hearing me admit that?"

"Yes."

"Why? Is it because you like knowing you have that
kind of power over me?"

"Yes, I guess it is. I'm only human." The image of
Egan's strong, long-fingered hands exploring my unconscious body made my skin tingle and my heart beat fas-
ter. My eyes, the tone of my voice, gave away what I felt.
Something flared like a lit match at the back of Egan's
hot, blue gaze.

For a long instant, we stared at each other, divining in
our locked gazes a million doubts, hopes and desires.
Then we closed our eyes and let our lips touch.

I hadn't admitted it to myself, but I'd been dreaming
of this moment. For years after Egan and I first parted,
I'd awake in the night with his image burning in my
mind. I'd lie there, remembering him and aching with
longing and guilty regret. If only I'd been honest with
him. If only I hadn't been such a stupid, selfish kid. Then
neither of us would have gotten hurt and maybe, just
maybe, we might have made something lasting out of our
love.

Seeing him again, I'd realized what he'd just admitted
to. Despite the years, I'd never gotten over this man. He
still had the power to drive me crazy, and maybe he always would. What did it matter whether I trusted him or
not? I had to know his touch again, even if it was just
going to be for one last time.

At first, our kisses were tentative, questioning. Soon
all our questions found answers. Physical sensations

washed away my doubts—the firm feel of Egan's mouth, the faintly salty taste of him. I could smell soap and grass and the wind from the lake. Egan's chin was prickly against mine, yet I liked the raspy maleness of that. It had been a long time since I'd made love, and suddenly my body gave way to a desire I hadn't even realized I was capable of.

As his kiss demanded more of me, my hands circled his neck. My fingers sank into the springy curls that clustered there. Their tips explored the fine, strong shape of his skull. It and his kisses felt both familiar and exciting. I moaned and tipped my chin up while his mouth explored my cheeks, the line of my jaw, my throat. After that, I lost touch with time and place. There was no world outside, no problems, disappointments or fears. All I knew was Egan's hard body against mine, his hungry, rewarding lips, the knowing touch of his hands.

Sometime while we were kissing, he turned off the light. "Is it all right?" he whispered.

"Yes," I whispered back.

Together, we sank into the warm darkness blanketing the sailboat's small cabin. Egan's mouth traveled over my body, nibbling and teasing. "You're even more beautiful," he murmured as he tasted the hollows of my throat. His hand slipped beneath my turtleneck and found my breasts. My nipples stiffened with desire as his fingertips fondled them.

I loved his kisses, but I wanted more, and knew from the way his body strained against mine that he wanted more, too. Finally, galvanized by the passion ignited between us, we all but tore off each other's clothes. His chest felt hot against my bare flesh. The hair on it rubbed my skin, but the roughness only excited me more. I was far beyond logic now. All I knew was the darkness, the boat swaying rhythmically with the water beneath us and Egan.

As we covered each other with more hungry kisses, his hands shaped my body. They explored me as if charting a wondrous new territory. My breasts swelled beneath his touch and I clasped him tighter.

"Katy," he moaned urgently.

I clung to him, drew his head down to mine. Then we melded, surging and falling on our own tide of long pent-up passion. When it was over, we collapsed against each other in perfect satisfaction. For many long minutes, we lay molded to each other's bodies. It was as if we were two parts of the same whole, long separated, now finally together.

Chapter Seven

It couldn't last forever. Egan drew back and studied me in the faint shaft of moonlight from the porthole. "I feel as if I'm in a dream."

"I don't think we're asleep."

He chuckled roughly. "No, I know the difference between reality and a fantasy. I've dreamed of this too often." As he spoke, his hand traced the line of my hip and then moved up my rib cage to the slope of my shoulder. I shivered with pleasure.

"Are you cold?"

"Hardly. Coldness doesn't seem to be my problem where you're concerned."

"Then we share a mutual problem. You're so beautiful, Katy. Do you have any idea what a lovely creature you are?"

"None whatsoever. Why don't you tell me all about it? I promise to pay close attention to every word."

In the murky light, I caught Egan's grin. "I can't believe you're still unmarried. Why, Katy?"

"Until recently, I was engaged," I said softly.

"Oh?"

"His name is Edward Brock. He was my boss."

"Is Brock the reason you're here and not in Detroit?"

"Partially."

"Since you're in my arms and not his, I suppose I should be happy about that," Egan replied, not sounding at all happy. "You told me you lost your job. But you wouldn't explain how. Did it have something to do with this Brock?" He said the name as if it had a bad taste.

I stifled a chuckle, the female in me amused by his obvious jealousy. "Yes, in a backward sort of way. I was involved in a sexual harassment lawsuit that cost the station a lot of money."

"Someone harassed you?"

"Not me. It was one of our secretaries. She was a very pretty young girl, and she was being stalked by the station's owner. He was a rich and powerful older man, with a wife and family and very high standing in the community, so no one would believe her—not even the police. When she came to me, I decided to give her the benefit of the doubt."

"You helped her?"

"Yes, I did."

"Even though you must have known it wouldn't do you any good at the station?"

"I guess I didn't think I had any choice. The situation outraged me. She had no one to defend her. I felt that as a woman I was honor bound to stick up for my sex. Brock didn't see it my way. He warned me to stay out of it. I ignored him."

"So, what happened?"

"I set up my own private investigation and got the goods on the guy. My evidence helped her prove her case, but it ruined my career. Edward finally bowed to pressure from the board of directors and asked me to resign."

"Couldn't you have taken them to court?"

"I suppose I could have. But it was obvious that my working relationships at the station were ruined. Besides, I thought I'd be better off getting a job at another station. When I started looking for other jobs, I found the word was out on the grapevine that I was a troublemaker. So far, I haven't even been offered an interview."

As Egan stroked my shoulder, I looked up into the darkness. "The funny thing is that Edward still doesn't really understand why his not sticking up for me ruined our relationship. In his mind, our professional and personal connection is completely separate. Knowing that I can't trust him to defend me when the chips are down professionally, how can I trust him personally? I can't, but he just doesn't get that."

"If a relationship is going to amount to anything, there has to be trust."

"That's right."

Egan sighed. "That brings things back to us, doesn't it? Do you trust me, Katy?"

I gazed at his face, trying to make out its expression in the shadows. "I want to," I whispered. I wanted to believe every word he'd ever said. But how could I really know the truth? The only thing I truly knew about Egan was that if I could lie in his arms like this forever, I'd be happy.

As if he were listening in on my thoughts, he groaned faintly. "Wanting to isn't the same, is it? Don't say any more. Let it wait until morning." Then his mouth came down hard on mine.

A COUPLE OF HOURS before dawn, sanity returned. "I have to go," I said as I picked up my jeans, "and you need to be in the house when Rex wakes up."

Egan sighed deeply. "I suppose you're right, but I don't like it."

After I finished pulling on my turtleneck, he reached for my hand. "This has been a beautiful night, Katy. I feel as if I stepped off the planet and into heaven."

I felt the same way. For a few all-too-short hours, Egan and I had been in a world where only we existed and made the rules. But the worries I'd crowded into the dark closets of my mind were sneaking out again. Gently, but firmly, I pulled my hand from his. "Pretty soon the sun will rise. If I'm not careful, so will the eyebrows of a lot of gossipy islanders."

He laughed and then reached for his own clothes. "I'll walk you home."

"Is that a good idea? What if we're seen?"

"Wagging island tongues really do terrify you, don't they?"

"Idiotic as it must seem, I would like to maintain what few shreds of good reputation are left to me."

Though I couldn't see, I sensed that Egan was rolling his eyes. "Listen, there are no other houses between your place and mine. We're going to be walking along the shore in the dead of night. I think it's safe."

Outside, it was chilly and breezy. My tennis shoes, still wet from the dunking they'd taken, squished in the dewy grass. "Compared to how dark it was inside your boat, it seems almost light out here." I gazed up at the sky, sprinkled with watching, waiting stars.

"The wind has blown away the clouds." He paused. "You aren't going to talk about it, are you?"

"Talk about what?"

"What just happened between us. What else? My God, Katy, after fourteen years apart, we just made love."

I swallowed. "I don't know what to say about it, Egan. What *is* there to say?"

Planting his feet on the ground, he put his hands on his narrow hips. "You could say you're glad."

"Of course I'm glad."

"Why? Because we finally got it out of our systems? And now that that's done, we can go about our business like normal human beings?"

I faced him. "I hope after this, we can stop sniping at each other. I hope we can be friends."

Egan's laugh held no humor. "Oh, Katy, dream on. We can't be friends. With us, it's either all or nothing. That's the way it's always been, and nothing's changed."

"I hope that's not true."

"I bet you do. And I think I understand the reason why. You're never going to be prepared to give yourself to someone like me, are you, Katy? In fact, you probably don't plan to be on Big Bass much longer."

"I don't know what my plans are, Egan. Honestly, I haven't made any."

"Oh, but soon you will. You'll want to move on to another glamorous job like the one you lost."

"I told you. My reputation's ruined. Word's out that I'm a troublemaker. It's not likely I'll ever get another job in broadcasting."

Egan shook his head. "A woman with your experience and talent? I'm sure if you keep looking, you'll find one. There is no future for us and never has been."

I didn't know what to say. When I'd made love with Egan, I hadn't been thinking about the future. In truth, I hadn't been thinking at all. How could I envision a future when everything about the present was so uncertain?

But Egan had sunk into a gloomy silence and didn't seem to require an answer. I started walking again and he kept pace at my side, a mute brooding presence. A short distance off, I could see the castle's turreted silhouette. As I looked at it, I thought of my grandfather and the doubts I still entertained about his death.

Egan finally spoke. "Do you accept what I've said regarding your accusations? I haven't tried to scare you. I haven't stolen from you or tried to cheat you."

We had reached the edge of my property. After the exquisite passion we'd shared in the *Nighthawk,* the bittersweet quality of this conversation made my heart ache. I couldn't tell Egan that doubts still nibbled at the edges of my feelings toward him. "Yes, I believe you."

"Well, that's something. Do you trust me enough to tell me what you found in the box your grandfather left you?"

I stumbled, caught off guard by the question. He put a hand on my shoulder to steady me and then turned me toward him. "What else did you find besides that one gold coin you mentioned last night?"

"Nothing of interest. Just a few scraps of paper and an old key. Oh, and a piece of crystal."

"Crystal?"

"Blue crystal."

"Are you telling me everything?"

Staring at him, I struggled silently. Somehow, I wasn't quite ready to tell him of the article about Spike Shawnaway. Despite everything that had happened between us this night, I was still far from trusting him completely. The realization hit me like cold water.

"You're holding something back, aren't you?" Cupping my chin with his left hand, he leaned down and planted a swift, hard kiss on my lips. "Why the hell did you come back?" he muttered, as if cursing me. Then he strode off into the darkness.

I SPENT THE REST of that night pacing around the castle, amazed by what had happened. After midnight, I'd set off for Egan's place, convinced he was my enemy. Then I'd wound up making frenzied, passionate love with him—after which, we'd parted on a sour note. How could things seesaw this way?

Obviously they could, but they shouldn't, I told myself as I opened the door to the cellar. I stood on the top step gazing down into the cool, dank room. As I pictured Grandfather falling into that well of darkness, a chill vapor seemed to seep up from the spot where he'd landed and taken his last breath. What if Grandfather hadn't been alone when he died? What if he'd been arguing with someone? What if that person had pushed him, either accidentally or on purpose?

Shouldn't I have warned Egan that I suspected the gold Grandfather had left him had been stolen from a government shipment by Shawnaway? Why hadn't I? My heart squeezed in my chest. I'd kept silent because I still wondered if Grandfather's fall had really been an accident. Despite my wild lovemaking with Egan, I still feared he might have been responsible.

When I finally did go to bed, I slept late. The afternoon sunshine streaming through the bedroom window woke me up. Groggy and disoriented, I glanced at the clock on the bedside table and groaned. If I wanted to get to the post office before it closed, I had just enough time to throw on some clothes and grab a cup of coffee.

A half hour later, I rounded the corner on the tree-lined lane that shaded the little brick building.

"What are you in such an all-fired hurry over?" Flo Hadditer demanded as I burst through the front door. She tapped my foot with the end of her cane. "Land's sake, you almost knocked me down."

"Sorry. I wanted to get my mail before the post office closed."

"If you're in such an infernal rush for your mail that you're willing to knock people down, you should start out for it earlier in the day." She peered into my face. "Been spending too much time out in the sun? Looks like you've got a bad burn there."

My hand flew up to my cheek. I felt blood creep up the back of my neck. My face wasn't sunburned. Egan's bristly chin rubbing against my skin as he kissed me had made it red. "I'll be okay," I mumbled.

"Better put some cream on that pretty face. Don't want it to peel." She followed me over to the boxes. As she unlocked hers, I undid mine. My heart did a little flip-flop when I saw the return addresses on the two business-size envelopes it contained. They were replies to the résumés I'd sent out. I couldn't resist tearing open my letters.

"Judging from the expression I see on that red face of yours, you didn't just win the lottery." Mrs. Hadditer leaned on her cane and studied me with speculative shoe-button eyes.

"You're right about that."

"Someone just send you a bill you can't pay?"

Tempted though I was to tell her that my mail was none of her business, I couldn't be rude to Flo. She was too old and too funny and too basically well meaning. "These aren't bills, Mrs. Hadditer. They're rejections."

"Rejections?" She quirked a silvery eyebrow. "You trying to write the great American novel?"

"Nothing so ambitious. I'm just trying to get a job."
After I opened the post office door for her and helped her
out, I held up the envelopes. "These are replies from
broadcasting stations to letters of application I sent out."

"Turning you down?"

I nodded. "Thanks, but no thanks. I guess I knew
when I saw them what they were. Good news usually
comes on the phone. It's only when the news is bad that
you find it in the mailbox."

"Makes no sense to me. I'd think a girl like you would
have no trouble whatsoever getting herself a job."

"Broadcasting is a very competitive field," I murmured. Especially when you've left your last job under a
cloud, I thought with a taste of bitterness.

"Nothing I can do about those letters. But I can offer
you a cup of tea and some homemade cookies. How
about stopping in for a few minutes?" Flo said a few
minutes later. It had seemed impolite to hurry on and
leave her alone. So I had walked along with her, slowing
my pace to match hers.

"Sure. That would be lovely."

Flo lived a block from the post office in a little cottage
with a wide, shady front porch. She led me to her compact kitchen and sat at the Formica table, directing while
I boiled water and assembled the ingredients for our tea.

"You'll find some nice chamomile tea in a glass jar in
that blue cupboard. Yes, that's right. And the cookies are
in the cookie jar. Put about a dozen on a plate. Nothing
I hate worse than a stingy-looking cookie plate. Now,
since the day's turned so pretty, there's no reason to stay
stuck here in this musty old kitchen. We'll have our treat
out on the porch where we can admire the tulips," she
declared.

I picked up the loaded tole tray and carried it ouside. After we'd filled our flowered cups, we settled back into a pair of old painted rockers. Slightly weathered hand-stitched cushions softened their thatched seats.

Enjoying the porch's shady coolness, I began to rock gently. The air smelled of spring leaves and fresh-cut grass. On the corners of the lawn, yellow banners of forsythia blazed. It wouldn't be such a bad thing to be an elderly librarian, if you had a spot like this in which to enjoy your declining years, I reflected. For a moment, I envied Mrs. Hadditer.

"Judging from what I read in the papers and see on TV," Flo said, "times are hard for everybody these days. Maybe you won't be able to find work on one of those news stations right off, but you're smart. You'll find something."

"Thanks for the encouragement, Mrs. Hadditer. Right now, I can use every kind word I get."

"'Mrs. Hadditer' is too much of a mouthful. Call me Flo. You know, if one of those letters had been a yes, you'd be leaving us, wouldn't you?"

"Well, I do have to support myself. Grandfather willed me the castle, but he didn't leave much else." I reached for one of her lemon cookies. It melted in my mouth. I was hungry. Except for the coffee I'd grabbed on the way out, I hadn't had anything to eat since yesterday.

"Have you tried to find a job here?"

I stopped midmunch and then swallowed. "No. I guess I didn't think anyone would want to hire me. As I recall, islanders aren't partial to hiring strangers."

"Well, you're really not a stranger. But I don't blame you for not trying. There's not much on Big Bass for a woman except maybe working the cash register in a gift shop. You've got too much education and ambition for that to satisfy you.'' She took a reflective sip of tea. ''Like I said before, you'll soon be finding something to suit you on the mainland. Meanwhile, I have a suggestion. Cy Clipson puts out the *Island Gazette* on an old press he keeps in that monstrosity he lives in. I know he's thinking about retiring. Why don't you offer to help him with the paper? Who knows, there might be an opportunity there for an enterprising girl like you.''

I opened my eyes at that. Such a thing had never occurred to me. But now that Flo made the suggestion, I was intrigued. ''Thanks. Maybe I'll considered that.'' Dimly, I remembered the *Island Gazette* from my first stay here. It wasn't much—a few ads, a chatty gossip column, profiles of some of the local characters and a healthy letters-to-the-editor section.

''How long has the *Gazette* been published?'' I questioned.

''Oh, ever since I can remember. And I first set foot on this island back in the twenties.''

''You did?''

''Came here to help get the library in shape, thinking I'd stay in this godforsaken place no more than a year. Then I met and married my husband. Been here ever since.'' She laughed. ''Even when Ben died, it never occurred to me to leave. Island life gets into your blood. That's hard to explain to outsiders, but it's the truth.''

''I know it is. Grandfather never wanted to leave. Since you came here in the twenties, you must have known him when he was a young man.''

''Sure I did. I suppose you'd like me to say he was handsome and charming,'' she said dryly.

''From the look on your face, something tells me he was no such thing.''

"Most arrogant, stubborn, self-important man I ever met. How he ever persuaded your grandmother to marry him, I'll never know. I never blamed your father for abandoning ship off the island soon as he could. It must have been hell to have Nate for a daddy."

I smiled. My father had never had much to say about Grandfather. But what he had said hadn't exactly been complimentary. "What was the island like back in the twenties?"

"A lot different from what it is now."

"I'll bet."

"Not so different in other ways, though. It's a drinking place now. Back then, people came here to drink and carouse, too. 'Course, then it wasn't legal and there was more money in it. Bootlegging was big business."

"Was there bootlegging on the island?"

"Is there lemon in lemonade? Big Bass was ideal for bootlegging. Rumrunners from Canada would cross over in fast boats and smuggle the stuff onto the island just about every night."

"Goodness."

Flo laughed at my expression. "Oh, midnights were busy times around these parts. Our men would store kegs in limestone caves, and then take the stuff onto the mainland on moonless nights. You can't really blame the islanders. At that time, there wasn't much tourist industry, and islanders had to make their bread somehow."

"Mrs. Hadditer—"

"Heaven's sake, didn't I ask you to call me Flo? Just because I've got more than half a century on you, doesn't mean we can't be friends."

"No, of course it doesn't. I'd be honored to be your friend ... Flo, did you ever hear of a man named Spike Shawnaway?"

Flo's eyebrows danced up. "Now, where did a young thing like you ever hear that name?"

"When I was cleaning the castle, I came across some old newspaper clippings."

"From back that far? Well, I guess I'm not surprised. That stingy old pack rat never threw anything away. Sure I heard of Spike Shawnaway. In those days, that was a name you heard whispered around here quite a lot. I think he was the man who paid the islanders off when they took liquor across the lake to the mainland."

She shook her head. "Lot of funny business went on at night, I'll tell you. Some of the islanders paid a heavy price for all that nonsense."

"Are you thinking of Betty Wiblin's grandfather?" I asked.

Flo gave me a sharp look. "Poor old Billy Wiblin. What a sad creature. You'd never guess, looking at him now, what a bright young fella he used to be. Always laughing and cutting up. A fast one with the girls, too. Oh, he and that devil, Rafe, they made quite a team bootlegging and chasing the pretty women."

"Do you mean Rafe Halpern, Egan's grandfather?" I asked.

"Who else? There was only one Rafe Halpern on this island."

Flo took another sip of tea and then fell silent. As she gazed out over the lilacs blooming in the corner of her yard, her usually sharp expression grew dreamy. Eager as I was to question her further, I hesitated to interrupt her silent musings. She was so obviously lost in a past I could never fully share.

"Now, there was a man who could truly be described as handsome and charming," she finally murmured.

"Rafe Halpern?"

"Oh, yes, indeed. More handsome than the angel he was named after and with a naughty way about him that made the girls swoon. He had a tongue smooth as silk. Could always talk himself out of whatever briar patch he'd got into. A fortunate talent for Rafe, because he liked nothing better than trouble and was always in it up to his neck."

"Always?"

Flo snorted. "Oh, yes. Tongues around here were always on the wag about Rafe Halpern and his doings. Egan looks a lot like his granddaddy did. But he never had Rafe's lying silver tongue. Maybe that's a blessing. Maybe Egan turned out solid because he couldn't talk his way out of trouble the way Rafe did. 'Course, since Rafe disappeared so young leaving a pregnant young wife behind him, we'll never know how he would have turned out."

"Rafe's wife was pregnant with Egan's father?"

"She was, and named him Rex, same as Egan's son. I sure hope the young Rex don't take after his granddaddy. Egan's father ran away from the island when he was a teenager. Became a merchant seaman and didn't come back until he was middle-aged and collecting a disability pension. That's when he married and had Egan. Drank himself to death shortly after, so Egan never really knew his daddy. If he had, I suspect he never would have named his son after the man."

I listened to all this curiously. But it was the story about Egan's grandfather that interested me most. "What do you think happened to Rafe?"

"Lord knows."

"Do you suppose he might still be alive someplace?"

Flo took a last sip of tea. With delicate precision, she set the flowered china cup and saucer back on the tray.

"It might surprise you to know how often I've lain awake nights wondering about Rafe. He wasn't the kind of man a person forgot. And for all his rakish, devilish ways, I guess I had a soft spot in my heart for him. I'd like to think of him alive and happy somewhere and still up to his tricks. But I can't."

"Why not, Flo?"

"Because Rafe was an islander, born and bred. You don't get that out of your blood. Oh, I don't put running away past Rafe. But he'd never have stayed away. If he were still alive, he'd have been back long before now."

"Then you think he died the night he disappeared and Billy Wiblin was injured?"

"Then or soon after."

"What do you think happened?"

"Can't say exactly. Maybe there was a fight. Maybe there was a bad accident. Whatever it was, my guess is Rafe found trouble he couldn't talk his way out of." She leaned toward me and lowered her voice to a whisper. "I'll tell you one thing. If Rafe Halpern died by violence, his spirit is still here."

I felt a shiver ripple up my spine. "You think Rafe Halpern's ghost still hangs around the island?"

"I think a lot of ghosts still hang around the island, and his is one of them."

"Why?"

"Can't say. It's just something I feel." She reached for the plate between us. "Have another cookie?"

I accepted the cookie and ate without really tasting it. Soon after, I said goodbye to Flo. When I left, she was still sitting on her porch, rocking and gazing at the lilacs with a faraway look in her old eyes. I could have sworn she was seeing the ghosts of the people she remembered so vividly.

Chapter Eight

After leaving Flo, I walked into town with a lot to think about. In my pocket, the crumpled-up rejection letters rustled and crunched against my hip. They reminded me of Flo's suggestion that I speak to Cy Clipson. On impulse, I veered left and headed toward his house.

Cy, a widower, lived in a remarkable house. It was the deckhouse of an old ore boat that had been broken up for scrap. He'd salvaged the most livable section and had it towed to the island. He'd dragged it up onto a spit of land he owned and named it Cy's Ship of Dreams. There its rusting hulk sat like a grounded gooney bird, outraging the islanders and intriguing tourists and passing yachtsmen.

Since spotting the Ship of Dreams the week before on one of my afternoon walks, I'd wanted to get a closer look. This was my chance.

I found Cy outside slapping a coat of red lead paint onto his unusual domicile's iron sides. He was a short, wiry, fit-looking man with a thick head of white hair and shrewd, humorous pale blue eyes. Now, as almost always, he wore baggy jeans and a plaid work shirt. He looked up when he heard my sneakers crunching on his rutted gravel driveway. Then he put his roller down in a paint pan, wiped his hands on a rag and stood.

"Hello, Mr. Clipson. My name is Katy Conroy." Though I felt it only polite to introduce myself, I was sure he knew who I was. Everybody on the island knew who everybody else was. By now, my having come back to live in my grandfather's house had probably been picked apart and talked into the ground.

"'Course I know who you are. Saw you in church last Sunday. Liked your pink dress. Looked good with your pretty yellow hair."

"Why, thank you," I said, smiling warmly. "Flo Hadditer suggested I speak to you. Have I come at a bad time? Would you rather I come back later?"

Cy's weathered face broke into a twinkly grin. "Now, see here, young lady, I'm not so old I'm going to shoo away a pretty girl who wants to speak with me. That doesn't happen so often these days. Besides, I was looking for an excuse to quit this infernal painting. Been doing it for the last couple of hours, and it's beginning to feel like work. What did you have on your mind?"

A bit hesitantly, I explained my background and Flo's suggestion that Cy might be interested in my help with the paper. To my surprise, he reacted enthusiastically to the idea.

"Well, it's about time the old girl made a useful suggestion. Mostly all she does is complain. You wouldn't believe the fuss she kicked up about my house here." He pointed at the Ship of Dreams.

"It must be wonderful to live in a real ship." I gazed up at the bridge.

"Almost like being at sea. Every morning, I wake up in the wheelhouse and feel as if I'm on an adventure. Flo wouldn't understand that. Not an imaginative bone in her body."

That wasn't true, I thought, recalling what Flo had said about the island's ghosts. But I didn't correct Cy. For the time being, I wanted to forget Flo's ghosts. "How do you get up on deck?" I asked. "Do you have to climb this ladder?"

"I've got a gangplank around the other side. Egan Halpern helped me rig it. Now there's a boy with a spark of imagination. Unlike some people, he understands what the Ship of Dreams is all about."

"I bet he does," I murmured.

I stayed with Cy for the next hour. It was sort of a combination house tour and job interview. While he showed me around his place, he talked about the newspaper. "Inherited her from old Abe Benson. He's dead now. 'Course, my wife thought I was crazy to take it over, but it kept me going after she died. That and moving to the Ship of Dreams."

He gave me another of his conspirator's winks and then led me to the final spot on the tour—his antique printing press in the dank recesses of the ship's hold. "Now, I don't mind if you wrinkle up your nose. I know it doesn't smell too sweet down here. Actually, it stinks like diesel. As you can see, my operation's pretty old-fashioned."

I looked around. Aside from the smell, the place was a rat's nest. Overflowing boxes and stacks of yellowed paper littered the floor. How Cy managed to get out a monthly publication in this confusion I didn't know. "It looks as if you've got back copies of every *Island Gazette* that's ever been published."

"Matter of fact, I probably have. See that stack over there? Dates back to World War I."

"Really?" I walked over to the old newspapers spilling out of a grimy box. When I touched them, they began to crumble. "You really ought to see if these can be preserved."

Cy chuckled. "What I really ought to do is toss them out. Been meaning to do that for years now. Maybe I'll get around to it this weekend."

While he talked, I checked out the series of boxes stacked nearby. One of them had copies of the *Gazette* from the twenties.

"If you really plan to toss these out, would you mind if I took some home to read?"

"'Course not. Be my guest. I guess you think this is a pretty amateurish operation," he added as I picked through the papers and then scooped up an armful from the mid-twenties.

"Maybe you could do a little modernizing. What about switching to desktop publishing?"

He shook his head. "I'm too old to change. Besides, I'm thinking of giving up the business so that during the winter months I can visit my daughter in Florida. But if you decide to come in with me and then get around to thinking you'd like to take over, you could do whatever you wanted. Still interested?"

"Yes, I am. I've got a computer and some publishing software. Maybe I can show you what I mean by desktop publishing."

"Maybe you can. It won't hurt me to take a look."

I GUESS MY FACE must have worn a cheerful expression when I left Cy's. A half mile down the road I ran into Betty striding along with a basket over one arm. She wore baggy canvas slacks and an orange T-shirt that emphasized her freckles.

"What are you grinning about?" she demanded. "Did you find a pile of gold in one of Nate's closets?"

This was so close to the truth that my mouth dropped open.

She cocked her head. "Hey, what did I say to upset you? A second ago, you were grinning. Now you look as if you just found a cockroach in your carrot cake."

I laughed. "I was just thinking about the assignment Cy Clipson gave me. He asked me to write an article on Doc Martin."

"He did? How did that happen?"

When I explained my new arrangement to help Cy with the paper, Betty nodded. "Sounds like a good idea to me. But there's not much money in it."

"I have to start someplace. Where are you headed?"

"Fern-picking. I thought I'd dig up some shoots and start a rock garden in my backyard. Want to come along? The spot is just a little way up the road."

"I'll walk as far as the west road with you. But then I have to take the shortcut home. This bag of old newspapers Cy gave me is heavy." I didn't explain that I felt light-headed with hunger and disoriented from interrupted sleep after my wild and crazy night with Egan. God, but I hoped none of the islanders got wind of it.

"That's quite a sunburn you've got," Betty said.

I clapped my free hand over my beard-reddened chin and changed the subject. "I've been talking with Flo Hadditer about the old times on the island. She told me more about the bootlegging days."

"Then she probably told you that before Gramps' accident, he was a bootlegger."

"She said that. She also said the island bootleggers used to hide the stuff in caves."

Betty nodded. "Makes sense. The north end of the island is riddled with them. I guess they would be ideal places to store booze, or anything else you might want to hide from prying eyes."

"Flo also talked about Egan's grandfather, Rafe, being a bootlegger."

"Well, that doesn't surprise me. Everybody knows he was never up to any good. Like father like son."

"You couldn't have known Egan's father. According to Flo, he died when Egan was young."

"Yes, but my mother told me he was a drunk." Betty gave me a thoughtful, sideways glance. "A while ago I found an old diary in Gramps' things. It's pretty interesting. Mentions Rafe quite a bit. In fact, it tells how Gramps and Rafe Halpern used to load a boat down with illegal hooch and deliver it to the mainland on moonless nights."

At that, my ears pricked up. "Would you mind if I read the diary, Betty?"

"Why do you ask?"

"I'm interested in island history, particularly that period."

She frowned. "Maybe I shouldn't have mentioned it to you."

"Why? Is there something in the diary you don't want me to see?"

"Well, not so far as I know. But I haven't finished it. It's not easy reading. Gramps didn't exactly have the best penmanship. And some of it's..." She hesitated. "Well, frankly, some of it's personal family stuff. I guess before I let anyone else look at it, I'd like to finish the thing myself. Then I'd like to do some thinking about it. Do you understand?"

"Of course I understand, Betty. Maybe you can answer this question, though. Does the diary say anything about a man named Spike Shawnaway?"

"Shawnaway?" She shook her head. "I don't think I've run across that name yet. I certainly have read a lot about the doings of Rafe Halpern, though." She grimaced. "From what Gramps wrote of Rafe Halpern, he was one wild and reckless bad boy. He'd roll over in his grave laughing if he could see what an upstanding citizen Egan has become." She snorted. "He probably wouldn't believe it, either."

"He wouldn't? What do you mean?"

"Only that around these parts, we tend to believe that blood runs true. No Halpern has ever stayed an upstanding citizen forever. It just isn't in them."

I took Betty to task. I told her she was being unfair and she agreed that she probably was. But even as I chided her, I wondered if she could be right and if Egan could be the grandson of the notorious Rafe Halpern in more ways than just looks.

THAT NIGHT I curled up on the Victorian couch in the living room and started reading through Cy Clipson's old *Gazettes*. It was different from reading the microfilm news pages in the Sandusky library. The *Gazette* didn't cover the news of the day but devoted itself almost exclusively to island gossip. I read about deaths, births and marriages, local disputes and barroom brawls. Rafe Halpern's name came up frequently in the last category. One article read:

Wild Rafe Halpern challenged all comers to an arm-wrestling contest at the Canopy Thurday night. Before the night was over, he'd vanquished a dozen of our brawniest boys. Clem Heavey claimed Rafe's methods were unfair, and the two went outside for fisticuffs, much to the enjoyment of all.

I closed my eyes and imagined the scene. In my mind's eye, I could see the men gathered around, laughing and shouting encouragement to whomever Rafe was taking on. There might have been women hovering on the fringes, too. According to Flo, Rafe had been a lady-killer. And no wonder, if Egan looked as much like him as she said.

Still tired from the night before, I drifted into a light sleep and began to dream. In my dream, I rose up from the couch and walked to the kitchen. As if in a trance, I put my hand on the cellar doorknob. The door swung open and I looked down. Grandfather's crumpled body lay at the foot of the steps. As I gazed down at him in horror, he opened his eyes and looked at me.

Then a voice echoed in my ear. It seemed to be coming from the house itself. "Revenge," it whispered.

I backed away from the door and put my hands over my ears. But the voice wouldn't be blocked out. Now it seemed to be coming from outside. In desperation, I ran outside onto the porch.

Some one hundred yards away, barely visible in the shadows, I saw Egan. His dark curls spilled over his forehead and his face was deathly pale. He wore overalls and a faded plaid shirt. As he gazed at me, my blood turned icy in my veins. Then he faded away and disappeared.

I woke up with a strangled scream and found myself still lying on the couch in the living room. As I stared around dazedly, the tall clock in the corner struck midnight. So I'd dreamed all that. None of it had really happened.

I should have been reassured, but the goose bumps on my forearms still stood out like miniature golf balls. I got up, hurried to the kitchen and flicked on the light. The cellar door was firmly closed. When I opened it, no body lay at the foot of the steps. Nevertheless, it took a minute before I could gather the courage to open the screen door and step onto the back porch. The night was quiet. I saw nothing in the shadows and heard only the faint moan of the wind in the treetops.

"WITH THAT LONG BLOND HAIR of yours blowing in the wind, you remind me of the young Ginger Rogers." Doc Martin winked.

"Why, thanks. Now if I could only dance like Ginger." Half my words got lost in the roar of the inboard engine. It was two days after my strange dream, and Doc Martin and I were speeding between Lee Cove and Piney View, two of Big Bass's small satellite islands. The communities on them were too tiny to support a resident doctor and would have no medical services at all if Doc didn't motor out to visit them once a week.

"I don't know what kind of a story you're going to get out of this," Doc said after we putted into the tiny harbor. It was a glorious spring day. Puffy clouds rode high in the deep blue sky. Pine and new grass scented the air. "Hope you're not wasting your time."

I stepped off the side of the boat onto a rickety wooden dock. Kneeling, I looped Doc's line around a piling. "Even if I weren't doing a story on you for the *Gazette*, this wouldn't be a waste of time. I've really enjoyed seeing you in action today. You're a hero."

"A hero? An old fool like me?" As he jumped onto the dock with his medical bag, Doc raised his bushy gray eyebrows. He was a short, square-built man with thick, iron-gray hair and a ruddy complexion.

"Of course you're a hero," I insisted. "Most medical types won't even make house calls much less boat calls."

Doc laughed this off, but it was true. Persuading him to let me accompany him on his rounds had taken some work. He just couldn't believe that what he did was worth my writing an article about. But what I'd seen today had really impressed me. Unlike so many doctors I'd known, Doc Martin hadn't isolated himself in a pricey office where he could rake in money from a specialty only the rich could afford. Instead, he lived modestly and helped working people who paid him what they could scrape together.

"Just what is it you're going to write about me?" Doc asked as we walked back to the boat from his last call.

"Oh, I'll describe how you checked out Linda, that poor pregnant young woman we just visited. I'll describe how you reassured her and how grateful she was. What would she do without you? Would she go to the mainland?"

"Only if something went badly wrong." He shook his head. "Fact is, if I didn't get into my boat and make these rounds, people like Linda would just go without medical help. That's what the islanders did before I came along."

"But didn't they have Grandfather? He was a doctor."

"He had the training, but he quit practicing when he was still a relatively young man. From what I was told, he wouldn't take a case unless it was a matter of life and death. Even then, he had to be begged. You know how proud the islanders are. They don't go in for begging."

I nodded, reflecting on this. "Why do you think Grandfather quit practicing?"

"Don't know." Doc handed me into the boat. "Asked him once, but he put me off. Just said he lost interest in ministering to humankind."

"That was a strange thing for him to say."

Doc nodded. "I thought so. It's no easy thing to get through medical school. Most medical students are idealists with pretty strong feelings about helping people. Apparently, something happened to your grandfather that made him change his ideas on that."

What, I wondered. "Doc," I asked, "did you examine Grandfather after he died?"

"I did." He set his medical bag down and looked at me sympathetically. "He was in good shape for his age. There are some durable genes in your family. If you take after Nate, you'll live to a ripe old age."

"That's good to hear, but it's not what I wanted to ask about. What did Grandfather really die of? Was it just the fall?"

"Anybody that age would have a frail ticker. The shock of the fall started him into a heart attack. That's what did him in."

"Not any other type of injury?"

"There were bruises and scrapes all over his body, including a bad one at the back of his head. All that contributed, of course."

"When Grandfather was found, was he lying faceup?" I couldn't forget my dream. In it, Grandfather had lain there staring at me.

"Can't say. By the time I got to the castle, he'd been moved."

"How do you think he came by that injury to the back of his head?"

"Could have been anything. Maybe he hit the edge of a step going down."

Or maybe somebody hit him on the back of the head, and that's why he went down in the first place, I thought. I didn't say anything. Obviously, it had never occurred to anyone, including Doc Martin, to think of my grandfather's death as anything but accidental. So why couldn't I get it out of my head that it wasn't? And who on the island would want to murder a man Grandfather's age?

Back on Big Bass, I helped Doc land his boat and then accompanied him to his simple white frame cottage about a half a mile down the shore road. "I think I've got everything I need for my story," I said as we turned up his gravel driveway, "but I wonder if you'd mind if I came in and took another quick look at your office?"

"Sure, come in and look all you want. It's a treat to have a pretty girl like you brightening the place up."

Doc showed me to the side door that patients used when they came to see him. Lilacs blooming in wild profusion next to it scented the air with spring sweetness.

"Not much on fancy decor, but it's functional," he said as he ushered me in.

On the other side of the door, the room was cool and quiet and smelled faintly of antiseptic, quite a contrast to the lilacs outside. I looked around, noting the pale green walls and the black marbled tiles on the floor. Antique medical instruments filled a white metal cabinet next to the reception desk. I walked over to have a better look and noticed the set of black-and-white framed photographs above it. Tipping my head back, I peered at them.

"Are these old photographs of the island?"

"Old enough to be antiques, I expect." Doc came up next to me. Together we stood gazing at the pictures. "I rescued them from a garage sale after old Pris Haworth died. Her daughter unearthed them when she was cleaning out the attic. I liked them because they show the harbor the way it used to be before it got prettied up for tourists." He pointed at a photo on the right-hand end of a row of four.

I stood on my tiptoes, squinting up at it. "Who are those men holding the fish?"

Doc shot me a mischievous glance. "Bet if you look at the tall one, you'll see somebody familiar."

The tall one in the middle did look familiar, but I couldn't believe my eyes.

"Here." Doc wheeled over a stool and got up on it.

"Really, you don't need to take the picture down," I protested.

"No, no, I think you'll find this interesting."

With a grunt, he lifted the frame off its hook and then stepped off the stool. After dusting the frame with his sleeve, he handed it to me. The photograph was obviously old. It showed a harbor barely recognizable from the one I knew. Instead of spiffy floating docks, there were narrow wooden finger piers, rickety and weathered. Instead of pleasure crafts, a gaggle of workboats jammed them.

"Those were the days when fishing was a serious business around here," Doc said. He pointed at boxes of silvery fish stacked on the deck of one of the fishing boats.

I nodded, but my attention was on the group of four men holding a string of freshly caught bass between them. "It can't be Egan in the middle," I said. "The picture is too old."

"Amazing resemblance, isn't it. Genes run strong in that family. That's Egan's grandfather, Rafe Halpern."

I stared at the tall man leaning against the hull of an overturned boat and grinning rakishly into the camera. He was the image of Egan. The same black curly hair and hawkish nose, the same wide shoulders and long legs crossed insouciantly at the ankles.

"The fellow next to him is Bill Wiblin, Betty's poor grandfather."

Reluctantly, I dragged my gaze from Rafe and focused on the shorter man standing with his arm draped around Rafe's shoulder. "Billy looked like Huck Finn," I commented.

"Does, doesn't he. Poor Billy. You'd never recognize him now from that picture. Betty has his freckles. She doesn't have that smile of his, though. Looks like the happiest young fella in the world there, doesn't he?"

"They all look happy."

"They do, don't they. Sometimes I think there's something sad about pictures like this. When this photo was taken, none of the people in it had any idea what the future held for them. They wouldn't have been grinning like that if they had."

That was certainly true of Billy Wiblin, I thought. I pointed at the tall, thin man in overalls standing on the other side of Billy. "Who's that?"

"Don't you recognize him?"

"No. Why would I?"

"It's Nate, your grandfather."

"Really?" I stared.

Doc Martin chuckled. "Well, there isn't much resemblance to how he looked at the end, but living ninety-odd years takes a lot out of you. Rafe Halpern, on the other

hand, he'll always be remembered the way he was there—
frozen in time."

"Frozen in time," I murmured as I returned my gaze
to Rafe's image. His eyes, crinkled in roguish laughter,
seemed to challenge me. A faint shiver rippled through
me. I was staring at what he wore—overalls and a faded
plaid shirt. He was dressed the same as the Egan look-
alike I'd seen outside the castle in my dream.

A few minutes later, I left Doc's and headed home. As
I strolled up the road, I noticed a couple of kids riding
bikes. I glanced at my watch. School must have just let
out. I rounded a bend and came across a small knot of
boys half-hidden by a grove of trees. They'd discarded
their lunch boxes in the grass behind them and were
shouting like bloodthirsty bullfighting fans. Something
exciting was going on inside the circle of their bunched
bodies.

I paused and listened. When I caught the name Rex, I
veered off the road and cut across the grass to get a better look. Closer up, I glimpsed a couple of boys going at
each other with fists in the center of the circle. They were
not evenly matched. The bigger boy was Betty's nephew,
Mark. The smaller kid was Rex.

"Hey," I shouted. "What's going on here? Break this
up!" At the sound of my voice, most of the audience
scattered. The two pugilists, however, were too en-
grossed slugging it out to pay attention to me. Both were
red-faced, their expressions set in masks of rage.

"Mark Wiblin," I screeched, "stop this at once! You
should be ashamed, picking on a boy smaller than you.
Wait until I tell your aunt!"

That got Mark's attention. Dropping a curse, he took
to his heels and streaked off through the woods. Rex
stood flushed and panting. Blood streamed from his

nose. Patches of sweaty dirt mixed with blood clung to his cheeks, elbows and hands.

"Rex, are you okay?"

He turned and might have run away from me himself, but I grabbed his arm. "Oh no you don't! Rex, you're a mess." Still restraining him, I searched through my jeans pocket. "Here, hold this tissue to your nose."

Reluctantly, he accepted the tissue and mopped at some of the blood spattering his upper lip. Meanwhile, I surveyed him. "Would you like me to take you to Doc Martin's?"

"Uh-uh." He shook his head. "I'm okay."

"Well, you don't look okay. You're going to be a mass of bruises tomorrow."

"So is he. I landed some good ones on the big jerk."

"About that, I wouldn't know. I do know it wasn't a fair fight. Mark Wiblin must have more than twenty pounds on you. How did the two of you get into a brawl like that?"

Rex's lower lip thrust out and his eyes avoided mine. "He was picking on me, calling me names."

"Calling you what? What names?"

"Trash, he said my family was trash."

"Oh, for heaven's sake!" I seized Rex's hand. "Come along with me."

"Where are we going?"

"I'm going to take you to your father."

"I can go home by myself."

"Is your father at home?"

"No, he's working in his shed."

"Then that's where we're going. I want him to see what that boy did to you and decide whether or not you should see the doctor."

As Rex explained to me, Egan worked in a big shed on a piece of property halfway between town and the airport. I commandeered Rex's pedicab, and he sat while I pedaled. "Dad isn't going to like getting interrupted," Rex muttered in back of me.

"I don't care what he likes. He should know what's going on."

"He does know. I tell him about the other kids teasing me."

I glanced over my shoulder. "Does he know that you get into fights like this?"

"I don't always tell him everything that happens, but I think he guesses."

"Just exactly what was the trouble between you and Mark Wiblin this time?"

Rex stared down at his feet. "Just stuff."

"What kind of stuff?

"He says my grandfather turned his into a vegetable and then ran away. It's not true. Nobody knows what happened way back then."

"No," I agreed. "Nobody does."

As we approached the shed, I heard the cutting grind of an electric saw. A garage-type door hung open, and Rex and I strolled right in. Inside, it was much warmer than out and I sniffed the combined odors of paint, fiberglass and freshly varnished wood. Egan was there with two other men. All wore paint-stained jeans. One had on a sweaty T-shirt. Egan and the other one were bare above the waist. As Egan knelt on a platform grinding at something, I could only stare at his broad naked back. A fine dew of sweat sheened his skin, and as he worked, his muscles flexed and rippled. For a moment, I could only stare and remember how it had felt to lie in his arms.

Perhaps sensing my hungry scrutiny, he straightened and turned. Embarrassed to be caught ogling him, I recovered enough to pretend to gawk at the boat they were working on. It was a magnificent creation that had to measure at least forty feet. They were buffing the layer of gelcoat on its sleek white hull to a high gloss.

Having caught sight of us, Egan switched off his sander and put it down on a bench. As he strode toward us, he pushed the plastic goggles protecting his eyes up onto his forehead and tore off the mask that covered his mouth and nose.

A quick look from Rex to me and back told him what the problem was. "Hey, buddy, what happened? Did you run into a buzz saw?"

"Nah." Rex shuffled his feet and looked down.

Egan tipped his son's face up and searched it. Rex had wiped some of the blood off, but there was still plenty left. "I've seen you look a lot prettier," Egan muttered. "What's this all about? Another fight?"

He glanced at me, and I began to explain. I was still explaining as he led the two of us into a small glass-and-wood corner booth that served as an office. A bathroom stood next to it.

"I've got some medical supplies in here. Let's get you cleaned up."

While I waited in the office, Egan herded his son into the bathroom. When they emerged some fifteen minutes later, Rex was considerably less bloody and Egan looked grim.

I studied Rex's face. Mercurochrome dotted several scratches and cuts and I saw the beginnings of a shiner on his left eye. "Well, it looks as if he'll live, anyhow."

"Oh, he'll live," Egan said. "Halpern men don't die easily. Believe me, he's come home with a lot worse than this."

As he spoke, Egan reached for the chambray shirt hanging on a hook next to his desk. I couldn't stop myself from following his movement—the graceful bend of his lean torso, the ripple of muscle and sinew as he twisted his shoulder. His work jeans rode low on his hips. I could see his flat belly with its washboard muscles, and my gaze traced the line of dark hair that marched from the center of his chest and dipped into his waistband. I remembered how it had felt to have his hard body cover mine. Suddenly, the memory of our intimacy was so acute, I had to clear my throat.

Egan hesitated and then looked over his shoulder at me. Knowledge of what I was feeling and a faint, but unmistakable glitter of masculine triumph came into his sapphire eyes. Deliberately, he poked one arm into his shirt and then the other arm. With tantalizing slowness, he began buttoning the shirt. As his muscled chest disappeared from view and his fingers dipped lower and lower, my cheeks flamed. I forced myself to look away.

"I haven't thanked you yet for stopping that fight and bringing Rex here, Katy."

"You're welcome." Why had I insisted on bringing Rex myself, I wondered. Was it really only that I wanted to make sure the boy was all right? Or had I been starved for the sight of Egan and ready to grab any excuse to be around him? Since the night of our lovemaking, I'd avoided him. That didn't mean I'd been able to get the man out of my thoughts and imagination. Seeing him like this, so vital and handsome, so good a father to Rex, I wanted to forget all the suspicions that plagued me. They had to be crazy, didn't they?

"As long as you're here, would you like to have a look around?"

"Yes, I would. That's a gorgeous boat you're building out there."

"Thanks. I'm pretty proud of it, myself. I'm building it for an East Coast restauranteur."

"He must serve good food. Not many people can afford to commission a custom yacht that size."

"It's going to get its first trial in the Annapolis-to-Bermuda race," Rex piped up. Glum and silent, he'd sprawled out on one of the office chairs. Now, animation returned to his thin face.

Together, the three of us left the office. Egan showed me around his construction area and introduced me to the two men who worked for him. Both were from island families whose names I recognized.

As Egan explained his design, the work already completed on the boat and the tasks that remained, two things impressed me. He stroked the boat's smooth keel with the same tender touch he'd used to caress me. Plainly, the man loved what he did. And what he did, he did very well. "The design is beautiful, and even I can see that the workmanship is impeccable," I commented. "This restauranteur is getting his money's worth."

"I hope he thinks so. I believe he will."

"Sure he will, Dad," Rex exclaimed. "For its size and class, this is the greatest boat anybody ever built."

While Egan laughed and ruffled his son's hair, one of the workmen came up. "Me and Tim are knocking off for the day," he told Egan. "See you tomorrow morning."

After the two men left, Rex turned to his father. "Are you still mad at me because I got into a fight?"

"No, son, I'm not mad at you. I just wish you'd do a better job of controlling your temper."

"Does that mean you're not going to welch on the picnic up at Cotton Bluff you promised?"

Egan shot me an amused glance. "Sometimes I think this boy was born for politics. He's a heck of a good negotiator."

"I can see that."

"No, Rex, I'm not going to welch on the picnic. It's ready and waiting in the refrigerator back home. All we have to do is pick it up and be on our way."

"Can Katy come with us?" Before his father could answer, Rex turned to me. "Would you like to come with us on a picnic, Katy? It's nice up at Cotton Bluff now and there's a great place to swim."

"I know there is." I remembered the spot well from the weeks I'd spent on the island years back. Egan had taken me there several times.

"You're welcome to join us," Egan said. His blue eyes searched mine. "It's a beautiful afternoon for an outing."

I hesitated, torn between desire and doubt. Desire won out. "Sure, I'd love to come."

Chapter Nine

Egan dropped me at the castle so I could grab my bathing suit. A few minutes later, armed with a huge picnic basket full of goodies, he and Rex picked me up and drove me to Cotton Bluff.

The bluff, named for its thicket of cottonwood trees, was on the north end of the island. Uninhabited because it was windswept and cold for much of the season, the north end remained much as it had been when the island belonged to Native Americans. The bluff overlooked the lake and a sheltered little white stone beach.

"Last one in's a wuss," Rex declared as he stripped off his jeans. With a whoop, he took off down the rough path to the stone beach.

"This time of year, it's going to be cold," I warned. Too late. Screeching with glee, Rex had already run in.

I turned to find Egan looking at me. "You going to take the plunge?"

"I put a bathing suit on under my clothes, so I guess that's my plan."

Egan grinned. "No time like the present." Seizing my hand, he guided me down the steep dirt path. We picked our way across the sheltered beach of white limestone pebbles smoothed and bleached by the lake.

Pulling free of him, I tugged my T-shirt up over my head. Then I unzipped my shorts and stepped free. Carefully, I folded my clothes. When I turned to lay them down, I found Egan standing behind me staring with narrowed eyes. He hadn't taken off his clothes yet.

"Does this bring back memories?" he asked in a low voice.

"If it didn't, I'd be brain dead, Egan." We'd had one of our first dates at this place. Egan had kissed me. It hadn't been my first kiss. Back home, I'd had several dates with other teenage boys. But Egan's kiss had been something entirely new. We'd lain on his blanket, our mouths blending, our young bodies straining and melting. *Not so different from what happened the other night,* I suddenly thought. I didn't regret that. How could I? But I didn't think it wise to repeat it, either. Looking away, I removed my sandals and tiptoed over the pebbles to the water.

It really was cold. I had to force myself to walk in over my knees and then strike out toward where Rex happily bobbed and dived.

"Rex," I yelled, "how do you stand it? I feel like an ice cube."

"It's great once you're in. Hey, Dad, did we bring my snorkel?"

"It's in the back of the truck. If you want it, you'll have to get it yourself."

Grumbling, Rex waded ashore. I watched him disappear into the trees. Suddenly, a hand closed on my waist. With a yip, I whirled. Egan was at my side. Water dripped from his hair, clumped his eyelashes into spiky black points and sheened his broad shoulders. Our dangling legs touched and tangled. As I back-paddled to free myself, he grinned. "For a city girl, you're doing pretty well. I don't remember your being such a strong swimmer."

"Back in Detroit, I belonged to a health club. I swam every afternoon," I said as I lazily backstroked toward the shore.

"Ah, that explains it," Egan said, sidestroking along side me.

"It doesn't explain how you and Rex can stay in this ice water. My nice indoor pool was heated."

As I spoke, I gazed into Egan's eyes. They were bluer than the sky. Without a word, we both stopped swimming and turned toward one another. With a will of their own, my hands went to his sun-warmed shoulders.

"I don't feel cold at all," Egan murmured.

His hand tightened on my waist and he drew me closer to him. His head came down over mine and we kissed. As our lips melded, I didn't feel cold anymore, either. I felt his hard belly pressed to mine. The crisp hair on his chest tickled the tender flesh above the top of my bathing suit. One of his strong hands went to the back of my neck and began to caress and rub while the kiss went on.

When our lips finally parted, we were both breathing hard. My arms were wrapped tight around his waist, my breasts crushed to his broad chest.

"Oh, Egan," I whispered as I felt his hardness against me.

"I've been having trouble sleeping. How about you?" he asked thickly.

"We shouldn't be doing this. Rex is going to come back."

As if to second my protest, Rex's shout pierced the air as he came swooping down the hill and emerged from the trees. "Got it, Dad!"

Egan and I untangled ourselves just as Rex came splashing out to join us.

"See," he exclaimed, "the water's fine once you get used to it."

"Fine for you two polar bears, maybe," I said. "Think I'll head back for shore and a warm towel."

On the beach, I spread my towel on the stones. As I soaked up rays of the late-afternoon sun, I watched Egan and Rex play.

"Hey, Dad, bet I can beat you to the black rock and back."

"We'll see about that."

"Hey, Dad, let's see who can hold their breath under-water longest."

"Okay, but no cheating. I'm going to keep my eyes open and watch you."

As their frisky voices rippled back to me across the water, I closed my eyes and heard other young voices from a time long past.

"Hey, Egan, it's over my head here."

"Don't worry, Katy. I won't let you drown."

Teasing. "How can I be sure of that?"

"I'd have to be crazy to let anything happen to the prettiest girl in the world. See, I've got my arms around you."

"Is that because you want to keep my head above water?"

"No, little Blondie, it's because I want to kiss you."

And Egan had kissed me. With my eyelids closed and the sun printing dazzle spots of red and gold behind them, I remembered that kiss. What a revelation his slick, strong body had been against mine. How the touch of his young lips had shocked and warmed me. No more than his kiss had affected me just now, though. Tasting again the kiss we'd just shared, my own lips began to glow and then burn.

My memories shifted to our lovemaking of just a few nights ago. Egan's mouth on mine, coaxing and then demanding, his urgent body staking a claim I couldn't deny. Reliving the experience, my whole being seemed to burst into flame.

"Warm enough now?"

My eyes flew open and looked directly into the azure depths of Egan's. Naked except for his wet bathing trunks, he was bending over me, his face mere inches from mine. Slowly, his playful grin faded. His lips thinned and tightened, his eyes narrowed. "Did I wake you?"

"No, I was just dozing."

"What were you thinking about?"

"Nothing."

His gaze dropped to my breasts. Under the thin damp fabric of my green maillot, I knew my nipples stood out like pebbles. Embarrassed by Egan's reading my erotic thoughts so easily, I suppose my expression grew mutinous.

He chuckled softly and extended his hand. "C'mon, beautiful dreamer. Time to get dressed and have our picnic."

An hour later, I said, "That was quite a spread. Don't tell me you fried that chicken and baked those wonderful homemade biscuits."

Egan splashed white wine into my plastic cup. "Hungry as I am for your approval, I can't take credit for the picnic. Mabel Perkins comes in three days a week to cook and clean. She fixed our meal."

I patted my full stomach. "For that feast, she deserves a medal."

I folded my legs under me and settled against the stripy trunk of a cottonwood. Propped on his elbows, Egan lay stretched out at my side. We were up on the bluff overlooking the beach. Below us, Rex tossed pebbles into the water. The sun was just beginning to show signs of setting. To the west, a brush stroke of pale pink and mauve glowed on the horizon.

"Do you come up here often?" I asked.

"When the weather is fine, Rex and I sometimes manage a picnic. He likes the swimming. I like the memories."

"Memories?" I swallowed the wine I had just sipped and looked away. "As I recall, this used to be a favorite make-out spot for island teens."

"Still is. We wouldn't have it to ourselves if we came here at night."

"You should know. You must have brought a lot of girls here."

"A few," he agreed. "But it's always you I remember."

My head snapped around and I stared. "Why?"

"Why?" He gave a rough laugh. "When I was a teenager, every pretty girl I saw turned me on. Then I met you. After you walked out on me—"

"I didn't walk out on you, Egan. It was more complicated than that."

"Okay, after your father and grandfather convinced you I was an immoral lout who only wanted your money, I couldn't look at a girl without comparing her to you."

"Is that the truth, or is it just a line?"

"I'm too old for lines, Katy. It's the truth."

"Hard to believe."

"But then, you've always had trouble believing me, haven't you?"

Now I certainly did. And maybe I'd had trouble believing him when we were kids, too. Oh, I'd wanted to accept the sweet words he'd whispered. But my teenage ego had been fragile. Could a guy as handsome and exciting as Egan really be as in love with me as he claimed? How, when he had a sexy dish like Debbie hanging around the sidelines? Because I'd been so unsure of myself, it hadn't been so tough for my father to persuade me that Egan only wanted my money.

"You say you were constantly comparing other women to me. Did that include Debbie?"

Egan closed his eyes. "Yes, unfortunately for both of us."

"Debbie was beautiful."

"True, but she wasn't you. No matter how hard I tried, I could never get your image out of my mind. Maybe Debbie guessed that. Maybe that's why she cheated on me."

"She cheated on you?" I was shocked.

Egan grimaced. "That just slipped out. Forget I said it."

"How can I? Egan, tell me what happened between you and Debbie. It's important for me to know."

He picked up a leaf and rubbed it between his callused fingers. As his eyes studied the leaf, he said, "Okay, but first there's something that's important for me to know. That night we ran away together, how did Nate find out in time to get your father to intercept us on the mainland? Did you leave him a note?"

"I swear I didn't. I have no idea how he found out. Did you think I'd tipped him off because I wanted him to rescue me from you?"

"You were young and scared. It seemed plausible—maybe even understandable. I went back to the island feeling like two cents. Thinking you might have wanted things to turn out the way they did, made it worse.''

"Oh, Egan, I know and I'm sorry. My dad said terrible things to you. He blamed you when the elopement was really my idea. But you must have gotten over me quickly. You and Debbie married not long after.''

"Debbie offered me comfort when I needed it pretty bad. I never thought we'd get married, though. Debbie was three years older than me and considerably more experienced. I thought she was on the Pill, so it came as quite a surprise when she told me she was pregnant.''

"Were you and Debbie happy together?''

"Happy?'' Egan's mouth twisted. "We tried to make a go of it. A lot of couples get married under circumstances like the ones we had, so I thought we could make it work. But we were both too young and carrying too much baggage.''

"Egan, I'm sorry.''

He gave me a surprised look. "You sound as if you mean that.''

"I do mean it. Was I... did your problems have anything to do with me?''

"Debbie knew I'd been in love with you and she was jealous. But there was more to it.'' He gazed out at the water below, where Rex still cavorted. His troubled expression told me these memories were painful.

"At first, we had to live with my mother. That was tough on Debbie. She had a miscarriage and wasn't feeling well for quite a while after that. Gradually, I started earning more money. When Debbie got pregnant with Rex, I was determined to have enough money so we could move into our own place. I talked my way into an apprentice position as a carpenter in a boatyard on the other side.''

"In Sandusky? That was very enterprising of you."

"I was damned if I'd be another 'no-good' Halpern," he said gruffly. "I wanted to make something of myself. When I wasn't working the carpentry job, I worked the fishing boats and the ferry. By the time Rex came along, I could afford to rent a house. Still, I was scrambling to pay the bills and couldn't be home much. That left Debbie alone with a baby most of the time. She didn't like it."

"She was awfully young herself."

"True, but other women stick out being home alone with their children and even get some pleasure from it." Egan shook his head. "Not Debbie. She was suspicious of my absences. Claimed I wasn't really working. Insisted I was having secret trysts with women. She even thought I might be meeting you on the sly. Of course, I only laughed at that. After your father sent you away, I never heard from you. I didn't even know where you were."

I hesitated and then admitted, "Actually, I wrote to Betty and asked about you."

"You did? She never said anything. Guess I shouldn't be surprised. Betty Wiblin McKenny has never exactly been a close pal."

"When she told me you'd married Debbie, I wrote back and asked her not to say anything to you about me. I thought it best."

Egan nodded. "It would have meant a lot to me to think you still cared enough to reach out a hand, Katy. But you were right. The way things were going in my marriage, knowing you had any interest in me at all would only have made matters worse."

"What happened?"

"Debbie started going with other men."

"While she was taking care of Rex?"

"She'd leave him with my mother and then go down to the bars on Main Street and pick up tourists—usually college kids." Egan ran a hand over his sandpapery chin. "She was lonely, I guess. Maybe in her eyes, it just seemed like harmless fun. That's how she died, in a boating accident with a couple of guys from the mainland over here on a drinking spree."

"Oh, Egan, I am sorry." I meant that. It was too sad a story not to pity everyone involved. "Poor Rex, to be left motherless at such a young age. How have you managed to raise him on your own and still build such a successful business?"

"My mother's been a big help. If it hadn't been for her, well . . ." Egan's voice trailed off. Then he pushed himself into a sitting position. "Anyhow, Rex and I are both survivors. Now he's old enough not to need a mother."

"Everyone needs a mother, Egan."

"Not everybody gets what they need," he said dryly.

The edge on his voice cut at me. "Egan, do you think I ruined your life?"

He stared. "There's nothing ruined about my life. Maybe it's not perfect. But I have a son, a home, a business I love. From where I sit, your life looks a lot less satisfactory than mine."

I felt my eyebrows shoot up. "In what respect?"

"You're alone—no family, no lover, no job. From where I sit, it looks to me as if you've made a worse mess of things than I have."

He had a point, but not one I liked. "You haven't answered my question. Are you still harboring resentments?"

"You can ask that after what happened between us the other night?"

"Yes, I can. Lust and rage aren't that far apart."

"Lust I understand, but rage? Katy, contrary to this fixed idea you've got, the offer I made on the castle didn't come out of some twisted desire for revenge. I wanted to help you."

"I think seeing the castle torn down would give you pleasure."

"Okay," he admitted angrily. "It's true. I would like to see that ramshackle old monstrosity bite the dust. All it does is ruin the view and hog a piece of the coast that could do the community some good. In its place, I'd like to see something that would give the islanders employment and opportunity. It's only mainlanders like you who find the island's past quaint and romantic and want to cling to it. Natives like me, who really love the island and have a stake in it, are much more interested in its future than its past."

"I have a stake in Big Bass," I snapped.

"Not if you don't plan to stay here. Do you, by the way?" Egan studied my face with almost surgical attention. The atmosphere between us, so relaxed earlier, thrummed with tension.

"I don't know what I'm going to do. I haven't made up my mind."

"Does that mean you're still considering my offer?"

"Maybe."

"You always were good at stringing people along, weren't you, Katy?" His tone was caustic.

"What's that supposed to mean?"

"It means I'm beginning to feel like a man who's stepped into a revolving door. Half a lifetime ago, you made me crazy about you. You let me love you and then turned your back and walked away."

As I opened my mouth to reply, Rex's voice floated up the slope. "Hey, you guys, come on down here. I found some really neat driftwood." He had left the water. A towel hung around his shoulders, and his wet black hair trailed in pixieish points around his face.

Egan jerked up onto one knee. "Time to pack up and go," he shouted down to his son. "I have a client call coming in at eight."

"Ah, Dad, I'm not ready to leave yet. Can't you get your call at home and come back and pick us up?"

"Katy has to leave, too."

"Do you really, Katy? Can't you stay here with me for another hour?" Rex pleaded. He aimed an appealing smile. "There are some really great places to explore."

Half in defiance of Egan, I shouted, "Sure, Rex. I'll stay with you."

Immediately, I regretted that. I had no right to interfere between father and son. As Rex whooped happily and telegraphed the high sign, it was too late to take it back. Surely, it was no big deal. It wouldn't hurt Egan to get us in an hour. Maybe by that time, he would have cooled off.

An instant later, I caught the tight expression on his face and wasn't so sure of that. "If you're going to leave the island, Katy, do it now. Don't play with my feelings, and don't play with my son's."

"Your son's?" I stared at him in shock.

"A while back, you said everybody needs a mother. You were right. Rex does need a mother. But it doesn't look as if he's going to get one. Don't make Rex fall in love with you, and then walk out on him, too. Understand? Don't do it. That I really won't forgive."

"Was Dad mad about something?" Rex asked after Egan roared off in his truck.

"I think he's just anxious not to miss his client call. Must be somebody important."

"Yeah. It's probably the guy who wants him to build a Chinese junk."

"A Chinese junk?" I pictured a gilded barge with a square red sail bellied in the evening wind. "Whatever for?"

As we walked along the water's edge, Rex scuffed his toe on a limestone pebble. "Oh, he wants it to take people on charter trips down in the Bahamas."

"The Bahamas, hmm." I picked up a fluted shell and skimmed it across the water. The setting sun had turned the lake into a rich purple, almost the shade of frothy grape juice.

"Dad gets jobs from all over the world, so he travels a lot," Rex continued. "I went with him to England last year."

"Really? I bet you liked that."

"Yeah, I did. But I got homesick."

"Homesick?" I stopped and studied Rex. "Do you miss the island when you're away from it, even though some of the kids here give you a hard time?"

Gingerly, he touched the bruised area around his eye. The poor kid was getting a prime shiner. "Sure I do," he replied cheerfully. "So does Dad. The island is our home."

"And there's no place like home?"

"Maybe it sounds dumb, but there isn't. You'd feel that way, too, if you lived here all the time. Are you going to live here?" He peered at me hopefully. For the first time, I wondered if there could be any truth to Egan's final accusation. "Rex, are you trying to talk me into staying?"

"Well, maybe. I mean, you're a nice person and the island needs nice people. Besides, Dad likes you and he doesn't have any other girlfriends."

"You surprise me. Your dad is a good-looking man. I'd think he'd have lots of girlfriends."

"It's not that ladies don't like him," Rex hastily explained. "It's just that he's picky. He likes you, though. I can see he likes you."

"I haven't made any plans for the future yet," I said gently.

"I know you'd like it here. I mean, the island isn't perfect, but it's pretty nice. Really, it has just about all a person could want. It even has cliffs with caves in them. See over there?" We were standing on the end of a stony spit, looking back at the curving shoreline. Rex pointed at a limestone escarpment covered by a thick stand of scrubby trees and bushes. "There's bunches of caves back in there."

I squinted at the rocky walls that rose almost straight out of the water. In among their folds and corners I glimpsed small stony areas. Someone who knew the island could drag a boat up and hide it there.

This must be where the Prohibition bootleggers had hidden their kegs of contraband liquor, I thought. The sun was down now, and the moon rode the top of a black wisp of cloud. As I glanced up at it, an eerie feeling crept over me. I pictured a shadowy skiff stealing silently up to the shore. A couple of men in dark clothes jumping over the side and guiding it onto the pebbles. There was a harsh rasp as its hull came to rest half out of the water. Quick and businesslike, the men began unloading their cargo. Only their low, hard whispers would disturb the rhythmic slap of the water and the tuneless thrum of the crickets.

"Have you ever explored the caves?" I asked Rex.

"Once with my dad, but he didn't let me do much. Years back, a kid got lost in the caves and died. Any kid who gets caught hanging around them gets a licking."

"That makes sense. Caves can be dangerous."

"Are you going to stay on Big Bass?" Rex asked again.

"I'm thinking about it."

"You should. I know Dad would like it."

"What makes you say that?"

Rex stuck his hands in his jeans pockets. "Oh, just a feeling I have."

WHEN EGAN RETRIEVED us a few minutes later, you'd never know he wanted me for a neighbor by the way he behaved. On the drive home, the conversation in the cab of the pickup was all between him and his son. Egan didn't speak a word to me until he dropped me off in front of the castle.

"Thanks for the picnic," I said.

"You're welcome."

"I'm sorry you had to go to the trouble of coming back to get us."

"It's nothing. Take care, now." Then he put the truck in gear and rumbled off.

Heavily, I headed down the path. Halfway to the castle's sagging porch, I paused and lifted my eyes. Silhouetted against the sky, the turreted roofline seemed to mock me. "Do you really think you can discover all the secrets buried in my heart?" it seemed to whisper. "Do you really think you can make me your home?"

A cloud cast a long shadow over its gingerbread dormers. As if it were a living, growing thing, the shadow stretched and lengthened. It crept past the porch and oozed over the lawn. Seconds later, it had completely engulfed me.

Inside, I restlessly fixed myself a mug of tea and carried it into the living room. There, I stood at the window sipping and thinking. Trees and a bend in the shoreline hid the lights of the Macaster place from me. I knew Egan must be brooding inside it, the same way I was brooding inside the castle.

Being with him and Rex this afternoon had been exquisite frustration. Even as we'd argued, I had wanted to touch him, to feel the heat of his skin and lips. Rex had been right to sense something between me and his father. During the taut, silent ride home in Egan's truck, the sexual electricity between us had hummed. Electricity was exciting. It had the power to light up your life. But under the wrong conditions, it could also burn you to death.

Sighing, I turned away and headed down the hall to Grandfather's study. I had a lot of work and a whole lot of thinking to do.

Close to midnight, I sat hunched at Grandfather's big old mahogany desk. The Tiffany lamp cast a circle of yellow light over a marketing plan for a desktop publishing business, which I'd spent the last several hours developing. Once again, I ran my cursor down the figures and asked myself if they'd really work. Suddenly, the skin on the back of my neck prickled. I knew I was being watched. My head jerked up and I stared out the window.

As the expressionless mask of Egan's face gazed back, I relived a nightmarish experience. I opened my mouth to scream, then everything changed. Egan grimaced. His face became human, mobile, warm. He tapped against the glass.

"What do you want?"

"I want to talk to you. Will you let me in?"

My heart thudded. "Yes, I guess so. Come around to the back door."

When I got to the kitchen, he stood on the other side of the screen. "Do you realize how late it is?" As I asked the question, I opened the door and watched him stride past me.

"Yes, I'm sorry. I know this is crazy. I came here to apologize."

"Apologize?"

"I feel bad about what I said up on the bluff. It's been eating at me. I couldn't sleep, so I took a walk and ended up here. I saw your light on and wondered if you couldn't sleep, either. So I investigated. Then I saw you sitting there framed by the window, and here I am."

"Do you realize that's the window through which I saw you looking in at me before?"

Egan rolled his eyes. He'd planted himself in the center of the kitchen floor. Under the overhead light, his shiny hair glinted. "Are we back to that? This is the first time I've looked in at you through that window."

"Egan, we're not back to anything. It's just that you gave me a start. Can I fix you a cup of tea? I think there might even be a beer in the refrigerator."

"I don't want anything. Katy, I came here to apologize. I had no business saying some of the things I did."

"Which one of them is bothering you? The remark about my messed-up life, the unpleasant bit about the castle or the implication that I'm deliberately trying to ruin your son's life?"

A dull red flush crept up his neck. "The stuff about Rex was out of line."

"Certainly sounded crazy to me. Where do you get off accusing me of trying to alienate his affections from you?"

"That wasn't what I meant, and it's not all that crazy. Rex took his mother's death very hard. He sees a lot of his gran, but she can't be a real mother to him. He wants a mom like the other kids have. Whenever I show the slightest bit of interest in a female, he gets excited. He's not stupid. He knows there's something between us and his hopes are up."

I knew from the conversation I'd just had with Rex that Egan wasn't just imagining things. "If it's true, I'm sorry. I'll steer clear of him, if that's what you want."

"My God, Katy. That's not what I want at all." He turned on his heel and paced to the wall, then paced back. "It's probably good for Rex to have a woman like you to talk to. He needs all the friends he can get. I just don't want to see the poor kid hurt and disappointed. He's had too many hurts and disappointments."

"I'll try not to do either. Honest. Is that what you wanted to apologize about? If so, apology accepted. Thank you very much."

While Egan stared at me, I held myself tightly. I knew I shouldn't have let him in so late. Half of me was still a little wary of him. The other half wanted to throw my arms around him. He looked tired. His eyes had a glazed look to them, and there were grooves between his dark eyebrows. But on Egan, tiredness was attractive. Even exhausted and irritable, he was more attractive than any other man I'd ever met—including Edward. How could I ever have imagined that I was in love with Edward? I knew now that I hadn't been.

"That's not enough for you, is it?" he said. "You want to hear more. Well, don't expect to hear me claim I'm sorry for what I said about the castle. This place has been here long enough." Slowly, he looked around. He did a lazy half turn, studying the age-spotted ceiling and the sagging lintel over the door. "You know, when I was little, my mother used to clean house for your grandfather."

"Oh?" I hadn't known that.

"I'd walk past the castle while she was working inside it and worry that she'd never come out. I thought your grandfather was a sorcerer."

"In a way, he was, I suppose. He did look a bit like Walt Disney's Merlin."

Egan shook his head. "Not a good sorcerer, an evil one, brewing up concoctions of spiders and toads. I was sure he had a dungeon, and I was afraid he'd throw my mother into it."

"You must have been an imaginative child."

"It didn't take much imagination to find this place scary. All these moldy turrets and spires. When I first met you, I saw you as the beautiful, golden-haired princess I had to rescue from the evil castle. Sometimes I still imagine you like that."

I stared at the odd glimmer in his eyes. "You're kidding."

"I'm not kidding. I'm perfectly serious."

At the fierce intensity of his tone, I felt my eyes widen. Strangely, I sometimes thought of myself as a prisoner of Grandfather's house. There were times, moments late in the darkest hours of the night, when I felt the house crouching over me, when its nocturnal creaks and moans sounded like the mutterings of an alien being.

"I'm not a beautiful princess, Egan. I'm just an ordinary woman with a cash-flow problem."

Egan grimaced. "That's another dumb remark I came to apologize for. I had no business telling you your life looked worse than mine."

"You were right." I shrugged. "I am an unemployed woman with no family and no lover. By most standards, that makes me a prime candidate for being considered a loser."

As his gaze skimmed me, I became conscious of my bralessness beneath my jersey T-shirt and of my brief shorts and bare legs. "You don't look like a loser to me. Are you still job hunting?"

"Yes. I'm also considering creating my own job. I'm thinking of starting a desktop publishing business."

When Egan raised an eyebrow, I elaborated a bit defensively. I hadn't yet mentioned my scheme to anybody else, and I felt unsure of myself. "One of the projects I have in mind is an island magazine geared to vacationers. That's what I was working on when you tapped on my window."

"Very enterprising." He no longer looked tired. As he took a step closer, I could feel his energy. It summoned an answering excitement in me. "Explain something to me, Katy, something I can't make sense of. Why is a woman as desirable as you are, alone?"

"I told you what happened with my fiancé."

"That doesn't explain why you haven't married long before now. You went to college. Don't tell me you weren't pursued by every eligible fraternity boy on campus. Nature created you for an upper-class suburb, with an overpaid lawyer husband and 2.5 blond, blue-eyed kids."

"Thanks a lot. I hardly dated at all when I was in college. I was too busy trying to get good grades. Later on, my career took all my energy. I simply never had much time for a social life."

"Why is that? You never struck me as a future-driven career woman when I knew you. What happened to turn you around?"

We stared into each other's eyes, neither of us blinking. I felt a trembling in my throat and swallowed to try to control it.

"Katy," Egan said in a low voice, "up on the bluff you asked me if you'd ruined my life. Now I'm asking you the same question. Did what happened between us change things for you? Is that why you never dated much in college? Is that why you never found anyone to marry? Is that why you're alone?"

The moment stood still. The urgency in his low voice, the way his blue eyes seemed to be looking through me and inside me—all had an unsettling effect. I felt the backs of my eyes burning. I clasped my hands together, as if by locking my fingers I could steady myself.

"After my father caught us, nothing was the same for me. I steered away from sex and love, as if they were a hot stove I'd burned my fingers on. I stopped flirting and thinking about clothes the way the other girls my age did. I put all my energy into getting good grades. My father thought it was an improvement. Maybe it was, I don't know. I do know my life changed."

"Oh, Katy," Egan said with a groan. He reached for me and drew me to him. I didn't resist. It felt so natural to flow into his arms and rest my head on his broad chest. As I pressed my cheek to the soft fabric of his shirt and listened to the steady thrum of his heart, tears leaked from my eyes.

Egan tightened his arm around my shoulders. With his free hand, he stroked the top of my hair. "It's as if we were both struck by lightning, isn't it?" he said softly.

Unable to answer, I pressed my face deeper into his shirt. I was ashamed of my tears, but I couldn't stop them.

"Are you crying?" Egan asked. He lifted my chin up so he could study my face. "You are. I'm sorry. I didn't mean to make you cry."

Mesmerized, I stared up into his eyes. "It's not your fault."

His answer was to lower his face. As his lips found mine, I closed my eyes. His lips felt warm and firm. Against them, my mouth was a weak barrier.

With a groan, both his arms went around my waist and drew me closer yet. Hungrily, his mouth explored my face. He kissed my forehead, my eyebrows, my cheeks, the line of my jaw. As his caresses rained down on me, I lost myself in them.

When his mouth found mine again, our lips and breath flowed into each other. I felt his tongue teasing mine. What had been a comforting warmth between us grew fiery.

As thrilling rivers of heat surged through me, my hands tightened on his waist. I felt his muscularity, his tension, the graceful, flaring line of his back. My hands crept up. They curled around his shoulders, and I crushed my breasts to his broad chest.

"Katy," he whispered fiercely. He turned me around and pressed me against the edge of the counter. Then his body leaned into mine. We kissed long and hard, clinging to each other like waifs in a storm. His legs tangled with mine. I felt the rough fabric of his jeans rub against my thighs. The sensation was exciting.

His hand slipped under my T-shirt and stroked the smooth skin on my back. "I knew you weren't wearing a bra," he said hoarsely. My breasts felt heavy, swollen. Their tips ached. The flesh there was filled with longing.

As his hands came around and cupped their undersides, I shuddered, then gasped. I wanted him, wanted him badly. Yet a warning flashed in my brain. I remembered the shock of seeing his face in the study window just minutes earlier. How could I make love again with a man I wasn't sure I trusted? "Egan, stop."

His grasp only tightened on me. "Katy, God, Katy!" His hands stroked my breasts, I felt his manhood pressed against me hard and demanding.

Everything that was womanly in me cried out for surrender. But I couldn't surrender again. Not when I had so many doubts.

"No, Egan. Please." With all my strength, I pushed him away.

His hands dropped to my waist, and he stared at me in disbelief. "What's wrong? Why? I thought—"

"I know, I know. It's my fault. I shouldn't have let things go this far again." Not wanting to look him in the eyes, I turned around and rested my elbows on the countertop.

There was a long, tense silence. "No, you shouldn't have," he finally said. "And I shouldn't have been such a fool. Good night, Katy. Sweet dreams."

I looked up in time to see him close the kitchen door and disappear off the porch into the darkness. "Egan," I whispered. "Oh, Egan." Then I sat down at the kitchen table and wept.

Chapter Ten

It's funny how everything looks different in the morning. When I opened my eyes the next day, puddles of sunshine warmed my cheeks. I padded to the window and peered out. Blue and serene, the lake sloshed gently against the stony breakwater. Between it and the house, several cherry trees bloomed, their gnarled branches frosted with white. Pinky-white petals drifted in the grass around them, making me think of bridesmaids' dresses.

I pushed the window open and stuck my head out. Somewhere nearby, a bird chirped. I inhaled the scent of lilacs. Turning my head, I looked toward the Macaster place. Where was Egan, I wondered. Still in bed? No, he'd probably been up and at work for hours. I didn't want to think about him. Thoughts of Egan had a way of turning complicated.

Downstairs, I fixed coffee and poured myself a bowl of cereal. The morning sun didn't light up the kitchen the way it had my bedroom. Like so much of the house, the kitchen felt dark and gloomy. Restlessly sipping orange juice, I paced its perimeter. I had a lot of work to do, but I still hadn't settled down from yesterday.

An hour later, I stepped aboard the ferry to Sandusky. Since it was midweek and early, I had the boat almost to myself. I spent the trip leaning against the railing watching foam fly up from the wake churned by the engines, and—despite my earlier self-warning—thinking about Egan. After he'd left last night, I'd ached with regret and frustration. Was I crazy to have allowed my largely ungrounded fears and doubts to overwhelm my desire for him? My thoughts ran wild until the ferry finally pulled into the dark.

By my previous big-city standards, Sandusky was no more than a sleepy little midwestern town. After two weeks on the island, it seemed like a bustling metropolis. I spent the next couple of hours browsing through the shops on Main Street. After treating myself to a bacon-lettuce-and-tomato sandwich at a quaint café decorated in rustic style, I headed for the jewelry store where I'd left my piece of blue crystal.

"Oh, it's wonderful!" I exclaimed when the proprietor brought it out and laid it down on a piece of black velvet. "You've mounted it beautifully."

"Crystal is popular these days, you know. All these New Age people like to wear it. They claim it has some sort of mystic power that gives them energy. I wouldn't know about that, but this piece is unusual. I've never seen a color quite like it." While the jeweler spoke, he lifted the crystal and slipped the chain around my neck.

As the gold links settled over my shoulders, the crystal slid beneath the rounded neckline of the blue jersey T-shirt I wore. The crystal felt cool and smooth and strangely electric—almost alive. It came to rest between my breasts, where I was intensely aware of it. It was as if it were sending and receiving signals. Quickly, I pulled the chain and took the crystal between my thumb and forefinger. It caught the light from the jeweler's overhead fixture. For a second or two, my eyes were dazzled.

"Looks real pretty with that blue top of yours," the jeweler commented.

"Thank you."

"You want me to wrap it up?"

"Oh, no. I'll wear it." My fingers closed around it tight. I didn't want to take it off.

As I walked out of the store, I remained conscious of the crystal dangling from my throat. I kept glancing at my reflection in storefronts, my eyes drawn to the spar- kling bauble. I'd heard the theory that crystals radiate energy and had laughed it off. But now I felt energized by Grandfather's blue crystal. Was it just my imagination, just the thrill of having a pretty new piece of jewelry?

So absorbed was I in speculating on this that I almost didn't recognize the driver of the burgundy Grand Am as it swung out of a parking lot on the other side of the street. But that hawkish profile and dark head of curls could never slip past me easily. "Egan," I murmured. My eyes followed the burgundy car until it cruised around a corner.

For a moment, I stood blinking, my hand instinc- tively clutching the crystal. I returned my attention to the parking lot. Ace Car Rentals, read a red and blue sign on a small white stucco building in the back of the lot. Why was Egan driving a rental car when I'd sold him my RX-7? With my breath coming harshly in my throat, I crossed the street and directed my steps to the building.

"Help you?"

"I thought I recognized a friend drive off your lot. Did Mr. Egan Halpern just rent a car from you?"

The clerk, a middle-aged man with clear plastic glasses and a head of thin, taffy-colored hair, glanced down at the form that lay on the glass counter. "That's right."

"Does he rent cars from you often?"

"Mr. Halpern is a regular customer here. Is there something else I can do for you? You need to rent a vehicle?" His Ohio drawl emphasized the "h."

"Not today, but maybe some time soon. What kind of cars do you rent?"

"All kinds, as you can see from what's on the lot. Just take your pick."

I went to the glass door and peered out. I saw a white Cavalier, a dark blue Geo, and three red cars of an American make I didn't recognize. Any of the red cars could have been the one that hit me.

"Does Mr. Halpern ever choose one of those red cars?"

The clerk's voice began to sound suspicious. "I suppose he might. Seems to me he's rented red cars from time to time. Depends on what we have available."

"Would you know if he'd rented one—" I gave the date when I'd been hit.

"It's possible. Can't say I've kept track, though."

I walked back to the counter. "You must have a record of the cars that have been rented recently and the people who've rented them."

"I keep records, but I don't go talking about them to anybody who walks in off the street. Is there something specific you wanted?"

There was, but the clerk was staring at me so distrustfully that I knew it would be useless to ask him to go through his files to determine for sure if Egan had rented a red car the day I was hit. "Have any of your cars come in damaged recently?"

"What kind of damage?"

"A dented bumper, that sort of thing?"

"Lady, we get dented bumpers all the time. Every one of our cars has a dented bumper. Now, is that all you wanted or can I write you up an order?"

"Not today, thanks. Maybe sometime soon."

As I walked off the rental lot, my hand crept up to the crystal swinging between my breasts. I held it, as if it could reassure me. It couldn't, though. I felt a sickness in the pit of my stomach that had nothing to do with the bacon-lettuce-and-tomato sandwich I'd recently eaten. *Oh, Egan,* I thought. *I can't believe you'd try to hurt me. I just can't accept it.*

Maybe I couldn't accept it, but I couldn't stop thinking about it, either. All the way recrossing the lake on the ferry, my mind churned like the engines that threw up a foamy wake behind the boat.

Back on the island, I hurried home and changed into jeans and sturdy sneakers. I packed a knapsack with sandwiches and a canned drink, and threw in a flashlight and small compass that I'd found in one of Grandfather's drawers. Then I climbed aboard one of the rusty bikes jamming the shed at the edge of my property and headed toward the north end of the island.

By now, it was late afternoon. The weather was still warm and fair. Fat buds covered those trees and bushes that hadn't already burst into bloom. As I pedaled, the warm air fanning my cheek felt thick with pollen and the promise of a golden summer to come.

As I passed yards, several people working outside waved to me. I caught sight of Flo Hadditer sitting on her porch. But she was busy rocking and dreaming and didn't seem to see me.

"Hi, there, golden girl!" Cy Clipson yelled when I pedaled by the Ship of Dreams.

"Hi, yourself!" I answered and slowed. "I'll have that article on Doc Martin ready for you by the end of the week."

"No hurry. These days, the only schedule I meet is the one for my heart medicine."

Laughing at his gallows humor, I finally pedaled past. The grin stayed on my face for at least a quarter of a mile. My first days on Big Bass had been lonely. The islanders, though polite, had been stiff with me and I'd felt like what I was—an outsider. Now I noticed some unbending, and it made me feel good. Their friendly greetings would have pleased me even more if I hadn't been so worried about where I was going and what I planned to do.

Since I'd heard about the caves and Rex had pointed them out, I hadn't been able to get the things out of my mind. Nor had I been able to stop thinking about Rafe Halpern's disappearance and Bill Wiblin's injury. Somehow, it was all connected with the objects in my black box. Surely Grandfather had left me those clues because he wanted me to solve this mystery. But why? I couldn't get it out of my head that his death was tied up with the answer. So, perhaps, were those caves. I intended to have a look at them.

It wasn't easy. The road swept away from the rocky promontory where they were hidden. I took what looked like a path headed toward them, but it petered out. Soon the trees were so thick and the terrain so impassable that I had to leave my bike behind.

After checking my compass, I set off in the direction I thought was right. I miscalculated. When I emerged from a stand of pine onto a stony ledge overlooking the lake, I was at least a quarter of a mile north of where I wanted to be. It was also getting late and I was hungry.

After unpacking my food and eating it, I considered my options. Really, I shouldn't have started off so late, in the first place. If I were smart, I'd head back and try this again in the morning. But I didn't want to do that. I grasped at the crystal, which still hung around my neck. Now that I'd come this far, I couldn't bear to turn back.

After stowing my sandwich wrappings and apple core in my backpack, I began making my way toward the area where Rex had said the caves were hidden. It was a rough climb. By the time I stumbled onto the mouth of the first cave, I was panting and dripping with sweat.

For a long time, I stood staring at the dark little opening in the side of the cliff face. What would I find inside? Animals? Snakes? Bats? What if I hurt myself with all this climbing, twisted an ankle or even broke a leg? Really, this was extremely stupid. I should have told someone where I was going. But there were so many secrets on the island. Who could I trust with my nebulous suspicions?

Switching on my flashlight, I ducked my head into the mouth of the cave. I didn't need to take more than a few steps inside. The cave was nothing more than a shallow declivity. It held nothing of interest. It was also too far from shore to have ever been used by bootleggers.

Drawing a relieved breath, I went back outside to search for another. It was a long and tiring hunt. Rex had spoken truthfully when he'd described the cliff as honeycombed with caves. It seemed as if I came across them at every turn.

Most were little more than shallow pockets in the side of the limestone, scooped out perhaps by a prehistoric glacier. Others turned into winding passageways. Eventually, however, all dead-ended.

Every time I ventured into a cave, I told myself, "This is your last one, Katy. After this, you head for your bike and go home."

But the caves fascinated me. Every time I stepped into one, it was like entering a secret world. I never knew what I might find. Some were empty. Spider webs bedecked others and occasionally I found the remains of small animals. Crystal formations sparkled on the walls of several. None of the crystals resembled my blue one.

I had been working my way down the side of the cliff, closer and closer to the stony coastline where a bootlegger might have dragged his speedboat up to unload. But the sun had been working its way down, too. As I stood before the entrance of a promising-looking new cave, I cast a worried look behind me.

The orangy-red rim of the setting sun lay on the watery horizon like a hot iron. Even as I watched, it began melting into the lake. I almost expected to hear a sizzle. Violet shadows lengthened and filled the hollows around me. Before my eyes, they transformed the cliff into an alien territory, a veiled landscape of mystery and menace.

That's when I saw him. A movement down on the rocky scrap of beach below me caught my eye. A man stood gazing up at me. I couldn't see much of him beyond his dark outline, but I knew it was Egan. I could tell by the set of his shoulders, the way his dark curls whipped in the wind that had suddenly come up. I opened my mouth to hail him, but something about the way he looked up at me made his name die on my lips.

I half expected him to call to me, but only the faint moan of the cool wind broke the eerie quiet. I squinted, trying to catch the expression on his face. But he was too far away and his features were lost in shadow.

"Egan?" I whispered.

His continued silence and something in his posture alarmed me. I noticed he wasn't wearing his usual jeans, but denim overalls. I'd never seen him in overalls—except in one of my nightmares. They reminded me of the ones I'd seen on Rafe in Doc Martin's photo. Why was Egan there? What did he want? It was growing darker by the second and this was such an isolated spot. An unnatural hush hovered over the barren landscape. It muffled even the pounding of the waves. How had Egan known to find me here?

He began to climb toward me. There was something strange about the effortless way he scaled the rocks, almost as if he weren't bound by gravity. I noticed that my skin was cold. Goose bumps stood out on my forearms. Fear, an animal knowledge of danger, surged through me. I turned and hurried back the way I had come. But every time I glanced over my shoulder, Egan loomed closer.

It was now so dark, I could barely make out my path. I tripped over a rock and then, as I righted myself, stumbled over another. Sprawling, I slid into the entrance of a cave. As I fell, I dropped the flashlight. "Damn!"

I felt around for it, but it must have rolled some distance away. That's when I heard the breathing. "Egan," I whispered again.

No answer came, but I knew I wasn't alone. The temperature in the cave seemed to drop several degrees. Lumps like golf balls pebbled my skin, and the short hairs on the back of my neck became rigid.

I scrambled up and pressed against a slick stone wall. My heart hammered like a pile driver. "Egan?"

Someone or something drew close. Though my straining eyes perceived nothing in the cave's inky pit, I could feel someone or something crowding in on me. An icy breath stirred tendrils of hair around my left ear, and I felt a cold finger ever so lightly touch my cheek. My legs buckled and I slid to the cave floor. Heart pounding with fear, I waited there, prepared to defend myself. But as my fear thickened around me, nothing happened and no word was spoken.

I STAYED RIGIDLY STILL for so long that my hip began to throb. In fact, my whole body ached. Yet it wasn't until something feathery and many-legged marched up my bare calf that I found the courage to move.

With a little yip, I sprang into a sitting position. Frantically, I brushed whatever it was off my leg. For several seconds, I crouched there, tensed like a threatened animal. My heart pounded and my breath rattled in my throat. Utterly disoriented, my eyes probed the blackness, which pressed in on me like a smothering hand.

Gradually, I heard things. Somewhere a bird called. In the distance, the soft slosh of the lake against the pebbled shore filtered into my ears. With a sick twist of my stomach, I thought about what had happened. Egan had followed me, chased me into a cave and then frightened me. But why? And why had he been dressed like his grandfather?

Moaning, I dropped my face into my hands. I sat there quivering for a while. I had to get out of here and find my way home. I lurched to my hands and knees and then to my feet. To my right, a pale glimmer beckoned. As I staggered toward it, my foot knocked against something hard and smooth. It was my flashlight, and recovering it was the first lucky thing that had happened to me all day.

I shone it toward the faint luminescence and discovered the outline of the cave's entrance. Outside, I stopped and glanced around apprehensively. But no one was there. I was completely alone.

During the trip back, I stumbled over every rock and root on the north end of the island. Twice I took a wrong turn and had to retrace my steps. Finally, however, I met up with my abandoned bike. By that time, I was half-hysterical.

Getting home didn't improve things all that much. Tossing the bike on the grass without even a thought for putting it away, I ran into the kitchen and threw myself onto a chair. For many long minutes, I just sat there gasping and shuddering. I'd felt awful before in my life, but this was right up there with some of my worst experiences.

At last, I pulled myself together and checked the time on the clock over the refrigerator. Eight-thirty. I'd expected it to be much later. I must not have been in the cave for more than half an hour. Why had Egan gone to so much trouble to terrify me and then simply turn around and leave? Had he hoped I'd never find my way out or that I'd trip in the dark and break a leg?

A surge of anger gave me new strength. I hobbled to the telephone and dialed Egan's number. Rex answered.

"Hello, Rex, this is Katy Conroy. Is your dad at home?"

"Oh, hi, Katy. Dad had to go to Cincinnati on business. He's been gone all day."

It took more seconds than it should have for my tired brain to assimilate this. "You aren't there by yourself, are you?" I asked lamely.

"Nope. Grandma's here. My dad called just a little while ago to say he's been delayed. He won't get back until tomorrow. You want me to give him a message?"

"Uh, no, thanks, anyway, Rex. I'll see him when he gets back."

Carefully, I replaced the receiver and tottered back to my chair. After lowering myself onto it with all the grace and flexibility of a ninety-year-old, I sat twisting and untwisting my fingers. Egan was in Cincinnati? But I'd seen him. He'd chased me. What did this mean?

No, no, this just didn't make sense. Somehow, I had to make sense of it. On impulse, I picked up the phone and dialed Flo Hadditer. She picked up on the fifth ring.

"Land's sake, who is it at this hour?" she demanded grumpily.

I shot a guilty glance at the clock. It was now nine, probably Flo's bedtime. "Mrs. Hadditer, Flo, I'm sorry for calling so late."

"Who is this? This wouldn't be Katy Conroy, would it?"

"Yes, I'm sorry. I hope I didn't wake you."

"Thought I recognized your voice. Well, you're mighty lucky I was having trouble sleeping tonight. Usually, I'd be in dreamland by now. What is it you called about?"

"This is going to sound kind of strange."

"At my age, girl, nothing sounds strange. Spit it out."

"A while back, you told me you thought Rafe Halpern's ghost was still on the island."

There was a little pause. "So I did. What of it?"

"Did you ever actually see him?"

The pause went on longer this time. When she spoke, her cranky old voice was sharp. "What's this about? Why are you asking?"

"I can't explain. Flo, I know it sounds crazy, but if you ever did see Rafe's ghost, I'd really appreciate it if you'd tell me."

She let out a gusty sigh. "I think I saw him once."

"You did?"

"It was down on the north end of the island, when my husband was still alive. We were out at Cotton Bluff having a picnic. As was his way, Ben fell asleep right after he finished off the beer and ate his potato salad. Though it was getting close to sundown, I decided to take a walk on the beach. While I was down there, the sun dropped like a lead weight and a storm came up. I was in one of those funny contrary moods you get into sometimes, so I stayed down there. I still remember how the wind howled around me. With the water all gray and wild, I felt as if I were in another world."

"How old were you?" I asked.

"Oh, this was many a year ago. I was still a young woman. Not more than thirty-five and not bad-looking, though you'd never guess it to see me now." She sighed. "It's funny how some things stick in your mind. I remember exactly how the wind felt, whipping at my skirt and sending my hair flying all around my face. That's when I heard someone whisper my name. Well, I thought it had to be Ben, so I turned around to tell him I was coming. That's when I saw him."

"Rafe?"

"Well, now, I suppose it couldn't really have been Rafe. Maybe I was just imagining it. But I swear I saw him lurking in the shadows, staring at me with the strangest look on his face. Gave me quite a turn."

"What happened then?"

"I called his name and he just faded away. Just disappeared. And when I looked down, my arms were covered with goose bumps, and I felt as if I were standing on a block of ice."

I began rubbing my own forearms. What she described sounded so much like what I'd experienced. "Flo, just one more question. What was Rafe wearing?"

"Hmm. Let me think. Why, he was wearing what he always wore. An old pair of bib overalls and a wrinkled plaid shirt."

Outside, the wind riffled through the trees. A branch clacked against the side of the house, and I heard the sound of eerie laughter, mocking me.

Chapter Eleven

The next day, I made it my business to be in town in time to do an errand and to meet the noon ferry. First, I stopped at the hardware store to arrange for new locks on my doors. The old ones were ancient and the one to the kitchen no longer worked. After making an appointment with a local handyman to have the locks installed as early as he could get to them, I went down to the public dock. As I stood watching passengers disembark, I felt like somebody with a multiple personality disorder.

Part of me didn't want Egan to be on that boat. Even after my conversation with Flo, I was far from ready to believe I'd seen a ghost. So part of me needed to confirm that I really had seen Egan the night before, that he really had chased me into a cave and scared the living daylights out of me. Yet another part of me preferred any explanation to that one.

Despite everything, when he came striding down the gangplank, looking incredibly handsome in a dark gray business suit, my heart leaped with joy.

I told myself to turn around and walk away before he saw me, but my feet had other ideas. They stayed planted where they were.

"Well, well, I wasn't expecting a welcoming party," he said as he walked up to me. A grin had creased his face the minute he'd spotted me. Now, as his blue eyes gazed into mine, they shone.

"That's not exactly how I'd describe myself." I looked at him closely. He certainly didn't look like a man who'd chase women into caves. In his business garb, he appeared successful, respectable and extremely eligible.

"Don't spoil my day, Katy. Pretend you're glad to see me. Smile."

I bared my teeth.

Egan laughed. "That's not a smile, that's a snarl." He cocked his head. "Is something wrong? I mean, something new and different?"

"I'm just in shock, that's all. I've never seen you in a suit before. It's very impressive." It really was. In paint-stained jeans, Egan had the bearing of a prince in disguise. Suited up in expensive English tailoring, he could hold his own with the Harvard-educated sharks on Wall Street.

"Don't be fooled by appearances, Katy. Beneath these costly threads, it's the same old Egan you know and don't love."

"What makes you say that?"

"What?"

"How do you know I don't love you?"

He stared at me and I stared back. I couldn't believe I'd said what I'd just said. What had gotten into me?

"Have you had lunch yet?" Egan asked, looking slightly discomfited by my remark.

I shook my head.

"Me, neither." He took me by the elbow. "There's a new place behind the tackle shop. Let's go there."

I allowed him to lead me up to the street and then steer me to the right where a complex of shops and eateries had been built on a long pier that extended over the water. A couple of minutes later, a waitress showed us to an outside table with an umbrella.

"We're lucky it's warm enough for this today," I said after we'd ordered.

"Let's not waste time talking about the weather, Katy. What did you mean by that remark?"

"What remark?"

"C'mon. That remark about how do I know you don't love me."

"I don't know what I meant by it, Egan. I've had a very stressful couple of days and can't be held accountable for what I say."

He let his breath out in a hiss. "So it was just another tease?"

"I'm not trying to tease you."

"Then what are you trying to do to me? Drive me crazy? Because, if that's your goal, you're succeeding."

While the waitress set our food on the table, we sat glaring at each other. Considering what had happened to me in the caves yesterday, Egan's remark seemed pretty ironic. Wasn't *I* the one being driven crazy by all these strange and threatening goings-on?

"What were you doing in Cincinnati?" I asked when we were alone again.

Egan paused in the act of unrolling his napkin. "How did you know I was in Cincinnati?"

"Rex told me."

Egan looked at me a quizzically. "Business. I have a client there. Actually, it's a corporation. I needed to work out some details with their CEO."

"You were there all day?"

Egan frowned slightly. "If you want my itinerary, I left before noon yesterday, rented a car in Sandusky and drove to Cincinnati, where I met with my client from three until well after we had dinner together. I spent the night in a motel and drove back first thing. Is there anything else you'd like to know?"

"Yes, as a matter of fact. Why did you rent a car when you now own my RX-7?"

"It's in the shop having its steering looked at."

"Do you rent cars in Sandusky often?"

"I have, but I don't expect to once I get the RX in tip-top shape."

"I thought it was in tip-top shape when I sold it to you. You must be a perfectionist."

"That's my big flaw. I only fall in love with the best. Trouble is, so often the best is unattainable."

As he said this, his gaze lingered on my face in a way that brought the blood to my cheeks. "Do you ever rent red cars?" I asked.

His expression changed, but instead of looking guilty, he was beginning to look angry. "What's this all about, Katy? Why are you cross-examining me?"

"Last week in Sandusky, a hit-and-run driver struck me."

"You weren't hurt, were you?"

"Not seriously, no."

"Then what...oh, I see. The car was red and you think I was at the wheel."

"I didn't say that."

"No, but it's obvious that you're thinking it..." Egan leaned forward over the small table so that our noses were only inches apart. So far, neither of us had touched our food. "Katy, I'm just an ordinary dumb male who doesn't understand women. But when it comes to you, my lack of understanding reaches new heights of bafflement. Would you mind explaining something to me? How can you tell me in one breath that you might still be in love with me? How can you do that, and in the next breath accuse me of trying to run you down in a rented car?''

I stared back in silence. How could I answer him when I didn't know the answer myself? ''I'm sorry,'' I finally mumbled. ''I never really thought it was you in that red car. Let's eat.''

''I don't think so. I've lost my appetite.'' With that, Egan surged to his feet, slapped down a twenty-dollar bill for the tab and strode off.

All the way home, I fumed and sputtered. Why hadn't I demanded that Egan explain what happened in the cave, I asked myself. Why had I allowed him to buffalo me again? How could I let him make me doubt my own sanity? It was high time we stopped playing cat and mouse.

It *had* to have been him frightening me in the cave. His face *had* to be the one I'd seen glowering at me through the window. I simply couldn't believe I was being harassed by the ghost of Rafe Halpern.

Yet I found myself recalling the picture of Rafe I'd seen in Doc Martin's office. He really had been Egan's look-alike. I shivered. No, I told myself. Haunted as the island and the castle sometimes seemed, I was not going to start believing in ghosts.

THE NEXT MORNING, Betty came to look over some of the old furniture I'd decided to get rid of.

''You're throwing away this linen press?'' she exclaimed. We were standing in one of the back bedrooms. ''It's solid oak.''

"I'm not throwing it away, Betty. But I'd be willing to let you take it for your new shop on consignment."

She cocked her head. "Well, I don't know. That fussy design with all the carved gewgaws goes in and out of style. But sure, why not? I'll give it a try. Now, what about the bedroom set? I can't believe you're dumping that."

We moved to the center of the room. The walls had been decorated with a design of latticework and roses. The paper was so old that the green background had faded to a dingy yellow. Brownish, damp patches marred several spots. Beneath our feet, the flowered wool rug had succumbed to moths and decades of dust. After giving it a cursory glance and wrinkling our noses, we surveyed the elaborately carved four-poster bed, chest of drawers and vanity. "They must be well over a hundred years old," Betty commented.

"More. Nobody's slept in this room for at least a century. My father had the smaller room at the other end of the hall. You wouldn't believe the layers of dust and cobwebs I had to clean out of here."

"Oh, I'd believe it." Betty was looking around speculatively. "This is where you want to set up your office?"

"Right. The room's big enough. I figure once the furniture's gone, I'll toss this wreck of a rug, strip the walls and paint them white. Shelves for supplies and software will go over there. Here, a long table for my computer, fax, scanner and laser printer."

"Hey, you sound serious. You also sound as if you know what you're doing."

"You're right on the first part, anyhow. I am serious. I've seriously decided to try going into the desktop publishing business. I got out my card file and made some calls the other day. Already, I've lined up a couple of projects. Now all I need is a stake to buy some of the equipment I'll be needing. I'm hoping to get that by selling some of these antiques."

Betty was studying me closely. "What does good old Egan have to say about this?"

"About me selling Grandfather's antiques?" I was nonplussed.

Betty snorted. "No, about your deciding to start a business on the island. Any dummy can figure out that means you're planning to stay a while."

"I haven't discussed it with Egan," I said stiffly. "Why should I?"

"Well, I'd guess he'd be interested," Betty drawled.

"What in the world makes you say that?" I could feel myself pokering up. Had somebody seen Egan and me together the night we'd made love?

Betty nudged my shoulder. "Oh, come off it. Everybody knows you and sexy Egan have a thing going. If you're anywhere in sight of each other, storm signals start flying."

"Storm signals?"

"Oh, you know what I mean. The air gets all charged up. The two of you give off more electricity than summer lightning."

I started to sputter a denial. Ignoring me, Betty wandered over to the vanity on the wall next to the window. "This piece alone should bring you a nice chunk of money. Tall oval mirrors like that fetch a good price. Sure you want to part with it?"

Nodding, I walked up alongside her. Side by side, we stood gazing at our reflections in the long mirror set deep into the well of the carved oak vanity. The mirror made me look taller, thinner and paler than I felt I really was.

Yet beside me, Betty looked shorter and plumper than she appeared in reality. Her red hair and freckles glowed more brightly. It was almost as if the mirror underscored what it saw, instead of reflecting an accurate image.

"Getting it out of here will be a relief," I admitted.

"It will? Why?"

"Sounds nutty, but when I first walked into this room, I thought I saw a stranger looking out at me from the mirror. It really scared me. I screamed and jumped a foot."

Laughing, Betty peered up into my face. "You mean, you didn't recognize your own reflection?"

"No, I didn't."

"Why not?"

I shrugged. I didn't know how to explain what had happened. All I knew was that for a moment, a face had looked out at me that wasn't my own. I had felt that it was the face of a woman from another time, another place. A split second later, I stood looking at myself, wondering if I were hallucinating.

"Are you really sure you want to stay in this house?" Betty questioned. "Frankly, it sounds to me as if it's getting to you."

"Well, it does get kind of spooky alone here at night." My hand went to the hard shape of the blue crystal. It hung out of sight under my short-sleeved blouse. I hadn't taken it off since I'd picked it up from the jeweler. "I keep hearing ominous creaks, as if somebody invisible is following me around. Overactive imagination."

"Hey, it wouldn't surprise me if it wasn't your imagination at all. Everybody on the island thinks this place is creepy. In fact, none of us would mind too much if it sank into the earth and disappeared." Betty got down on one knee in front of the vanity and opened a middle drawer.

"I'm sorry I haven't emptied out all the drawers yet," I apologized. "I just haven't gotten around to it."

"Have you sorted through all this stuff?"

"I've glanced through." Odds and ends filled the drawers—tarnished silver card cases, yellowed lace handkerchiefs, wooden knitting needles and button-hooks, bits of crochet, boxes of old combs and tortoise-shell hair ornaments from a bygone era.

"Hey, antique silver buttons like these are hot items," Betty exclaimed as she opened a small box filled to the brim. Her fingers thrashed through the mismatched buttons. Then she laid the container aside and reached into the drawer again. "There's another button box at the back, but I can't get the drawer open all the way."

"It's sticky. I had trouble with it, too."

Betty yanked and pulled. "Hey, you know what? I think something's catching on the slide. Let's take out the bottom drawer."

Once we'd done that, Betty reached up and felt with her hand. A moment later, she pulled out a slim wooden box. "It was taped to the bottom. Hey, look, it's locked."

"Well, I haven't got the key." As I spoke, I thought of the key that had been part of Grandfather's mysterious legacy. This was definitely one lock I hadn't tried that key on.

"Doesn't matter. The lock's rusted. See, it comes right apart. What's this?" She lifted out a square object decorated with incisings.

I leaned forward to get a better look. "It's a card case. I've found several like it. People used to carry calling cards in them and leave them when they dropped in on neighbors."

"All my neighbors leave now is potholes in my driveway," Betty commented. She flipped open the tarnished silver case and pulled out a square of folded paper. "What have we here? A treasure map?"

Eagerly, I snatched the paper from Betty's hand. Hurrying to the window, I unfolded it.

"Hey, I'm the one who found it," she protested.

"If it's really treasure, I'll cut you in," I muttered. I was only half joking. For days now, I'd wandered the house, hoping to find something that would make sense of the clues in Grandfather's black boxes. My instinct told me this might be it.

"What is it, anyway?" Betty had joined me. I felt, rather than saw, her standing on tiptoe to peer over my shoulder.

"It is a map of some kind. But it's so faded and the paper's so old and crumbly, I can barely make it out."

Faint pen lines showed a series of linked objects. Words had been written over the objects, but the print was so tiny and blurry, I couldn't read it.

"What you need is a magnifying glass," Betty said. "Here, I think I saw one in the vanity's top drawer."

While I stood poring over the mysterious drawing, my heart beating with excitement, she walked away. Seconds later, she thrust an old magnifying glass into my hand. "Does that help?"

"Yes, I think it does."

"What do those words say?"

"Hmm, rooster, eggs, target, uh, let's see, either horse or force. Doesn't make much sense, does it?" When I glanced at her, she was gazing at me quizzically.

"One of the caves is called Horsehead, because from a distance its mouth is sort of shaped like that. I think another is called Chicken, and the two little ones next to it are called Eggs."

"Oh, really." I refocused on the map. The markings could be a diagram placing the network of caves on the north end of the island. I'd only read off the words that were most legible. Now I concentrated on the blurrier, more difficult-to-read names. One in the corner and near the top caught my eye. "Ue stal. Bue csa." I must have stared at it for several minutes before I guessed what it said. Blue Crystal. As the letters took shape and leaped out at me, my free hand went to the ornament nestled against my skin. With sudden intuition, I knew it had come from the cave named on this diagram.

"Katy, what's wrong? You've got the oddest expression on your face. You've gone pale as a sheet."

"Have I?" I tucked the map into my breast pocket and then wandered over to the edge of the bed and dropped onto it. Instead of feeling elated at my discovery, I felt confused and frightened. In fact, I felt like crying. "I'm just tired, that's all. These last few weeks have been difficult."

"Sure they have. I mean, they started off with your grandfather's funeral, right?" Betty had followed me. Now she sat down on the bed beside me. "But it's more then that, isn't it?"

"What do you mean?" When I glanced her way, she was scrutinizing me with such comprehension and sympathy that I had to blink to keep back the tears.

"Now, don't try to kid good old Betty. There really is something going on between you and Egan, isn't there?"

"Maybe, but I'm not sure what." I felt weak and weepy. I badly needed to spill my troubles into a sympathetic ear.

Betty chuckled. "Kiddo, maybe you're not sure, but nobody else around here has a doubt in the world. The two of you always had the hots for each other. With you back on the island and with both you and Egan being single, the flame has been rekindled. Am I right, or am I right?"

"You're partly right." I massaged my aching temples. "But it's a lot more complicated than that."

"You don't want to go the stepmother route?" She nodded her comprehension. "Well, I can understand that. Right now, my own kids are driving me batty."

I laughed despite myself. "Oh, Betty, it's not that. I like Rex. It's not Rex, it's Egan. I'm not sure he's ever really forgiven me for what happened when we were kids and tried to elope."

Betty grimaced. "Katy, I'm sure you're wrong. Egan is a stubborn cuss, but my guess is that all you've got to do is throw your arms around him, and he'd be willing to forgive you just about anything."

She gave me an amused smile, but I couldn't smile back.

"Strange things have been happening, Betty."

"What strange things?"

I didn't want to talk about my more peculiar encounters with Egan or my suspicions about him. Somehow, I couldn't bring myself to put those things into words. But I couldn't resist the pressure building inside me, urging me to confide, either. "Betty," I blurted out, "has it ever occurred to you that my grandfather's fall might not have been accidental?"

She leaned back in shock. "Katy, for heaven's sake, what else could it have been?"

"Why would he have gone down to the cellar at all? There's nothing down there but moldy preserves."

"Who knows why Nate did half of what he did. Katy, the man was over ninety. You're the only one who's inherited property from him. Why else would anybody bother to kill him?"

Actually, I wasn't the only person with property from Nate. Egan had been given a big stack of gold. I chewed my lower lip, then said, "Old as he was, Nate probably knew a lot of island secrets. Maybe he was blackmailing somebody."

"Well, that's a fascinating idea. Who? Old Mrs. Hadditer? Maybe she had an affair sixty years ago."

I giggled nervously. The idea of blackmailing Flo over an imagined, ancient love affair sounded pretty ridiculous.

This time, it was Betty who didn't laugh. She gazed at me thoughtfully, then heaved a big sigh. "Katy, all this time I've been thinking I should keep my mouth shut and let sleeping dogs lie. I mean, what's the point after all these years? But maybe it's time I told you something."

"Told me what?"

"Remember that family diary I mentioned?"

"Your grandad's diary?"

Betty nodded. "Billy Wiblin, boy loser's personal daily record. Well, I finished reading it. Toward the end, it's got some pretty interesting stuff written in it."

"Like what?"

"You asked me if I'd ever heard the name Spike Shawnaway. In the last fifty or so pages of his diary, Gramps started writing about somebody named Spike. Apparently, Gramps and Rafe were on Spike Shawnaway's payroll. They were running bootleg liquor from Canada for him, hiding it on the island, then taking it to the mainland."

"That didn't come as any surprise, did it, Betty? I mean, you'd already guessed as much."

"Yes, but I hadn't guessed who else was in cahoots with them." Betty's voice was now edged with spite.

"Who?"

"Nate Conroy." She spat the name out.

I stared at Betty. "Grandfather? But he was a doctor. Why would he get involved in running illegal liquor?"

"How should I know? Maybe island doctoring wasn't all that good a paying job back then. Maybe he just liked the adventure and the company. Boys will be boys, you know. I can tell you for sure, though, the old coot was definitely in on it. And there's something else I can tell you."

"What's that?"

"For half a century, everybody on this island figured Rafe Halpern got into a drunken brawl with Billy Wiblin. He coshed Gramps on the head and ran away leaving him for dead. Well, now, I've got another theory."

"Which is?"

Betty leaned forward, her hands tight on her knees. "Maybe the night all this happened, there was a third party involved."

"You mean Grandfather?"

"Exactly. What if Rafe Halpern didn't run away? What if he was never seen after that night because his body is lying at the bottom of the lake and Nate Conroy put it there? A few years back, Egan started shining up to your grandfather. He even admits it was because he wanted to learn more about island history in general and his family in particular. What if he wormed this story out of Nate and it made him mad? Push Egan hard enough and he has a temper."

"You're saying that if anyone had a motive to push Grandfather down those steps, it was Egan Halpern?"

Solemnly, Betty nodded. "Yes, I guess that's what I'm saying."

AFTER BETTY LEFT, I ran around the castle in fast-forward mode. I sorted, cleaned and scrubbed until sweat poured down my arms and pooled in the hollow between my breasts, until my hair hung in dusty strings over my eyes and cobwebs and grit were embedded in my knees.

Anything to keep my mind off what Betty had told me. Her theory didn't make enough sense to be seriously considered, I told myself. But no amount of busy work could keep it at bay forever. By nightfall, I fell onto an old glider on the porch. Too tired to fix myself a real dinner, I'd slapped together an egg salad sandwich and mixed myself a tall glass of instant lemonade.

As I sipped the lemonade, I rocked back and forth and listened to the slap and slosh of the waves against the breakwater. Periodically, I glanced in the direction where the Macaster place lay hidden by trees. Could Egan have killed my grandfather in a fit of rage? I had reason to know that Egan had a temper. But I had no reason to think it was violent in that way. Then I remembered the terrifying incident in the cave and shivered. My heart told me no. The man who was such a tender lover couldn't have killed a helpless old man—no matter what the provocation.

Yet, my head kept scripting horrible scenarios. I kept picturing Egan's big hands on my grandfather's frail back. I kept seeing the old man pitch headfirst down those steep stairs to the stony floor below.

Finally, with a groan of pure misery, I set the lemonade and my plate on the porch floor and lay back on the glider. Closing my teary eyes, I massaged my aching temples. As if in sympathy, the lake kept up its soothing background lullaby.

When I woke up, it was midnight. I knew from the chiming of the tall clock in the hall. "Oh, my God," I muttered as I pushed myself into a sitting position. Inside, I turned off the kitchen light and went upstairs to my bedroom. Like an automaton, I went through the motions of undressing, washing up and getting into bed.

But as I lay with moonlight streaming in through my open curtains, I couldn't sleep. Too much confusion still swirled inside me. Painfully, I tried to sort through it. One thing was very clear. Coming back to the island had reawakened all my old feelings for Egan. He, obviously, wanted more than the brief night of lovemaking we'd impulsively shared. I admitted to myself that I wanted more, too. At this very moment, I ached for him. Remembering our kisses, my lips burned. But there was no way I could give in to those longings—not until I knew for sure that he hadn't been responsible for my grandfather's death.

Ghosts haunted our relationship, I thought sadly. Not just the ghost of our teenage love affair, but also Grandfather's, Rafe Halpern's and—in a strange way—poor Bill Wiblin's. The tragic threads of their decades-old story had become entangled with ours, and Grandfather still pulled the strings. I couldn't give in to my feelings for Egan again until I'd straightened it all out.

Restless, I swung my legs over the side of the bed. I padded to the window and looked out at the moonlit lawn. Then I headed for the door and walked down the hall. As I descended the staircase, I mulled over my conversation with Betty.

I couldn't accept her reluctant suggestion that if anyone had had a motive to kill Grandfather, it was Egan. I wanted to believe his death really had been an accident. That meant he'd been going down the cellar steps for a reason. What? Earlier, I'd taken a look around down there. It was not a pleasant spot, and despite my good intentions, I hadn't lingered to explore with any real care. What if I'd overlooked something?

In the downstairs hall, I grabbed a flashlight off the table and walked to the kitchen. The clock struck two. Perhaps because of the lateness of the hour, I was reluctant to turn on a harsh overhead light. My eyes had adjusted to the darkness, anyway.

In the kitchen, I glanced at the back door and wished it had its new lock. Then I switched the flashlight on and followed its narrow yellow track to the cellar door. For a moment, I stood hesitantly in front of it. With all my bad feelings about the cellar, this was a crazy time to go down there. I should wait for bright morning sunshine. But I knew I wouldn't be able to sleep until I'd satisfied my sudden burst of curiosity.

Opening the door, I aimed the flashlight's beam down the rickety wooden steps, then carefully descended them. At the bottom, I rubbed the goose bumps on my bare arms. Up in the kitchen, the spring night had been pleasantly warm. Down here, it was cold and clammy. It didn't smell too great, either.

The cellar only went under the kitchen section of the house. The roof was so low, I had to stoop slightly to move around in it. The slick earthen walls smelled of mold and decay. Some relative from a bygone era had built rough wooden shelves against the east wall and filled them with jars of preserves.

The beam of my flashlight picked out fruits and vegetables, now colorless and mushy from age. I couldn't believe Grandfather had come down here because he was after any of those. I told myself what I should really do is donate those jars for medical research. Who knew what great undiscovered cures those molds might contain?

A movement near my face made me squeak and jerk my flashlight up. Caught in its light, I saw a huge black spider. It squatted in a web only inches from my hair. Its legs moved and it plunged onto me. Strung tight with nerves, I shrieked, dropped the flashlight and jumped back.

"Ugh, yuck, uuh!" Frantically, I brushed at my body, trying to make sure the spider wasn't crawling on me. Then I started feeling around for the fallen flashlight. When I found it, it was broken.

"Oh, great, Katy," I muttered. Without the flashlight, the cellar was a pit of blackness. I'd jumped around so much trying to brush away the spider, that I was now completely disoriented. I had no idea where the stairs were.

I probably didn't spend more than ten minutes feeling around in the dark for the stairs. But it seemed like hours. When I finally located them, my legs were trembling and my breath was coming in short, half-hysterical pants. I felt nauseated. As I inched my way up the narrow steps, I was seriously afraid that I might faint, tumble backward and meet the same fate as my grandfather.

At the top of the steps, I reached out for the doorknob. At the instant my fingers found it, I heard a creak and then a soft *swish swish,* as if slippered feet were tiptoeing past on the other side.

Dear God, I thought, *someone's sneaking in through the kitchen door.*

Chapter Twelve

I stood there, my hand frozen on the doorknob, my ears straining. I kept hoping I was wrong, but I wasn't. A few feet away, on the other side of the door, stealthy footsteps crossed the kitchen floor. They whispered into the hall, then faded like a deadly snake disappearing into tall grass.

For another minute, I stayed petrified, unable to think what to do. Who was there and what did they want? Should I go out and confront them? Since I didn't know who they were, that didn't seem wise. My instincts told me to stay put, and for several more minutes that's what I did. Yet, standing there with a thunking heart, wondering what was going on in my own house was unbearable. Then I thought of the phone. I could call for help.

Before I'd given myself time to really think this through, I'd turned the knob and slipped out into the dark kitchen. The phone, like everything else in the castle, was an old-fashioned model. It sat on the counter on the opposite wall.

Ears straining for noises from the front of the house, I glided over to it. When I picked it up, I realized that calling for help on the island wasn't going to be so simple. You couldn't just dial 911 as on the mainland. I even wondered if there would be an operator on duty at this hour.

With my heart in my throat, I picked up the receiver. In the silence of the dark kitchen, the dial tone seemed to roar. Nervously looking over my shoulder, I dialed 0. It rang eleven agonizing times before I heard the click of a pickup.

"Help you?" a sleepy voice inquired.

"This is Katy Conroy," I whispered. "I need help."

"Speak up, please," the operator said in a nasal tone. "I can't hear you."

"I can't speak up. There's someone in my house, and I need help."

"What city are you calling?"

"I'm not calling a city. I need you to call the sheriff."

"I'm sorry, ma'am, you need to speak up. I can't hear you."

Somebody else had heard me, though. My ears detected footsteps pounding down the hall in my direction. Then I heard another sound. Little as I knew about guns, I recognized it immediately. The distinctive snick of a revolver being cocked stabbed the darkness.

Instantly, I dropped the receiver. Ignoring the operator's plaintive twang, I ran to the back door. But I was too late. Even as I yanked it open, my intruder was upon me. Fists up to defend myself, I half turned. "Egan," I started to say as I opened my mouth. Then lightning exploded behind my eyes. Awash in a wave of pain, I crumpled to the floor.

How long was I out cold? Long enough for whoever had hit me to drag me across the kitchen floor and push me down the cellar stairs. When I regained consciousness, I was lying at the foot of them in an aching, pain-wracked heap.

"Ohhhh," I moaned. For several minutes, I lay with my eyes tightly closed, unable to even entertain the thought of opening them. My head felt as if it had been split open. Then I started to smell it, the acrid odor of smoke.

That yanked my eyelids up as almost nothing else would have. Opening them made little difference. Around me, I saw only inky darkness. As my fingers splayed out, I realized I was lying on packed dirt. That told me I was back in the cellar where my grandfather had died. Perhaps I was lying in the very spot where he'd breathed his last. How long had I been here, and who had pushed me down? Egan? Oh, God, I prayed, please don't let it have been him. But who would do this to me? And why?

I heaved myself to my knees and tested various parts of my body. Though everything hurt, nothing appeared to be broken. A sulfurous stench made me cough. I turned toward it and bumped up against wooden steps. At least I knew where to climb to get back up to the door, I told myself.

But climbing in my bruised and scraped condition was no easy matter. I heard the whimpering of a wounded animal and realized with a kind of detached horror that it was me.

At the top of the steps, I grabbed the knob and tried to turn it. Nothing happened. Whoever had pushed me down here had locked me in. And I knew why. Though I couldn't see the choking smoke leaking through the cracks around the door, I could smell it. In the distance, my ears picked up a faint, ominous crackle.

I YANKED ON the doorknob, then hammered and screamed. "Help, somebody! Anybody! Egan! Please, please!"

Thick skins of smoke snaked through the cracks around the door. I wanted to back away, but the door was my only exit and my only hope. I banged on it, calling desperately. My eyes burned. Tears blinded me. They leaked down my cheeks and into my mouth. It was getting hot in here. The realization jacked up my terror, and I hammered and screamed more desperately still.

Suddenly, I heard a voice call my name. It was Egan's voice. The door yanked open. A pale reddish glow, dominated by a tall dark shadow, filled my tear- and smoke-blinded gaze. I recognized Egan, but didn't know whether to be glad or afraid. I can only imagine what he saw—a filthy, disheveled, smoke-blackened sniveling creature.

"My God," he exclaimed as he reached for me. I was too weak to resist him. Whatever fate he had in mind for me had to be better than being cooked alive in the cellar.

"Hold your nose," he commanded. He swung me up into his arms, pivoted and rushed through the billows of hot smoke jamming the kitchen. The trip to the door couldn't have taken more than a second or two. Yet, it seemed to go on endlessly.

Then we were outside and my lungs filled with air instead of smoke. Gently, Egan laid me on the grass. I heard excited voices around me, the roar of cars pulling up. Then I slipped into unconsciousness and heard nothing at all.

"POOR BABY." A woman's voice.

"She's had a bad time, all right." Egan's voice.

"Do you think she's going to be okay, Dad?"

I opened my eyes and looked into the concerned eyes of an older woman with thick, salt-and-pepper hair. I lifted my gaze and saw Egan standing behind her. He looked tired, dirty and concerned. His face was grimed with sweat-streaked soot. I saw a raw, red weal on his forehead. A burn, I realized.

Next to him, Rex danced into view. His hair stuck out around his face. He wore pajamas and a worried expression.

I returned my gaze to the woman with the graying hair. She smiled at me, then leaned forward and patted my shoulder. "Hello, Miss Conroy. I don't think we've met. I'm Egan's mother."

"I remember you," I tried to say. All that came out was a hollow croak.

"Now, don't try to talk. You've had a bad time of it and breathed in a parcel of smoke. Doc Martin's already been and gone. He says what you need is a solid piece of rest. He left a sedative and some medicine for your eyes and throat. Right now, you're safe and sound in my son's house. He brought me here to take care of you. So, don't worry about a thing."

Strange to say, I went back to sleep after that and didn't wake up until late the next morning. When I did open my eyes again, I was in a sunny room. It was painted butter yellow and furnished with a maple bureau and wardrobe. There was a green braided rug on the floor and matching chintz curtains on the window. Next to the bed where I lay, Rex teetered on an old-fashioned rocking chair painted green.

When he saw me looking at him, he hunched forward. "Are you awake?"

Since the answer to that seemed obvious, I replied with a question of my own. "What are you doing home from school?" My voice still croaked, but the words came out recognizably.

"It's Saturday. Gran said I could sit here and tell her when you woke up." He jumped to his feet and hurried to the partly open door. "Grandma, she's awake," I heard him call down the stairs.

He came back grinning. "My gran will bring up your breakfast in just a minute."

"That's kind of her, but I don't want to put her to any trouble."

"She doesn't mind. She likes to cook. Did you sleep okay last night? I mean, you were in pretty bad shape."

"I don't remember, Rex. I hope I didn't put you out of your room."

He shook his head so energetically that his curls appeared to be dancing. "This isn't my room. It isn't even the room Grandma uses when she stays over. We have five bedrooms in this house. There's enough space in this house that a really big family could live here."

"I can see that."

Rex looked guilty. "I shouldn't talk about our house when yours burned down. I'm sorry, Katy."

"Did mine burn down?" I'd guessed that, but I'd been afraid to ask. The news didn't make me feel much. Maybe I was still in shock.

"Dad says a big part of it did."

"Where is your dad?"

"He saved your life." Rex looked proud.

"I know he did. I need to thank him."

"Dad had to work, but he'll be back later." Rex came close to the bed and studied me with bright blue eyes, hauntingly like his father's. "What are you going to do now, Katy? Where will you live?"

"Don't know. Maybe the castle can be fixed. I won't know until I see it."

"Dad says it's pretty bad. You can stay here as long as you want. We've got plenty of room."

"I don't think your dad would care for that."

"Yes, he would." Again, Rex nodded emphatically. "I know he would."

"Now you stop badgering that girl." Mrs. Halpern bustled through the door bearing a tray with a teapot and a bowl of chicken soup. She looked at Rex sternly. "You shouldn't be making her talk. I know that throat of hers has still got to be sore. This might make it feel better, though." She brought the tray over so I could see it. "Nod if you feel up to it," she said to me.

Nodding hard, I pushed myself into a sitting position. After Mrs. Halpern tucked a pillow behind my back, I began spooning up the soup. It tasted delicious.

"I was just telling Katy that since her house is burned down, she can stay here if she wants to," Rex said. "We've got tons of room."

"Rex, why don't you go downstairs and see to that chore your dad left?"

"Aw, Grandma, now?"

"Yes, now. I want to have a word or two with Miss Conroy."

"Katy...please call me Katy."

Mrs. Halpern smiled. "And you call me Alice."

After Rex had shuffled out, Alice said, "You look better than you did last night, but you're still a bit peaked. How are you feeling?"

"A little ragged around the edges and my throat is sore, but otherwise I'm fine. Thanks for breakfast. It was wonderful." I had poured myself a cup of tea. Gingerly, I took a sip.

"Now, don't talk if you don't feel up to it." Alice Halpern settled herself in the rocking chair Rex had occupied and folded her hands in the lap of her loose print dress. Though years of hardship had marked her hands and face and thickened her middle, she was still a handsome woman. Her long gray-black hair was caught in back with a simple clip. She wore no makeup, but her gray eyes needed little emphasis. They looked out at me from thick black lashes. Now I knew where Egan had gotten his beautiful sooty lashes.

"I'm no great gabber myself," she said in her pleasant contralto, "but things being the way they are, I don't mind if you don't hold up your end of the conversation. Best you let that throat of yours rest up. I sent Rex away because I thought it was high time we met."

"You did?" I was surprised and wary.

She nodded. "It's a shame we never met before. When you and Egan first went around together, I didn't pay much attention. Egan knew so many pretty girls. It was only afterward that I realized you were something special to him."

"How did, I mean—"

"Oh, he told me about the elopement. Of course, he just shrugged it off. That boy has never been one to let his feelings show. But I'm his mother. I could tell what happened between you two cut a lot deeper than he let on. Then you came back and I started hearing about you from Rex. He's not closemouthed like his dad. When he's excited about something, he chatters." She clucked and then smiled wryly and shook her head. "Egan, being Egan, he never said much. But I could see the change in him. I thought I should come over and introduce myself. I was planning to, too. I'm real sorry I didn't do it before this happened. I just wanted to let you know that."

I opened my mouth, but nothing came out. "I don't know what to say," I finally murmured.

"Don't say a thing, dear." She took my tray. "Just tell me what I can do to make you more comfortable."

After Mrs. Halpern removed the food, she came back up with the clothes I'd had on yesterday, freshly laundered. I had awakened wearing one of Egan's T-shirts. How it had come to replace the grimy shorts and shirt I'd had on when Egan rescued me, I had no idea.

Things seemed better after I'd showered, washed my hair and put on fresh clothes. When I came out of the bathroom a little while later, I felt almost human. For the first time since last night, I could think about what I needed to do next. First, I had to check on the castle.

Downstairs, I told Mrs. Halpern I intended walking over to have a look at my property.

"In your condition?" She looked me up and down.

"I'm all right, really."

"I don't know how you can say that with those scrapes, scratches and purple bruises all over you."

"I know I look a sight, but I'm okay. Alice," I added politely, "I really need to see the castle. Rex tells me it's in pretty bad shape. I can't rest until I see it for myself."

Her expression softened. "Well, now, I can guess how that is. If you'll just wait, I'll call Egan and he'll drive you over."

At that, I shook my head, thanked her and, over her protests, hurried out. I wasn't ready to see Egan yet. I was too confused. Before I spoke to Egan, I needed to revisit the scene of last night's disaster and rethink what had happened.

I'd hoped to slip away from Egan's house without running into anybody else, but no such luck. "Katy,"

Rex called as he came darting down the driveway. "Sheriff Creech is here. He wants to talk to you."

"Rex, you come in here and do your room," Mrs. Halpern called from the open door.

"Aw, Grandma!"

"Don't make a face like that. Come in here this minute!"

As Rex dragged his feet toward the house, I proceeded down the driveway. Ralph Creech, Big Bass's one and only year-round lawman, was just climbing out of a battered Chevy. He was somewhere in his fifties, with thinning gray-blond hair and a babyish face. As he sauntered toward me, he pushed his hat back on his forehead. He was in uniform, his khaki pants loosely belted below his impressive paunch.

"Well, well," he called, "you're looking pretty spry for a girl who nearly woke up as burnt toast."

I was not in the mood to appreciate Ralph's gallows humor. "I'm just going over to see the castle now," I said as I approached him.

He shook his head, wobbling his jowls. "'Fraid you're not going to like what you see. A shame. It was a fine old house. Island won't seem the same without it."

"Was? You mean nothing is left of the castle?"

Ralph scratched his ear. "Oh, there's some left. But it'll be a job to piece it all together again. You'll soon be seeing for yourself."

"Yes, I will. Sheriff Creech, thanks for rescuing me."

He looked surprised. "Wasn't me who rescued you. Egan Halpern did that."

"I know Egan came in and carried me out when my house was on fire. But I thought you must have brought Egan with you after the operator called you and told you I was in trouble."

He had the grace to look faintly sheepish. "Well, now, our island operator that night was Francy Pierce. Francy knows I don't like to get unnecessary calls in the middle of the night, so she gave your nearest neighbor a buzz. That happens to be Egan Halpern. He's the one who came over to check on you."

My mouth dropped open. It was unbelievable that an operator wouldn't want to wake up the sheriff when someone had dialed for help. But that was Big Bass for you. The place was a world unto itself.

"Have you determined how the fire started?" I asked.

"Rich Sisk, he's head of our volunteer fire department, said he'd come over and take a look this afternoon. But I don't know what he'll find. It's no easy thing figuring out where a big blaze like that got its beginnings. Most likely it was electric. A lot of old houses on the island have burned from wiring that's gone bad."

"Faulty wiring didn't start the castle burning last night," I said flatly. "Someone got that fire going deliberately."

Creech looked astonished. "What makes you think a thing like that?"

"Someone came into my house in the middle of the night. That person hit me over the head while I was trying to call the operator for help and then threw me down the basement steps and locked the door so I couldn't get out."

"Look here, are you serious?"

"Dead serious."

"That's crazy. Who on this island would want to do a thing like that?"

"I have no idea. You tell me."

Ralph's meaty face turned red. "Look here, I'd keep a story like that quiet if I were you. Don't go spreading it around until I've had a chance to investigate."

I felt as if I'd had the breath knocked out of me. "Are you saying you don't believe me?"

"I'm not saying nothing of the kind. I'm just telling you to be careful until we get the facts on this straight. A woman living alone in a big old house like that can get nervy. Sometimes the wind rattling the timbers on an old house can start all kinds of creepy imaginings."

"I didn't imagine being locked in the basement, and I didn't imagine last night's fire."

"All kinds of little things can start a fire. You'd be surprised. Kettle left on the stove, oven not turned off. I hear tell you'd been doing a lot of cleaning in that house, lately."

"Yes, I had. So what?"

"Maybe you were trying to clean something with gasoline and spilled it where you shouldn't. That attic must have been full of old newspapers and rags. It could have been spontaneous combustion."

I looked into Sheriff Creech's mud-brown eyes and realized that he was humoring me. He didn't believe for a minute my story that I'd been attacked last night. It made me furious. I wanted to scream and kick him in the shins. How dare he imply I may have set my own house on fire by leaving a kettle on the stove! But arguing with him wasn't going to do me any good. I needed proof of what had really happened.

"If you'll excuse me," I said coldly, "I want to walk over and take a look at my property."

"You do that," he agreed. "But you be careful, now. Don't go wandering around inside and put a foot wrong.

Old houses that have been burned can be mighty dangerous.''

I HURRIED ALONG the shore, steaming. I was also deeply alarmed. It had never occurred to me that anyone would doubt my story. But as I mulled it over, I realized how bizarre it must sound to island ears. Here, everyone knew one another. Families had been intermarrying for generations. Except for the occasional unruly behavior of a drunken tourist, there was no crime. I was an outsider on the island, an unknown quantity. Of course they'd be more likely to think I was crazy than to take seriously my claim that one of them had stalked me and tried to burn me alive.

Suddenly, I felt as if I were wandering through a murky and threatening maze. Everywhere I looked, I saw danger and deceit. ''You need to be careful, Katy,'' I muttered. ''You need to know what you're doing.''

As I rounded the bend in the shoreline that opened onto my property, I expected to find the castle burned. Yet nothing could have prepared me for the reality.

''My God,'' I breathed as I stared at the derelict hulk that had once been home to generations of Conroys. The cornices were charred and blackened by smoke, and sections of the roof were missing. One of the turrets seemed to pierce the sky like a ruined firebrand. The porch, its wood singed and smoke-stained, sagged to one side. Next to it, part of the structure of the bay window in the dining room had fallen down on the scorched grass.

As I walked toward it, I saw pieces of melted glass from its panes sitting in black puddles left by the fire hoses. When I bent and picked up a lump of melted glass, it was still warm. An acrid odor hung over everything, burning my eyes and nostrils. What would I do now? Was the house even insured? I doubted it.

Gingerly, I approached the porch. Beneath the thin soles of my sandals, its timbers were warm. Inside the kitchen, the heat and smell of burning was heavy. Smoke and water had ruined everything—cabinets, furniture, a century's accumulation of antique china, glass and cookware. I picked up a copper pot that had sat on a ledge over the sink. It was coated with burned-on soot. It, too, felt warm.

I should have turned around and left. But I couldn't. All the way over, I'd asked myself why someone had sneaked into my house and then tried to cremate it. What had they been looking for, and what had they wanted to destroy? One possibility had occurred to me. Before I'd gone to bed, I'd left the old map of the caves in Grandfather's study. I wanted to see if it was still there.

Nervously, I made my way to the front of the house. There wasn't as much damage in the hall as in the kitchen. Yet, as I glanced into the front parlor, I heaved a groan. Smoke coated all the fine old antiques. Their upholstery was sodden. Paper, scorched and shriveled by the heat, hung off the walls.

A pall of smoke hung in Grandfather's study, and my nostrils burned from the odor of singed books. The room itself, however, had come through relatively unscathed. I'd left the old map in the top drawer of Grandfather's desk.

"Ah!" I exclaimed when I saw it wasn't there. So I'd been right. My attacker had been after the map of the caves. I frowned. The only person who'd known about the map was Betty. Surely she couldn't have been the intruder who'd tried to kill me. *Correction,* I thought. *If Betty knew early in the afternoon, then half the island knew by nightfall.* Anyone could have heard that I'd found that map—including Egan.

As this possibility hit me, my hand trembled on the drawer pull. Was I absolutely certain that I'd put the map in the top drawer? Could I have put it in another? I searched, finding nothing until I yanked out the bottom right-hand drawer. My eyes widened as I stared inside. Sitting on top was Grandfather's black metal box.

As I gazed down at it, the blue crystal that I still wore around my neck seemed to heat. Through the thin fabric of my shirt, my hand grabbed it. With my free hand, I lifted the box out and set it on the desk. When I took off the top, I gave a little gasp. All the objects it had originally contained were still there. But now the map had joined them.

Carefully, I took the map out. As I unfolded it on the desk, my mind worked double time. Whoever had torched the castle last night was the same person who'd taken the box. Why had they returned it? Why had they put the map inside? Had they studied the map before placing it in the box? Of course, they must have, I thought. I focused my gaze on the faded pencil marks locating various caves. Whoever had attacked me must have made a copy. Now they knew as much about Grandfather's riddle as I did.

As this realization struck me, I refolded the map and stuck it in my pocket. Then I straightened and stood with my arms crossed over my chest, rubbing my forearms. So distracted was I by my churning thoughts, that it was a moment before I registered being cold. Cold? The house was still overheated from last night's blaze. Seconds earlier I'd been sweating. I couldn't be cold.

Yet, I was. I stared down in amazement at the goose bumps prickling my skin. Suddenly, the top of my head was brushed by an icy breath. An inexplicable dizziness enveloped me. That was when I felt it—the gentle brush of a hand across my throat.

With a strangled shriek, I whirled and stared about me. "Who's there?" I heard myself croak. I saw no one, yet I knew I wasn't alone. Somebody or something was in Grandfather's study with me. Nausea crept up the back of my throat. The room revolved around me. Far away, I thought I heard faint cries. Cries of anger, cries of distress.

A dark web floated across my eyes. I lost my balance, stumbled and started to sink to the floor. As I struggled to regain my balance, I saw a hand holding a gun. It was a man's hand, and he gripped the old revolver I'd found in the hall. As I watched in horror, the hand aimed the gun at me. It squeezed the trigger and fired a silent shot. Then blood seemed to rain from everywhere.

When my vision cleared, I struggled to my feet. I had to get out of there. Like a wild thing, I darted through the door. The hall, glazed with smoke, was dark and claustrophobic. As I dashed down it, I felt as if I were choking, as if my very lungs were burning out. Was something chasing me, dogging my heels and preparing to snatch at me?

Gasping, tears of terror blinding me, I sprinted through the scorched cavern of the kitchen. As I threw open the door, a dark shape loomed up in front of me. It reached out long arms to seize me and I screamed.

"Katy!" Egan said as he grabbed my shoulders. "For heaven's sake, Katy, what's wrong?"

Chapter Thirteen

I don't know how long I stood sobbing and shivering against Egan's chest. When I recovered enough to step back, I could feel his eyes on my ruined face. "Here," he said, drawing a clean white handkerchief out of his pocket. "You need this."

I certainly needed something. Tears still half blinded me. My soggy cheeks felt like a swamp. As I swabbed at them, Egan guided me off the porch to a glider, which had somehow found its way to a spot on the lawn under a tree. While I struggled to pull myself together, he watched closely, waiting for me to speak.

After a while, I crumpled his handkerchief into a ball between my fingers, dropped my hands in my lap and looked at him.

"Katy," he said, laying a gentle hand on my shoulder, "I'm sorry about the castle. Obviously, seeing it like this has upset you. I know it looks bad, but it's not beyond repair."

"It isn't?"

"It'll take time and effort. The lower floor is a mess. But fixing it won't be impossible."

"It's impossible if you don't have the money, and I don't."

"Insurance?" he asked hopefully.

"I doubt it very much."

Egan grimaced. "That's too bad, but listen. I'll help you."

I stared at him in amazement.

"I'm a pretty fair carpenter. In my spare time, I'll help you put the castle to rights."

This was the last thing I expected to hear from Egan. For an instant, I felt disoriented, overloaded with conflicting emotions. I shook my head. "Egan, I'm not happy to see my house in ruins, but that's not why I came running out of the castle in hysterics."

"Why then? What's wrong?"

As I studied him, I didn't know where to begin. His blue eyes looked so concerned. I wanted to lay my head on his shoulder. I wanted to feel his hands on my body, comforting me. "Egan," I whispered.

"Katy." His gaze fastened on my lips. "God, Katy." His head bent toward mine and our mouths met. For a long, wonderful moment, I melted into him. While the kiss lasted, I felt safe and protected.

At last, we drew apart, and I looked up into his face. "Egan, do you believe in ghosts?"

His expression became worried again. "Depends on what kind of ghost you're talking about. I feel the past haunts the present and the future. Growing up on Big Bass, it's hard not to feel that."

I shook my head. "That's not what I mean. I mean real ghosts, the kind you read about in horror stories."

"Katy, what are you talking about?"

Unconsciously, my fingers kneaded the handkerchief still balled between them. "I just had a very strange experience in Grandfather's study."

"You shouldn't have been in there. Parts of a house damaged like yours could give way at any moment. You could be trapped, crushed."

"I know. I just..." As my tongue stumbled, I realized that much as I wanted to tell Egan about the map, I didn't feel ready to discuss it with him yet. If he already knew about it from Betty's gossip, let him bring the subject up. "I needed to go in there and see if some records had been burned. While I was in there, I sensed I wasn't alone."

"You thought somebody was in there with you?"

"Somebody I couldn't see or hear. Somebody I could only feel."

"You mean a ghost?" The corners of Egan's mouth lifted. Awkwardly, but gently, he patted my shoulder. "Well, I wouldn't be surprised if old Nate haunts this place. He'd be mighty displeased at seeing it in ruins like this."

I wanted to protest that it wasn't Grandfather's ghost I'd felt in the study, but I could see from Egan's expression that he was humoring me. It affected me like an icewater shower. I drew back from him. "You think I was imagining things, don't you?"

"In a situation like this, who could blame you? What happened last night would send anybody around the bend."

"Around the bend? Is that where you think I am?"

"Of course not. Katy, I only meant—"

"Why did you leave work to come here? How did you know where to find me?"

"Sheriff Creech stopped in to see me. He mentioned—"

"Oh, now I see," I interrupted. "Creech told you what I told him about being hit on the head and thrown down the basement stairs."

"He said you thought your house was set on fire deliberately and that someone had tried to kill you."

"I suppose he also told you that he thought I was crazy."

"You've got to admit, an accusation like that is going to sound pretty farfetched to a lawman who's never seen any crime on this island beyond an occasional drunk from the mainland breaking windows."

"And what do *you* think, Egan? You're the one who rescued me last night. You know that I couldn't get that basement door open. Somebody must have locked it."

"Katy, that door doesn't have a lock on it. When I came in, the warming pan above the lintel had fallen and was wedged against the knob. That and the heat from the fire would have helped stick the door inside its frame."

I stared at him, hardly believing my ears. I had hammered with all my strength against that door. But, a traitorous part of my brain whispered, "You were weak and out of your mind with pain and fear at the time."

"Are you telling me you think I was locked in the basement accidentally?" I demanded.

"I have no idea how you got stuck down there. Why were you downstairs at that hour of the night, in the first place?"

"I was restless. I couldn't sleep. I wanted to see the place where my grandfather died."

"What in the world were you looking for down there after midnight?"

"I'm not sure what I was looking for. Some clue. Something that might tell me what really happened the night Grandfather fell down those stairs."

"What really happened?" Egan stared at me. "Katy, what are you saying?"

"I'm saying I can't get it out of my mind that Grand-father's death wasn't an accident."

"You think somebody pushed Nate down those stairs?"

"After what happened to me last night, yes."

"But why? And who?" Suddenly, Egan's expression changed, became wary. "My God, you suspect me, don't you?"

Our gazes locked and held. I couldn't lie. The time had come for some honesty between me and Egan. "I can't imagine why anyone would want to kill my grandfather. But you're one of the few people I know of who might have had a motive. Egan, what were you doing down in the basement that first night I was back on the island?"

"Looking for an old photo album Nate promised me. It was supposed to have had pictures of my grandfather in it."

"Rafe Halpern?"

"Yes, but Nate died before he could give it to me. He mentioned he thought it might be down in the cellar. He'd promised it to me, and I wanted it for Rex. I was afraid once his estate went to his heirs, I'd have no chance at it."

"Did you find the album?"

"No, I didn't." Egan's eyes narrowed. "Do you hon-estly think I'd murder your grandfather over something like that?"

"No, no, I don't." I clutched at his sleeve. "Egan, I don't want to believe ill of you."

Ignoring my denial, Egan said, "Katy, you've been suspicious of me ever since you came back, haven't you? My God, even the night we made love, you were sneaking around my property looking for evidence against me.''

I felt a deep flush rise on my neck. What he said was true, and I hated that it was. "Egan, I couldn't stop myself from putting two and two together."

"And every time you added two and two, you came out with my name, didn't you?" His voice was cold, his eyes wintry. "Tell me the truth. Last night, did you think I was the one who'd locked you in the basement?"

When I gazed at him, tongue-tied, he expelled a long breath. "You did. Katy, that kitchen was a hellish wall of flame and smoke when I went in. I did it because I couldn't bear the thought of any harm coming to you. God help me, I'd do it all over if I had the chance."

"Oh, Egan," I cried. "I don't want to suspect you. But so many strange things have happened. I know there's more than what you've told me. I can feel it. Let's be honest with each other. What do you know about a man named Spike Shawnaway?"

Egan stiffened. "He was a gangster during Prohibition. How did you come up with his name?"

"I did some research in Sandusky. I read that just before he was gunned down, he stole a shipment of government gold. Was the gold Grandfather left you in the black box part of that shipment?"

"Possibly." Egan's voice was tight, guarded.

"What was Shawnaway's connection with both our grandfathers and Billy Wiblin? How did my grandfather wind up with so much of that stolen gold, and why did he leave it to you?"

Egan's expression had become hard and unyielding. His voice, when he finally replied, was flinty. "Katy, this is island business."

"No, Egan, it's my business. I have to know the truth. Please, if you care for me at all, tell me the truth."

"Let's turn that around, Katy. If you care for me at all, trust me. Believe me, as soon as I know the answers, I'll tell you. In the meantime, go back home and stay there."

I pointed a frantic finger at the castle. "Egan, my home is burned."

"I meant my home. As long as you stay there, no harm can come to you. Katy, for God's sake, just give me a little time and trust me. Consider what we've been to each other and believe in me. Is that so impossible?"

"If you won't tell me the truth, I'll find it out for myself," I said bitterly. Before Egan could react, I leaped to my feet and dashed blindly toward the road. I wasn't sure what I was going to do. But as I flew past Egan's truck, I spotted his keys dangling from the ignition. In that moment, I knew exactly.

"Katy," Egan yelled. I had already yanked the truck's door open and climbed in. He came racing after me, but he was too late. By the time he had reached the truck, I had switched on the ignition and put the vehicle in gear.

With Egan's angry voice echoing in my ears, I headed his pickup out onto the main road and pointed it north. My free hand fumbled in my pocket until I felt the ragged edges of the map I'd stuffed there. Somehow, I had to find the truth. I couldn't go on with my mind clouded by ugly suspicions and doubts. I had to know. And there was one place that might tell me.

I drove north along the coast road that led to Cotton Bluff and the spot where I'd have to get out and make my way to the caves on foot. As the truck rattled along, I glanced through the windshield at the sky. The afternoon had become overcast. A storm might come up later. How many hours of daylight and decent weather did I have left? The last thing I wanted was to return to the caves where I'd had a terrifying experience. But part of that terror had been the darkness, I reassured myself. As long as I had daylight, it wouldn't be so bad.

Nevertheless, as I drove along, cold dread crept over me. I kept looking back over my shoulder, half expecting to see Egan in hot pursuit and half hoping that I would, so I needn't go on with the scheme forming in my mind. He wouldn't be able to follow me without a car, I told myself. He'd have to borrow one. But that shouldn't be so difficult.

Even then, how would he know where to look for me? He might guess, but he wouldn't know unless he also knew about the map. And if he'd known about the map...my brain stopped, paralyzed. I refused to speculate. I couldn't believe that Egan was behind any of the bad things that had been happening to me. How could I accept such a notion when I was falling in love with the man all over again? I had to find the truth. Nothing else would do.

I drove to the spot closest to the coastline harboring the caves. As I approached it, I looked around for a sheltered place to leave the truck. There was none. I followed the road another quarter of a mile until I came upon a shady spot behind a large outcropping. After parking where passersby couldn't easily see the truck from the road, I explored the glove compartment. It held a medium-size flashlight. I stuck it in the waistband of my shorts. Doubling back, I set off along the trail.

Doc Martin's painkillers were wearing off. Aches and pains from the beating I'd taken the night before began eating at me. Nevertheless, I plowed on. As I hurried along the uneven dirt track, I kept chanting to myself, "I've got to find out, I've got to find out."

At the limestone plateau next to the cliffs that hid the caves, I pulled the map out, unfolded and studied it. Since my head ached and my eyes smarted, it was several minutes before the faded markings on the aged scrap of paper made any sense to me. I kept looking from the map to the craggy wall of limestone facing the lake and back again.

Finally, I began to make correlations. When I'd explored the caves before, I hadn't climbed very high. Assuming that anyone toting heavy kegs of bootleg liquor and in a hurry to unload them, wouldn't want to go rock climbing, I'd stuck with the caves easiest to reach from the shore. But if my map made any sense, the cave marked Blue Crystal was much higher up on the escarpment.

For several seconds, I stood frowning over this. From where I stood, Blue Crystal looked virtually inaccessible. How would the island's bootleggers have gotten their cargo up there? Then I thought of the complicated rigging on Egan's boat. Island men were sailors. Ropes, pulleys.

Bootleggers could have hauled their contraband up the side of the cliff with a system of ropes and pulleys. Only one man would have needed to climb to the cave marked Blue Crystal. The others could have stayed on an easy-to-reach spot well below it.

After refolding the map and stuffing it back into my pocket, I squared my shoulders and set off for the small stony beach where the bootleggers would have dragged their boat. Once there, I surveyed the cliff wall hiding the caves. Slowly and carefully, I began to ascend.

By now, I was in real pain. Every bone and muscle in my body throbbed. Squealing with anguish, I lost a handhold and slipped to my knees on a pile of jagged rocks. *I should be home safe in bed,* I thought as I tried to stop the flow of blood from my new scrape. *Rock climbing is the last thing in the world I should be doing.* But I had no home now. The only bed I had was in Egan's house. And, I acknowledged with a sick feeling in the pit of my stomach, I was far from being certain that either the castle or the Macaster place was safe for me.

As I struggled along, I kept a lookout for spots the bootleggers might have used for a platform when they'd hauled their kegs up the cliff. At the cave where I'd had such a bad experience, my heart wedged in my throat.

As if pursued by Furies, I hurried past the cave's mouth and pushed myself up a sharp incline. At the top, obscured by scrubby growth, I found a flat area large enough for at least three people to stand on. Would the bootleggers really have carried their contraband this far, I asked myself.

Uncertainly, I gazed out at the lake. As I listened to the slap of the gray, wind-tossed waves below, I tried to picture how it would have been. Crossing the lake so often, the bootleggers might expect to be chased by federal agents who were on to them. Agents would have come to the island to make spot checks. The lawbreakers would have wanted a hiding place that lawmen weren't going to find easily.

This climb had been tough on me, but I was a woman in a weakened condition. If the bootleggers had been Rafe Halpern, Billy Wiblin and my grandfather, they would have been strong young men in their early twenties. Spurred on by greed and adrenaline, this climb might not have seemed too arduous, especially when so much depended on the liquor not being discovered.

I started to look around. Of course, after more than a half century, I couldn't expect to see remnants of the rope and tackle they must have used to haul their kegs.

Where was Blue Crystal in relation to this spot? I turned my attention to the cliff face and peered up. Then I took out the map and studied it. No matter how far back I craned my head, I couldn't see any sign of a cave. Yet the map showed Blue Crystal directly above this spot.

Where, I wondered. And how had the third man got himself up there? I saw no handholds, nothing that could be used for steps. Yet there must be some way. I felt certain this had to be the place. Wind tossed my hair and whipped at the hem of my T-shirt. Glancing over my shoulder, I saw a scarf of dark gray cloud shrouding the horizon. A storm was definitely on its way and this was no place to be in a storm. My hand went to the crystal beneath my T-shirt. As I rubbed it between my fingertips, strength and conviction seemed to flow from it to me.

Ignoring the storm signals, I began to explore. The left side of the flat area was clearly impassable. The right side ended in a jagged spine of limestone. *I'll get cut to ribbons on it,* I thought. Nevertheless, flattened like a spider, with my arms and legs splayed out at sharp angles, I inched around it.

When I almost lost my grip, I came close to turning back. But I didn't. Something, some inner conviction, urged me on. As I hauled myself around the edge of the spine, I spotted a series of weathered cuts in the rock. From anywhere else, they'd be invisible. From my vantage point, it looked as if they could be used as steps.

A quarter of an hour later, sweaty, scratched and panting from exhaustion, I pulled myself up onto a narrow ledge. It was difficult to gain purchase, as a scrubby pine had somehow rooted itself in the rock. Its spiny branches sprawled every which way. Giving it a swipe, I managed to push enough of it aside to balance myself on the ledge.

For several minutes I sat there gasping for breath. By now, my body was such a mass of cuts and scrapes, I felt like hamburger. Getting up here had been a nightmare. A cold wind lashed at my face and hair and dark clouds massed on the horizon. I didn't even want to think about how I was going to descend.

I started looking around. Aside from a splendid view of the incoming storm, there really wasn't much to take in. Cave Blue Crystal, where are you? There was no sign of an opening. Had I gone through all this for nothing? "Damn," I exclaimed. Sharp needles grazed my knee and I gave the pine bough they belonged to a kick.

Instead of springing back as a living branch would do, the bough dropped and lay motionless. I stared. Then I rolled over, got to my knees and gave the branch a tug. It came loose in my hand.

Nerves prickling, I investigated further. The tree itself looked rooted. But the branch I'd just kicked, and several others besides, had been cut away from the trunk, and the cuts were fresh. I soon saw why. The pine was growing in the mouth of an opening. When I'd pulled the freshly sawed branches away, I'd opened a space just large enough to slip through.

After realizing this, I stood breathing hard, my heart thumping. One hand went back to the crystal, and the other went to the flashlight still tucked in my waistband. Who had cut the branches and then stuffed them back to hide the opening? Might that person still be in there? And did I really want to go poking around in there and find out?

I hadn't come all this way not to. Swallowing back the lump in my throat, I took out the flashlight, switched it on and squeezed through the opening. Immediately, I was in a different world. Outside, storm clouds rode a high wind that scrubbed at bleached rock and heaving water. Inside, I stooped in a low, narrow passage plagued by darkness and a musty, unpleasant closeness.

The passage wound into the side of the rock without appearing to widen much. Playing my flashlight over the walls, I followed it. There was no sound except the beating of my heart and the rasp of my breathing. Was I alone in here? All my instincts shouted danger. Yet I walked on, determined to see this through to the end. Truth had become more important to me than even my own safety.

I rounded a slight bend and the passage widened. Above me, something caught the beam from my wavering flashlight and glinted. I glanced up and blinked in surprise. A thousand glittering points of light winked at me. It was an elaborate crystal formation. When I directed my flashlight over the facets, shafts of opalescent blue shone back at me. Blue crystals, the same shade as the one I wore around my neck. I was in the right place.

The realization sent a shock wave of pure terror rippling up my spine. I took several faltering steps past the crystals and shone my flashlight over the low, musty chamber for which they served as portals. A thick layer of dirt covered the floor of the cave. In the center, someone had been digging at it. Freshly heaped dirt lay mounded up around what appeared to be a sizable hole. In the corner, a large garden spade lay abandoned against the wall.

Gingerly, I approached the mounded dirt and peered over the edge and into the hole. Stepping closer, I probed it with my light. "Oh, my God!" I whispered.

The lower part of a skeleton lay exposed. Though it was nothing but bone now, it still wore a pair of bib overalls. A leather shoe dangled from what had been an ankle. I knew instantly whose skeleton it was.

"Rafe Halpern," a voice said behind me.

I whirled. Betty Wiblin blocked the entrance I'd just passed through. She was carrying the revolver stolen from the castle, and she was pointing it at me.

"Betty," I breathed.

"It's me, all right."

"How did you get here?"

"I've been here all along. I saw you coming and put the pine branches back. I hoped you wouldn't get this far or that, if you did, you wouldn't find the cave entrance. But you're one determined woman, Katy Conroy. I give you credit for that much."

Her voice was cold and stark. The lines of her face stood out harshly in the wavering light of my flashlight.

"It was you last night," I exclaimed.

"That's right. All I wanted was to return the box and have a look at the map. Why'd you have to be wandering around making phone calls like that in the middle of the night?" In her other hand, she held a flashlight of her own. She switched it on, blinding me.

"Betty, why?" I exclaimed as I covered my eyes to shield them from the glare.

"Why? A good question," she answered bitterly. "But here's a better one. Why should the Conroys have lived like kings for half a century, when the Wiblins could only barely manage to scratch along? Why should my mother have watched her life drain away taking care of a helpless wreck like Gramps? Why should I have to do the same and raise three boys on pennies? I found the answer to those questions when I read Gramps' diary. It was then that I learned how your grandfather cheated and ruined us.''

"My grandfather?''

"Oh yes— Nate Conroy, may he burn in hell. I hope he's there right now.''

Venom flooded her voice and a horrible certainty filled me. "Did you push him, Betty? Did you kill him?''

She stiffened. Her head went up, and I thought I saw her gun hand tremble. "It was an accident. When I found Gramps's diary and read it to the end, I was plenty mad. It was late at night, but I was too pissed to stay put until morning. I stormed over to the castle loaded for bear.''

"What were you after?''

Her eyes blazed. "The gold, my share of the gold Nate had been sitting on all his life like a nasty old spider. Of course, he refused to tell me where it was. I didn't mean to kill the old coot, though Lord knows he deserved worse than he got after what he did to Rafe Halpern and my grandfather.''

"Did he kill Rafe?''

"Shot him down for Spike Shawnaway's loot, obviously.'' She pointed at the skeleton behind us. "Like I said, I read all about it in Gramps' diary. The three of them, Gramps, Rafe and Nate, had been doing a great job running liquor for Shawnaway. Just before he got killed in a shootout on the mainland, he decided to trust them to hide his stolen money. Your grandfather shot Rafe here in the cave and covered his body with dirt. That's where the diary ends, but the rest is easy enough to figure out. Nate and Gramps must have argued. Somehow, Gramps got hit on the head so bad that Nate left him for dead. But Gramps didn't die. All those years he was a living reproach to your grandfather and a living hell to his family.''

"Well, now you've had your revenge."

"What revenge? All Nate's life, the Conroys lived in the lap of luxury. Now it's the Wiblins' turn. That gold is ours."

"Betty, was it you who ran me down with a red car in Sandusky?"

"I wasn't trying to kill you. I only wanted to hurt you, so you'd stay out of the castle long enough for me to search it. I figured Nate had the gold hidden there someplace, but I never got the chance to really search. You're hard to keep down, Katy. You weren't gone long enough for me to find anything."

"Did you think you'd find the gold here?"

"When I saw the map, I thought I might. But it's not buried with Rafe, so it must be somewhere in what's left of the castle. Don't worry, I'll find it yet."

"That gold is the government's. I don't know what the law is, but probably most of it will have to be returned to the federal government."

A cunning expression came over Betty's face. "Not if they don't know I've found it."

"The coins are dated. They can be traced."

"Gold that's been melted down is untraceable. I'll do what Nate must have been doing all these years. When I find the main stash, I'll melt it down. And there won't be anyone around to tell what I've done. Now," Betty said, taking a step closer, "that leaves the question of what I'm going to do about you."

"What are you going to do about me, Betty?"

"Isn't it obvious? I'm sorry about this, Katy. It's nothing personal. Although, I must admit, I never did like you much once you started dating Egan. It was like a slap in the face, and I was only too happy to bust up your marriage plans by warning your grandfather. Still, if you hadn't insisted on sticking around, if you hadn't been so darn nosy and asked so many questions..." She shrugged and raised the muzzle of the revolver.

My reaction was automatic. I hurled my flashlight at hers. Normally, I can't hit the side of a barn. This time, fear guided my hand to its target. My flashlight knocked hers away from her hand. Both went crashing to the stone floor, sending beams of light shooting crazily up at the ceiling.

There was a deafening crack. Something whizzed past my ear. A bullet, I thought, as I darted past Betty and sprinted for the cave's entrance. She caught up with me just as I reached the end of the passage. Flashes of lightning and the windy roar of the storm now battering the cliff filtered through the half-torn screen of pine. Realizing I couldn't escape, I turned and dived at her. I had to get the gun away from her before she could use it again.

"Oh no you don't," she screeched as I grabbed at her wrist. She tried to aim the weapon at me, but I managed to hold it away. Together, we crashed to the floor. Scratching and struggling, we rolled back and forth. Desperately, I fought to keep Betty from aiming the revolver at me. But she was a strong, athletic woman, and I was weak from the ordeals of the last few days.

Gradually, she began to wear me down. Her wrist twisted in my grip, and the barrel of the revolver swung toward my head.

"Betty," I screamed, "don't!" Then there was an eerie electric crackle. A flash of lightning bathed both our faces in intense white light. It forced Betty, who was looking into it, to close her eyes. Her grip on me eased enough so that I tore away. Blindly, she grabbed at me, but I managed to elude her and scramble past the broken pine. Once outside, I had no place to go. While the wind pummeled me and rain beat at my face and body, I pressed myself against the cliff face. I stood on a six-inch ledge, nothing between me and a sheer twenty-foot drop.

I looked to my right and saw Betty emerge from the cave entrance, gun in hand.

"I'm sorry about this, Katy," she said over the scream of the wind. "I really am." Slowly, she raised the barrel of the gun and pointed it at my midsection.

I braced myself and wondered what it would be like to die in this lonely place the way Rafe Halpern had. At that instant, another flash of lightning ripped the darkness open and spilled out a light so bright, it momentarily blinded me. When I was able to see again, I focused on Betty. I expected her to shoot me. But she wasn't even looking my way. Her head was turned. Glancing past her, I saw a man standing on the ledge. He wore bib overalls and an awful expression. If he hadn't been pale as death, he would have looked like Egan.

As he started to move toward her, Betty screamed and took a step in the opposite direction. It was the wrong thing to do. She stumbled and fell. When I looked down, I saw her sprawled on the ledge below. When I looked up again, nobody but me stood on the ledge.

Chapter Fourteen

"Are you sure about this, Egan?" As I climbed down the cellar steps, I gazed at him quizzically.

Waiting for me at the foot of the stairs, he stood surveying the dank, gloomy space that lay beneath the castle's seared hulk. "We've searched every inch of what's left of the rest of the castle and found nothing," he replied. "After I buried what remained of my grandfather's body, I dug up the entire floor of that cave. The gold has to be down here."

"Not necessarily. It could be buried someplace on the property. It could even be in a safe-deposit box somewhere on the mainland."

Egan shook his head. "Knowing Nate, not a chance. He was a possessive devil. He would have wanted it where he could get at it easily. Keep in mind, all these years he's been holed up in the castle living like a cranky old lord of the realm. The other islanders always assumed he had family money—stocks, bonds, that sort of thing."

"No, there was only the house for me to inherit. Nothing else. Egan, as far as I know, Grandfather never lived ostentatiously. He paid his bills on time, but even before Grandmother died, he never traveled or entertained. And he certainly never gave the impression he was happy. He must have spent most of his life feeling wretchedly guilty. Otherwise, he wouldn't have left us those black boxes. Surely he did it because he wanted us to learn the truth."

"The truth." Egan grimaced. "We'll never know the truth of what happened in that cave. We'll never be able to do anything but guess."

"Frankly," I said, "I have a hard time believing that Nate and Billy deliberately plotted to kill Rafe. I think your grandad must have been shot accidentally."

Egan nodded. "That's what I think, too. Maybe they got into an argument over the gold and fought. The gun went off and Rafe died. Nate and Billy panicked and buried him. Afterward, Billy may have had second thoughts and wanted to go back and bring Rafe's body home."

The scenario made sense to me. "Grandfather would have been desperate to protect his reputation," I added. "After all, he was the island doctor. He would have objected. Perhaps he and Billy struggled over the issue, the struggle got violent and Billy ended up the way he is now. All these years I've always wondered why Grandfather gave up his practice—maybe it was because of guilt."

Egan's strong jaw firmed. He set the battery-operated lantern he carried on the floor and switched it to high. "And all for the sake of that cursed gold," he muttered. "The sooner we find it and get rid of it, the better for everyone on the island. Katy, while I dig, you take those moldy old preserves down and see if there might be some sort of secret compartment behind the shelves."

"Okay." As I walked over to the cobwebby shelves, I reflected on what had happened three days earlier. Minutes after Betty fell, and I'd found myself standing alone on the ledge outside Rafe Halpern's cave, Egan had appeared on the beach.

"Katy!" he'd yelled up to me over the wail of the storm. "Are you all right?"

I tried to answer. But my wavering voice was lost in the wind lashing at me and the cliffs. Wasting no more words, Egan started to climb. I watched in terror, afraid one of the lightning bolts cracking the boiling sky around us might strike him, afraid that he'd lose his grip on the rain-slick rocks and fall to his death.

Fortunately, Egan was surefooted and sure-handed. Twenty minutes later, as he reached the plateau where Betty lay sprawled, the storm began to abate.

"How is she?" I called down. "Is she..." I couldn't bring myself to say the word.

"She's okay," Egan answered. He was kneeling over Betty, his hand on her wrist, his head close to her chest. "Breathing's normal, heartbeat's regular. She's out cold, though, and it looks to me as if she might have broken a leg."

Hoping it was no more than that, I put a hand over my own rattling heart. I didn't want Betty to be seriously hurt—there had already been enough tragedy.

"Will you be all right up there long enough for me to go get help for Betty?" Egan asked.

"I'll be fine."

"Sure?"

"Absolutely." I tried not to look at the mouth of the cave behind me where Rafe Halpern's bones lay exposed.

"Don't suppose you can tell me in a sentence or two what's been going on up here?"

"No, it's too complicated. It's quite a story, though."

"Sit tight and don't move. I'll be looking forward to hearing it when I get back."

As I watched Egan start down to the shore, I noted his outfit—the same jeans and faded blue polo shirt that he'd worn when he'd kissed me on the glider back at the castle a few hours earlier. I hadn't expected anything different. I already knew that the face I'd seen in my window and the man in overalls who'd distracted Betty on the cliff wasn't Egan. No, that pale, unearthly face and those glowing eyes had belonged to Rafe Halpern's unquiet spirit.

Now, three days later in Grandfather's cellar, Egan read my thoughts. "Still convinced you saw my grandad's ghost?" He paused in his digging long enough to take a swipe at his sweaty forehead.

"Yes, I am."

Shaking his head, Egan jammed his shovel back into the hard-packed earth. "Well, since ghosts are out of my area of expertise, I won't try to argue you out of the notion. But answer me this. If you really think you're being haunted by Rafe Halpern's ghost, why are you sticking around his island? Why aren't you running for the mainland?"

"Why do you ask? Are you in such a hurry to get me out of your spare bedroom?"

His head jerked up and he looked at me intently. "You know I don't want to get rid of you. Ever since you came back, I've been praying you'd stay. I knew it was foolish, but I couldn't stop myself. Even now, after all that's happened, I can't stop myself. Tell me the truth—does Rafe Halpern's ghost scare you so much that you'll be packing your bags?"

I shook my head. "It'll take more than a ghost to scare me off these days. Besides, it's not his island. Big Bass belongs to everyone who lives on it, including me. Anyhow, now that your granddad is decently buried, I don't think he'll be doing anymore haunting."

Egan gave a short chuckle. "Are you psychic?"

"No, but I sort of felt it when we laid him to rest. It was almost as if he were heaving a sight of relief. Anyway, I'm not afraid of his ghost. I don't think he really meant me any harm. I just think he was upset because of the way he died and because everyone blamed him for Billy."

Egan's gaze stayed pinned to my face. "Katy, when I spotted you up on that cliff, I was so scared you might fall and hurt yourself. I'm ashamed to say it, but until I had you down safe and sound in my arms, I was shaking. I knew if anything happened to you, it would be my fault for not telling you everything."

With that, I agreed heartily. "Egan Halpern, you should have told me you suspected Nate was involved in your granddad's death. You should have let me know that you thought he might have that shipment of gold squirreled away someplace. If we'd joined forces, we could have both avoided a lot of trouble."

Egan sighed. "Maybe I have too much pride for my own good. I didn't want to share my theory until I'd proved it. I couldn't be sure I was right, and I hated the idea that if I was wrong, more bad information might come out to rake up the family disgrace and hurt Rex. It never occurred to me that Betty was involved in Nate's death, or that she was a threat to you."

"Me, neither, until I actually saw her pointing that old gun at me. It must be the gun that killed Rafe."

Egan nodded. "They've matched it to the bullet they found in Rafe's skull, so there's no doubt."

"What about the watch and knife Nate left in your box? What was their significance?"

"Apparently, they belonged to my granddad and Nate was too much of a skinflint to bury a good knife and watch with Rafe's body. He must have kept them all these years, then decided they should go to me."

"I suppose in some strange way, he felt he was making up for what happened to Rafe by seeing that Rafe's grandson inherited those things. Egan, what about Betty? How is she?"

"Last I heard, she was safe in the hospital outside Sandusky. What happens next depends on you and Sheriff Creech. Do you plan on charging her with Nate's murder?"

"After speaking to a lawyer, I don't think so." Emphatically, I shook my head. "It would be impossible to prove, and from what she said, it sounded to me as if it was an accident, anyway."

"But she admitted she tried to run you down."

"There's no way to prove that, either. Now that she's talked to a lawyer, she'll never sign a confession. I think the best we can hope for is to force Betty to seek treatment and leave the island. That will be punishment enough."

"Considering that she came close to killing you up in the cave, that's big of you, Katy."

"Realistic is more like it."

Nodding, Egan went back to work. He'd dug up a large patch of the cellar floor already and found nothing. While he attacked a new section, I surveyed the rows of ancient jars now sitting on the hard earth at my feet. They were so gritty with layers of dust and spider webs, it was disagreeable for me to even touch them. I wiped my grimy hands on my shorts and tried not to look at the disgusting preserves floating inside the things. The thought of eating any of those moldy gray fruits made me gag. I imagined that if I opened up a jar, it would smell horrible.

"Make out anything like a secret compartment over there?" Egan asked.

"Sorry. From what I can see of the wall, it looks solid."

"Let's shine some light on the subject." He dropped his shovel, picked up the lantern and crossed to where I was working. Holding the lantern high, he peered down behind the shelves, then grunted with disappointment. "You're right. It looks solid."

But the searching beams of the electric lantern had picked out something else. Despite my reluctance to look at the contents of the jars, a metallic glint drew my eye to them. I knelt for a closer inspection, then held up one of the containers to the bright light and, for the first time, studied it closely. I saw yellowish objects coated with a thick layer of crumbly, brown vegetable matter.

"Egan," I said, "I think I know what happened to the gold."

It was two weeks later. May's lilacs had faded and roses were beginning to scent the air. The summer sun worked hard to make the lake tempting for swimming.

"Shall I put the swimming ladder over the side?" Egan asked.

"Yeah, Dad, that'd be great!" Rex gobbled the last chocolate chip cookie in our picnic lunch and then leaped to his bare feet and stripped down to his bathing trunks. "How about you, Katy? You coming in, too?"

"Maybe in a little while. Right now I think I'll just soak up a few more rays and watch."

"You, Dad?" Like a puppy eager to frolic, Rex looked hopefully at his father.

Egan's strong white teeth flashed in a grin. "Sure thing. First one in gets to take the tiller on the way home."

"Yay!" Rex screeched as he ran for the side and jumped in. Five minutes later, I lay alone on the deck of the *Nighthawk.* As I watched Egan and Rex splash at each other, I pushed myself farther into the shade of the sail and took another sip of soda. A lot had happened since Egan and I had found the gold and turned it over to the federal government.

We were married now. We'd gone to the mainland and had a simple civil ceremony, very similar to the one we would have had if our elopement had worked the first time. Now we planned an extended honeymoon in the Bahamas, as soon as Egan could finish the boat he was working on. In the meantime, I intended to replace my ruined computer and get my fledgling desktop publishing business back on track. So far, it was going well. With all the computer networks available to me, living on the island didn't mean I was isolated from the outside world at all. Every night, I communicated with people all over the United States, many of them business contacts and potential clients.

My new career excited me, but nowhere near as much as my new husband did. Everyday, I seemed to fall more deeply in love with him. And every night, well, the nights were heated magic.

"What are you smiling about?" Egan asked. Rex still played in the water, but Egan had climbed up off the swimming ladder. Now he stood dripping in the center of the teak deck. With his navy blue trunks clinging wetly to his lean flanks, and the June sun gilding his hard thighs and tanned, well-developed shoulders, he was a sight that would have gladdened any female eye. Mine was far from being an exception.

"Oh, nothing," I answered as I gazed up at him. I tried not to stare, but I couldn't take my eyes from the line of dark, wet hair that arrowed from his muscular chest down his flat belly and into his bathing suit.

A gratifed masculine smile lit Egan's blue eyes. "You look mighty pretty all stretched out there in that pink bikini."

"Not half as pretty as you, sir. Right now, you look as if you could model for one of the marble gods in the Parthenon. Do you have a secret gym you work out in?"

"I spend my days working as a carpenter, remember? Hard labor has its benefits." Chuckling, Egan draped a towel around his shoulders and sank down beside me. We heard a splash and then a whoop as Rex surfaced clutching a rock covered with zebra mussels.

"Hey Katy," he shouted, "come on in. Water's great."

"In a minute," I shouted back.

Egan and I smiled at each other. "He's really thrilled to have you for his new mother, you know," Egan said. "But nowhere near as thrilled as his dad is to have you in his bed with a ring on your finger." Suddenly, Egan leaned down and kissed me passionately. "Oh, God, Katy," he whispered in my ear. "I love you so much."

Many kisses later, Egan finally asked, "Have you decided yet what you're going to do about the castle?"

"Not yet, but soon. In fact, tonight I think I'll go over there, confront Grandfather's ghost and make a decision."

Egan looked worried. "You haven't seen anymore ghosts, have you?"

I laughed and reached out to smooth the frown from his eyebrows. "No, but that doesn't mean they're not around in some form or other. Don't worry, I'm not afraid of ghosts anymore, even the ones that look a lot like you. Ghosts are part of the past. It's only the future I'm thinking about now."

That evening, my new husband and I ambled over to the castle. Little had changed since the fire. Though wind and rain had washed away the sulfurous pall that had blanketed the place, it still squatted on the haunches of its foundations, charred and derelict.

Moonlight gleamed on its eyeless windows and picked out the jagged profile of its turrets and peaked black roof. As I gazed up, it made me think of the carcass of some huge prehistoric beast, once magnificent, now fallen to ruin. It made me think of Rafe Halpern's skeleton and of the whole sad secret history that my grandfather had hugged to his chest all the years of his life. Obviously, he'd left the boxes to Egan and me because after his death he'd wanted his evil secret exorcised. But how unhappy and guilty he must have been while he was hoarding it!

Turning, I looked at the tall, dark man standing quietly at my side. The breeze off the lake ruffled his hair and then, as if it meant to tease, tweaked at a lock of mine. Silver threads of moonlight picked out his long legs, trim waist and the wide wedge-shaped block of his shoulders.

A month ago, I might have been afraid that he meant me harm. Now, as Egan reached out to me, I felt only happiness and anticipation.

"You have some thinking to do, don't you, Katy?" he said. "Do you want me to go away and leave you alone?"

"No, Egan, I'm glad you're here." I smiled as his hand closed over mine. In that instant, I felt warmer and safer than I'd ever felt before in my life.

He looked at me searchingly. "Have you made a decision?"

"I have. As soon as you can arrange it, you can have the castle torn down. Then, if you're still interested in building on the property, you can. Do you still want it?"

"I still want it, Katy, but there's something else I want much, much more..." He drew me to him and enclosed me in the strong circle of his arms. Our faces silvered by moonlight and patterned by shifting shadow, we gazed at each other.

"Egan, there's something I want to tell you. Betty told me she was the one who warned Nate about our running away together. She was jealous of me and hated you because you were a Halpern, and she thought the Halperns were responsible for what happened to her grandfather."

"Oh, Katy," Egan said on a harsh sigh. "It doesn't matter. You're the only thing that matters. I love you so much. I think I've always loved you." His head swooped and he took my mouth in a fierce, hard kiss.

I yielded to his lips gladly. Our arms tightened around each other, and we lost ourselves in the taste of our love. Kissing Egan, I seemed to dissolve into a world composed solely of sea, sky and desire. When we finally drew apart, I nuzzled the hollow of his throat and then burrowed against him. With a groan, Egan rested his chin on the top of my head.

"There've been so many times over the past couple months that I've been afraid."

"Afraid of what?"

"Of losing you again, Katy. It was hard the first time. I didn't think I could stand having it happen all over again. Oh my darling, if you go away now, I think I'll die."

My hands were splayed across his shoulder blades. Beneath my fingertips I felt him tremble. The discovery that his emotions were so strong shocked and thrilled me. I pushed off from his body so I could look up into his face. "I'm not going anywhere, Egan," I whispered with all the earnestness I possessed. "This time I'm here to stay."

"You're sure?"

"Absolutely."

And with that pledge between us, our mouths blended once again. As we lost ourselves in the sweetness of each other, the hulk of the castle, with all its dark secrets, seemed to fade away and, with it, the ghosts of the past. Only the future and our newfound love remained.

HARLEQUIN®

Don't miss these Harlequin favorites by some of our most distinguished authors!
And now, you can receive a discount by ordering two or more titles!

HT #25551	THE OTHER WOMAN by Candace Schuler	$2.99	☐
HT #25539	FOOLS RUSH IN by Vicki Lewis Thompson	$2.99	☐
HP #11550	THE GOLDEN GREEK by Sally Wentworth	$2.89	☐
HP #11603	PAST ALL REASON by Kay Thorpe	$2.99	☐
HR #03228	MEANT FOR EACH OTHER by Rebecca Winters	$2.89	☐
HR #03268	THE BAD PENNY by Susan Fox	$2.99	☐
HS #70532	TOUCH THE DAWN by Karen Young	$3.39	☐
HS #70540	FOR THE LOVE OF IVY by Barbara Kaye	$3.39	☐
HI #22177	MINDGAME by Laura Pender	$2.79	☐
HI #22214	TO DIE FOR by M.J. Rodgers	$2.89	☐
HAR #16421	HAPPY NEW YEAR, DARLING		
	by Margaret St. George	$3.29	☐
HAR #16507	THE UNEXPECTED GROOM by Muriel Jensen	$3.50	☐
HH #28774	SPINDRIFT by Miranda Jarrett	$3.99	☐
HH #28782	SWEET SENSATIONS by Julie Tetel	$3.99	☐

Harlequin Promotional Titles

#83259	UNTAMED MAVERICK HEARTS	$4.99	☐
	(Short-story collection featuring Heather Graham Pozzessere, Patricia Potter, Joan Johnston)		

(limited quantities available on certain titles)

	AMOUNT	$
DEDUCT:	10% DISCOUNT FOR 2+ BOOKS	$
	POSTAGE & HANDLING	$
	($1.00 for one book, 50¢ for each additional)	
	APPLICABLE TAXES*	$ _____
	TOTAL PAYABLE	$ _____
	(check or money order—please do not send cash)	

To order, complete this form and send it, along with a check or money order for the total above, payable to Harlequin Books, to: **In the U.S.:** 3010 Walden Avenue, P.O. Box 9047, Buffalo, NY 14269-9047; **In Canada:** P.O. Box 613, Fort Erie, Ontario, L2A 5X3.

Name: _____

Address: _____ City: _____

State/Prov.: _____ Zip/Postal Code: _____

*New York residents remit applicable sales taxes.
Canadian residents remit applicable GST and provincial taxes.

HBACK-AJ

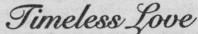